TELL ME IT'S WRONG

KATIE WISMER

Tell Me It's Wrong

Copyright © 2025 by Katie Wismer

All rights reserved. Printed in the United States of America. No part of this book may be used or reproduced in any manner whatsoever without written permission of the publisher, except in the case of brief quotations embodied in critical articles and certain other noncommercial uses permitted by copyright law. This work does not contain any AI-generated content.

For more information visit: www.katiewismer.com

Cover design by Najla Qamber
Proofreading by Beth Attwood

Standard Paperback ISBN: 978-1-958458-08-2

Alternate Paperback ISBN: 978-1-958458-09-9

First Edition: April 2025

Also by Katie Wismer

Find your next read here: https://www.katiewismer.com/books

Sign up for My Author Newsletter

Sign up for Katie Wismer's newsletter to receive exclusive content and be the first to learn about new releases, book sales, events, and other news!

www.katiewismer.com

This book contains material that may be triggering for some readers. Reader discretion is advised. For a complete list of trigger warnings, please visit katiewismer.com/trigger-warnings

Playlist

Listen on Spotify: https://shorturl.at/K6ckK

Off My Mind — Joe P
Penthouse — Kelsea Ballerini
Bye Bye Bye — *NSYNC
dont let me go — mgk
Faint of Heart — The Strike
PINCH ME — young friend
Spectator — Friday Pilots Club
Strange Love — Halsey
You and I — We Three
hurt less — LØLØ
Lone Survivor — The Wrecks
Good As It Gets — Little Hurt
Don't Go — YUNGBLUD
Oracle — Chris James
Tissues — YUNGBLUD
Moon — The Cab
Can't Help — Parachute
Overrated — Landon Conrath
Glad To Be Here — Friday Pilots Club
I Think I Like You — The Band CAMINO
I Wanna Be Yours — Arctic Monkeys
Somewhere Only We Know — Keane
Animal — The Cab
Fresh — Artist Vs Poet
Stay Away — MOD SUN, mgk, Goody Grace
Please Don't Go — Mike Posner

Guilty as Sin? — Taylor Swift
Less Than I Do — The Band CAMINO
I Can See You (Taylor's Version) — Taylor Swift
Yours — Sueco, Bea Miller
See You Later — The Band CAMINO
BLEED — The Kid LAROI
Out Of My League — Aidan Bissett
Won't Go Home Without You — Maroon 5
I'd Rather Overdose — honestav, MOD SUN
The Bolter — Taylor Swift
MakeDamnSure — Taking Back Sunday
Til It's Over — Old Dominion
Over My Head (Cable Car) — The Fray
Mess — Noah Kahan
Bed Chem — Sabrina Carpenter
Without You — Parachute
the mood i'm in / jsyk — The Maine
Can We Pretend That We're Good? — Daniel Seavey
spiraling — The Maine
I'd Do Anything — Simple Plan
Stutter — Maroon 5
Lost — Blake Rose
WE MADE PLANS & GOD LAUGHED — Beauty School Dropout
I Don't Wanna Live Forever — Taylor Swift, ZAYN
I Did Something Bad — Taylor Swift

Chapter One
CHRISTINE

There is nothing more pathetic than a woman getting drunk at a bar alone.

That's what my husband always says—ex-husband.

A hysterical cackle bursts from my lips as I finish off my glass of Riesling. How fitting that I ended up here on the day we finalized our divorce.

And I do mean day. That's definitely sunlight coming through the windows.

I've passed this bar a hundred times on my way to the yoga studio down the street, but I've never been inside. Julian wouldn't have been caught dead in a place like this, and since he owns half the other bars around here, we usually ended up at one of those.

Not that we had many nights out together.

I hadn't planned on coming here. After leaving the lawyer's office, I was driving back to the hotel I've been living out of these past few months. But then I remembered I'd be there alone.

My son, Casey, has been staying there with me, but Liam,

his half brother—who is closer to my age than his by a landslide—offered to take him for the weekend while we finalized the divorce. I hadn't realized how much I needed that until now. I just don't have it in me to put on the *everything's fine* face today.

Julian has barely been involved in his life as it is. But now? And like most seven-year-olds, Casey doesn't know any better and worships his father.

I don't know how much longer that'll last.

Driving through town after that meeting was its own kind of torture—my ex-husband's last name plastered on every other building.

Until I came across this shabby little place. There was just something about it that drew me in today.

Maybe because it reminds me of another life.

The neon lights, the pool tables, the shitty cracked leather barstools—it's the kind of place I would've gone before him. Before this current version of me.

If past me could see me now... I let out another laugh. She'd fucking choke.

The bartender sets down the cup he'd been drying when he notices my empty glass and heads over. He barely looks old enough to be in here.

"Can I get you anything else?" he asks.

I tap the top of my wineglass.

He nods and pulls a new bottle out. His eyes flick from the glass to me as he pours. They're nice eyes. Unique. Somehow green and brown at the same time. Is that considered hazel?

"Rough day?" he asks as he slides the glass to me.

I snort out a humorless laugh as I take a sip. There's no way this poor kid wants to hear my middle-aged sob story. Is thirty-two considered middle-aged? Everyone spent the last seven years preening over how young I was next to Julian, but now without him in comparison...

But then again, there's no one else in the bar, so maybe he's bored.

I swirl the wine around in my glass. "I just became a multi-millionaire. I should be thrilled."

A million for each year we were married, per our prenup. Plus the twenty grand monthly child support. I could have asked for more—assets, properties—probably would've gotten it too. Maybe a younger version of me would have.

His eyebrows lift, and his eyes flick around the room. Slowly, a smirk tugs on the corner of his mouth, and he leans closer to me. "And you're drinking *here?*"

I snort, and that smirk turns into a grin.

He has nice teeth too. Is that a weird thing to notice? Very white, very straight.

"So are we talking a lottery win or a bank robbery?"

I sigh and rest my chin in my hand. "Divorce."

He winces. "Sorry."

I shrug. I'm sure a lot of people are thinking I got what's coming to me, marrying for money like that.

That's a real easy thing to say if you've never had to go without it.

"How long were you together?"

I blink, surprised he's still standing here. Most would run before having to hear any more.

"Seven years." I roll my eyes. "Which I'm pretty sure is the average for marriages that end in divorce. Even statistically I'm a cliché."

He shakes his head with a smile. "You seem about as far from a cliché as they come."

I cock my head to the side, not sure if he's just trying to be nice or he really doesn't know who I am. He carded me when I first sat down—something that definitely fluffed my poor beaten-down ego—but maybe he hadn't paid attention to the last name on there. Seems like everyone knows everyone around here—and everyone's business.

But maybe that's just the circle I run in.

Ran in.

"That's a big assumption for a stranger I've exchanged half a dozen sentences with."

"Fletcher." He extends a hand over the bar for me to shake, and he clasps my hand firmly, not the wimpy way some men do when they shake hands with a woman. "Now we're not strangers. Well..." He raises his eyebrows as he waits for me to fill the silence.

"Christine."

His smile returns. "I'm also good at reading people. I've seen plenty of clichés walk through that door. Don't think you're one of them, Chris."

Now it's my turn for my eyebrows to shoot up. Is this twentysomething bartender *flirting* with me?

Before I can respond, he ducks beneath the bar and returns with a tall cup. He meets my eyes as he grabs the soda gun and fills the cup with water.

"Passive aggressive," I mutter, but pull it toward me anyway, then frown as the light catches my ring.

The ring, for some reason, I'm still wearing.

"How many drinks could I buy with this?" I ask, slipping it from my finger.

He lets out a low whistle. "Think you could buy the bar."

I glance around the musty, dark space, and my upper lip curls.

Fletcher laughs, the sound deep and rich, an almost musical quality to it.

I press the ring to the bar, my finger in the middle, and spin it around and around.

It's giant and expensive and hideous. I've always thought so.

It's white gold, for one, which I never wear. The emerald cut does not complement my fingers at all, and the band is thick and gaudy with all of the extra stones crammed into it.

A ring someone who didn't know me at all would buy.

But I didn't care. At least, that's what I told myself at the time. Because I'd done it. I'd found a man who could take care of me for the rest of my life. I would never have to worry again, and I'd done it all before the deadline my mother and I set when I was five.

I can't remember the first time she brought it up, me needing to marry for money. It must have been around there.

Your beauty is your best asset, Christine. Use it while you can, because it won't last.

The only thing she talked about more was how she regretted not doing the same thing for herself.

I could have had everything, she'd say. *Don't you dare repeat my mistakes.*

Her mistakes being...me, mainly. Having me at seventeen, marrying my dad. Him leaving less than a year later, never to be heard from again. And the two of us struggling day in and day out on food stamps, other people's couches, and eventually another man's paycheck until I packed my bags at sixteen and never looked back.

"I think there are way more fun things you could do with that money though," Fletcher says lightly, pulling me out of my thoughts.

I sip my wine. "Oh, really? What would you do with it?"

He hums thoughtfully. "An African safari. Swim with dolphins. Super Bowl tickets. Ooo, rent out an entire cruise ship."

"What would you possibly need an entire cruise ship for?"

He shrugs. "Bring people you like with you. All you can eat and drink. You'd never have to wait in line. Don't have to worry about someone peeing in the pool."

"Is that something you worry about often?"

He frowns and tilts his head back and forth in a *more than you'd think* gesture.

I chuckle and shake my head. "I will take those suggestions under advisement. Thank you."

He salutes me with two fingers and heads back to where he was cleaning the glasses. "I'll be here all night."

Chapter Two

FLETCHER

The bar fills pretty quickly once five o'clock rolls around, as it usually does.

But Christine doesn't leave.

Every time I get pulled aside by another customer, by the time I make it back to peer at her spot, I keep expecting her to be gone, but she's not.

At least half a dozen men have taken the seat beside her at this point, trying to flirt and buy her a drink.

For some reason, my shoulders tense every time.

But they don't last long. After a few minutes, they leave, and Christine sits there sipping her wine with a smug little smile on her lips.

God, what I wouldn't give to be a fly on the wall for those conversations.

It's obvious why they all keep flocking to her despite witnessing the failures of the men before them. She's like a neon light sitting there, everything about her screaming she doesn't belong in here. From the blatantly expensive dress and purse, to the shiny blond hair and perfect posture, to the jewelry I'm a little afraid someone is going to mug her for in the parking lot...a green-skinned alien would blend in better than her.

Something about her is so damn familiar, but I can't put my finger on it.

After a *seventh* guy strikes out with her, I make my way over.

"How are you doing?"

She smiles up at me, and that's how I know she's drunk. Even when I'd gotten her to laugh earlier, the corners of her mouth never quite passed the middle line, like they were fighting against it. Her eyes are a little glassy now, and I double-check she still has that baseball of a ring on the bar and no one swiped it.

But no, it's there. She's still spinning it around and around.

"No more for me," she says, pushing her half-full wineglass toward me.

"Glad we agree on that."

"Thank you for talking with me earlier," she says, her words starting to slur. "That was nice of you."

"I enjoyed it. You're the most interesting person I've had in here in a while." She rolls her eyes, and I lay my hand palm up on the bar top. "But I'm going to need your keys."

She purses her lips like she knows I'm right, but makes no move to give them to me.

"I can call you a cab," I add.

"I don't want to leave my car here. My hotel is only a few blocks away."

"Come on, you know that's not a good idea."

"Didn't I see on the news you keep having break-ins in your parking lot?" Her nose scrunches. "No offense."

She's not wrong. People have definitely caught on to the

number of cars that get left here overnight and taken full advantage of that.

I sigh and glance at the clock, then the second bartender who showed up an hour ago. "Which hotel are you staying at?"

"The Ridley."

Damn, that is really close.

"All right." I curl my fingers for the keys, and her lower lip pushes out a little in disappointment. "I'm going to drive you. Come on."

She blinks, a crease forming between her eyebrows. "You won't get in trouble for leaving?"

I shake my head. "It'll take less than ten minutes."

"But how will you get back?" She seems genuinely baffled.

I chuckle. "I've got it taken care of. It's me or the cab. Your pick."

Slowly, she pulls her keys from her purse and drops them into my waiting palm.

Thank God she's not leaving her car here. This thing must have cost at least a hundred grand. It wouldn't have stood a chance.

It's nothing too flashy—a sleek black SUV. I would've taken her more for the sports car type, that is, until I open the back seat to toss my skateboard inside and notice the car seat.

Damn. She seems really upset about the divorce as it is, but that adds a whole new layer to it. I have a million questions I want to ask, but I don't know where the line between friendly ends and nosy begins.

She climbs into the passenger seat with a sigh, and I drop the ring she left on the bar into the cupholder.

"Oh." She stares at it as I adjust the seat. "Oops."

A laugh gets stuck in my throat. That ring looks like it was a million dollars. *Oops?* Who the fuck is her ex-husband? God?

"Are you even old enough to drive?" she says as I pull out of the parking lot.

"I am *not* that much younger than you."

She scoffs. "I could be your mother."

My head whips toward her. Is she *serious*? "How old do you think I am?"

She frowns and squints at me. "Sixteen?"

I give her an unimpressed look. "And bartending? Try again."

"Eighteen?"

"That's more legal, but still no."

She purses her lips. "Twenty-one."

"Twenty-three," I admit. "But you can't be that much older. Definitely not old enough for the age jokes."

She groans and covers her face with both hands. "Try ten years."

Huh. Looking at her, I would've guessed less, but still. "That's nothing."

"That's a *decade*."

"So?"

She shakes her head like she can't believe I just said that.

All too soon, I pull into her hotel's parking lot, and I find myself grasping for something else to say to make her stay longer.

"You have your hotel key?"

She frowns and digs in her purse until she finds it.

"Phone?"

She digs for that next.

"Wallet?"

She throws her hands up, but then she sees me smirking at

the cupholder and presses her lips together like she's trying not to smile.

"So I forgot one thing," she mumbles as she fishes the ring out. It takes her a few tries, but she gets there.

I grab my skateboard from the back and hop out to get the door for her. She stares at me for a moment before climbing out.

"These too," I say, slipping the car keys into her purse.

"Thank you," she says softly.

"For what it's worth, coming from someone with zero knowledge of the situation, your ex-husband must be an *idiot*."

She blinks up at me—blue eyes. I hadn't been able to tell in the bar lighting, but yeah, they're definitely blue. The deep kind, like the ocean. She was beautiful sitting there in the bar, but up close? She's fucking breathtaking. Down to every little detail—the curve of her lips, the freckles on her nose. Without a doubt, she's the most beautiful woman I've ever seen.

I'm seized with the sudden urge to kiss her, but that would probably be the worst possible thing I could do right now. If she were sober…I'd probably try to get her to invite me inside.

Reluctantly, I take a step away. "I should get back."

She blinks and takes a step back too. "Of course. Thank you. For the ride."

"See you around, Chris." I set my board down and kick off with a wave. "I work Thursday through Monday!"

Even as I round the corner and her form disappears into the dark, I manage to catch her smile.

"I'm never going back there!" she calls.

I smirk. We'll see.

Chapter Three
CHRISTINE

I watch the other children all but shove their parents or nannies away at the drop-off, eager to be free of them. Since when did kids start getting embarrassed of their moms at seven years old? Doesn't that usually start in the teenage years?

But Casey—my poor sweet, sensitive Casey—has a death grip on my hand. I walk with him to the front door of the elementary school where his summer art camp is being held for the next two weeks. There's a group of volunteers at a folding table beside the front door, smiling as they sign everyone in.

A few moms lingering off to the side look me up and down when we reach the front of the line, and I pretend not to notice.

It was only a matter of time until news of the divorce spread around here.

I give Casey's hand a reassuring squeeze as we collect his name tag, and I squat down to attach it to his shirt.

I force a smile that's much sunnier than I feel. "I can't *wait* to see what you make in there."

"I'll make something for you," he promises.

"You're going to have so much fun and make so many new friends."

The first hint of worry scrunches his face together.

Casey is the most bubbly, outgoing kid I've ever seen... around adults. For some reason, when he's with kids his own age, he shuts down.

He has friends—the kind you invite to birthday parties and have over to your house for playdates.

But they've never been the kind he's begged me to let stay over a little bit longer. Instead, I usually have to remind him to get back out there and keep playing with them instead of coming to see me. I don't know if he's ever met another kid he actually *likes*.

I tug him a step away from listening ears.

"I want you to go in there and have fun. If you do that and just be yourself, they're going to love you. I promise. And I'm your mom, so that means I know everything."

He smiles, and I ruffle his hair before pulling him into a hug. "I love you. I'll see you this afternoon, okay?"

He nods and casts one last look at me over his shoulder before letting go of my hand and taking the volunteer's instead. She gives me an understanding smile as she escorts him inside.

I slide my sunglasses on and hurry to the car. *I will not cry. I will not cry.*

The tears fall as soon as I close the door behind me.

I cried taking Casey to preschool, to day care, to his first day of kindergarten, his first playdate—I don't know why I thought today would be any different.

Today feels so much heavier though. I just really, *really* hope this goes well. That the other kids are nice to him. That he likes the camp counselors. So much in his world is falling apart, and it's my fault.

"Christine?"

A fist pounds against my window, and I jump.

Jesus fucking Christ.

Lola Bartlett peers in at me, far too close to the glass for comfort. She's in a matching neon pink workout set, and her face is bright red like she just left the Pilates studio.

I roll down the window.

"Oh." She smiles and stands up straight. "I thought that was you. How are you?"

"I'm good, Lola, thanks. But you know what, I'm actually in a hurry. I'm heading out to see this house, so..."

I have several hours before I need to be there, but she doesn't need to know that.

"Oh! I didn't know you were on the hunt already! I could've put you in touch with our real estate agent."

I give her a closed-lip smile. "Yeah, you know, I'm just looking around right now."

She hums and nods understandingly as she pops her hip out to the side and readjusts the bag on her shoulder. "Well, anyway, I was going to call, but then I saw you as I was dropping Nolan off and figured I'd run over here to let you know book club is canceled this week." She pushes her lower lip out and sighs dramatically. "Stephanie has the flu, Maryanne's taking her in-laws to a Broadway show, and Chelsea's house is getting fumigated, if you can believe it! So we all thought it would be better to reschedule. Wouldn't want anyone to get behind or be left out of the discussion!"

"Oh. Yeah, of course."

As if we ever actually discuss the books.

She smiles and waves before heading off.

I suck my teeth as I roll the window up. I would bet every penny of my divorce settlement that she's full of shit.

I just got kicked out of fucking book club.

"Fully updated kitchen, and there's a *beautiful* view of the ocean back here."

The Realtor shifts her weight restlessly as I pace around and take in all the details.

Downsizing doesn't even begin to cover it, but even after eight years, I'd never gotten used to living in that museum of a house. This one, at least, has the chance of feeling like a home. A four bed and three bath, which is more than enough space for me and Casey. The location is perfect—close to his school, the beach, and town.

It's an older house, which I'm trying to convince myself makes it *charming* instead of *outdated*. Appliances that are older than my son, yellow-orange wood, floral wallpaper in all the bathrooms.

But there aren't a ton of other options to choose from.

If the circumstances were different, I'd be long gone by now. I know how this town sees me. I was the gold-digging whore who married someone twice her age. But he's the man who pulls all the puppet strings around here, so at least while I was married to him, no one ever said anything to my face. I had invitations everywhere, every door standing wide open.

That'll forever be what these people know me as. It would be easier to take the money and start over someplace new.

But Casey.

His school is here, his half siblings. His life.

I glance at the time on the stove and chew on my lip. I need to get out of here within the next few minutes if I'm going to pick him up from camp on time.

The woman—I already can't remember her name—watches my every move as I pace from the kitchen to the laundry to the living room. It'll take a nice chunk out of the divorce settlement, but not too much. I know I need to be smart about making it last. I'm a single mother who's been unemployed for eight years with no discernible skills. Running out of this money is not an option.

"It probably won't stay on the market long at this price…"

I wave her off before she can launch into whatever sales pitch she's been preparing. I've known since the moment I drove up that this was as good as it was going to get.

"I'll take it."

In my thirty-two years of life, I've somehow been lucky enough to never have this happen to me.

Today, that feels a lot more like bad luck though, because I have no fucking idea what to do.

I pull the car as far onto the shoulder as I can manage without careering into the ditch, the flat tire thumping obnoxiously. I climb out of the car and frown at the offender—the back right has a nail sticking out of it.

Of course.

I don't know how to change one myself, I have no idea what number to call, and it would probably take too long for them to get here even if I did.

Do I call a ride and leave the car here and hope it's okay when I come back for it later?

I could call Casey's camp and tell them I'll be late, or see if

Liam's able to pick him up. I'd rather get hit by a semitruck right here and now than call Casey's dad.

But I want it to be *me* he sees walk through that door. There's been so much change in his life, and he's doing the best he can with it, but I've seen the light in his eyes dwindling these past few months.

I told him I would pick him up. He's expecting *me*. So that's who it needs to be.

I jump back a step as a truck slows and pulls in behind me—

—and freeze at the sight of the man who steps out of the car.

Is that...that can't be...

But yes, even in the daylight and with sunglasses covering his eyes, I can tell that is most definitely Bar Guy.

I don't think he's seen me yet. He glances both ways down the road, then at my car, his head tilted to the side like he's inspecting it. "You all right?"

I swallow hard past the sudden dryness in my throat. "Flat tire."

He stops midstep. Looks up. Looks at *me*. His mouth twitches like he wants to smile, but instead he says, "You have a spare?"

I nod.

"You need some help?"

"I—yeah," I admit on a sigh. "If you don't mind."

"Not at all. You have a jack?"

"I have absolutely no idea."

He smirks and gestures to the car. "Pop the trunk. Let's have a look."

I do as he says and definitely don't stare at him as he gets closer. I don't know why I thought his hair would be lighter in the sun, but it's still dark as night. He shoves it out of his eyes with one hand as he opens the well beneath the trunk to get the spare. Luckily, there are some tools I never knew were in there too.

If there's one thing my drunk memory did *not* do justice—he most certainly doesn't look like a kid now. I was mostly joking with the age cracks to begin with, but had he—did he really look like *this* the whole time?

Jesus fucking Christ.

The longer we don't acknowledge this, the weirder it'll get, so I say, "It's Fletcher, right?"

Amusement tugs at his lips. "Didn't know if you'd remember me."

He says that like I was blackout. "I wasn't that drunk."

He glances at me sideways with a crooked grin. "Did you forget I was the one serving you?"

"How long is this going to take?" I blurt. "Not that I'm not grateful for the help. I'm just in a really big hurry, and I'm already late."

He turns the corners of his lips down, considering, and shakes his head. "Not my first rodeo. Give me ten minutes."

"Do you want me to—can I help?"

"No offense, truly, but you'll probably just get in the way. I've got it. Do you have the parking brake on?"

"No."

He smiles in a way that would probably be condescending on anyone else, but his just looks genuine. "Can you do that then, please?"

I hop back in the car and hit the brake. "I hope you weren't headed somewhere important," I call.

"Nah. Would much rather be your knight in shining armor again anyway. Are we making this a regular thing?"

I make an unintelligible noise in the back of my throat and

climb out of the car. "You're not nearly as charming as you think you are."

All I catch is a flash of white teeth as he grins and sets the tools on the ground.

Not knowing what else to do, I venture as far from the road as I can get without wading into the weeds, sit, and watch.

So I can know how to do it if this ever happens again, I tell myself.

Not because his arm muscles flex as he jacks the car up then gets to removing the bolts or whatever holding the tire. *Not* because I can also see the definition of his back through his thin T-shirt as he removes the first tire and sets it aside. *Not* because the veins in his hand and forearm are standing out as he tightens the bolts on the new tire.

I am *not* eye-fucking this twenty-three-year-old on the side of the road. Not in the slightest.

The way I keep catching glimpses of his smile when he turns his head, he fucking knows it too.

I must be ovulating or something.

"You're all set." He climbs to his feet, wipes his hands on his jeans, and starts packing everything back into my trunk.

"Thank you. Really. I don't know what I would've done if you hadn't showed up."

I don't know why I admitted that aloud. I brush off the dirt on my clothes and find him watching me with a strange look on his face.

"Give me your phone," he says.

I frown, but I do it.

"I'm going to give you my number," he says without looking at me. "You don't have to use it. But just in case something like this comes up again and you need some help, I want you to have it. I'm sure you have a million people you'd rather call first, but in case everyone else is busy…" He hands the phone to me. "I'm happy to be a last resort."

The truth is, I don't have a million people. I don't even have one.

And somehow, I think he knows that.

For the first time since pulling up, all the teasing and amusement is gone from his tone. And the intensity in the way he's looking at me right now…it's too much.

I wag my phone in the air. "Of course you turned this into an opportunity to slip me your number." My voice doesn't come out as light as I'd been hoping, but it does the trick.

That grin slaps back into place, and he waves as he heads to his car. "You're welcome!"

Chapter Four
FLETCHER

Something is burning. And God, it's hot.

Something pounds in the distance—what is that tapping noise?

I roll over in bed and try to kick off the sheets sticking to my sweaty legs. Where the fuck is the air-conditioning?

Joan probably forgot to pay the bills again.

My lungs itch and constrict, and I cough, but the sensation doesn't subside.

"Fletcher! Fletcher, please," a small voice wails somewhere near my ear.

I sit up straight in bed, my hand shooting up to clutch my chest as I gasp in a breath. The air is clean, but the ghost of that suffocating feeling lingers behind.

I throw my legs over the side of the bed and shove myself out of the room as if I can physically leave the nightmare behind. It's still dark through the windows as I stumble down to the kitchen.

4:25 AM blinks at me from the stove, and I sigh as I turn on the coffeepot.

Same time as always.

Once I pour a cup, I head out to the single chair sitting on the newly finished deck, my breaths still coming in a little too hard. I hang my head between my shoulders for a second, waiting for my brain to catch up with my actual body temperature and realize we're not burning up. The morning air brushes across my chest, cooling the sweat clinging to me.

But it's the voice that won't stop echoing in my mind.

That voice.

It hasn't faded with time at all. Or maybe it has. Maybe I have it all wrong now and can't tell the difference.

I shake my head, forcing myself to focus on the yard in front of me. It's an absolute mess.

I don't even think twenty-four hours had passed since I wrapped up the renovations on the house before Mom showed up with a truck full of gardening supplies and a wide smile, eager to get to work—her idea of a housewarming gift. There was only so much she could do when I lived in an apartment, and now she's making up for lost time, I guess.

If there's a method to where she left everything, I can't see it. Bags of mulch, fertilizer, a wheelbarrow, shovels, pots, stones. I'm a little afraid to see what she plans to do with all of it. In the places she and Dad have flipped in the past, she's always done something elaborate and high-end. I don't know if she even knows *how* to rein herself in.

Coffee still untouched, I head inside to hunt down my phone. I can't remember what time she said she'd be back today. She's always been an early riser though, and it's probably best to start before it gets to the hotter parts of the day.

The phone's plugged in on the kitchen island where I left it yesterday afternoon. A dozen or so notifications wait for me on the screen, and I quickly scroll through to make sure there's nothing important. An invite to hang out from my best friends

Liam and Leo, a reminder from one of my bosses about the schedule this week. A smirk pulls at my lips as I realize half are from my mother. One to let me know she'll swing by at seven, and the rest are links to house listings she thinks I should look into.

I text her that maybe *she* should look into them.

She responds immediately. *Your dad and I wanted to give you first dibs!*

I smile a little and shake my head. A single solo flip under my belt, and now she thinks she's convinced me to follow in their footsteps.

I enjoy working on houses, I do. And I'll probably do another at some point, and help them out when they need some extra hands. I know she sees it as better money—a way for me to quit working my other jobs. But I'm not so sure that I want to.

I frown when I remember what time it is and text her again. *What are you even doing up so early??*

She sends me a string of emojis that's impossible to decode, followed by: *Early bird gets the worm!!!*

She, thankfully, doesn't ask me the same question.

She already knows the answer.

I shower then tidy up the house before Mom gets here, because if I don't, she'll feel the need to. I've barely finished unloading the clean dishes from the wash when there's a knock on the door. I glance at the clock.

6:30 AM.

Should've known she wouldn't make it until seven.

I swing the front door open, and my mother smiles sheepishly at me from the other side, two coffee cups and a brown paper bag in hand…and a dog at her feet.

"Mom…"

It's a *beast* of a dog. It's half as tall as Mom sitting down, and judging by the gray around its snout, it's a senior. No leash, no collar. Just big brown eyes staring up at me.

"Oh, that's Charlie," she says as if this is perfectly normal, then juts her chin. "Can we come in?"

I step aside, eyes still on *Charlie*, and he politely waits for my mom to go inside before slowly pushing to his feet and ambling after her.

"I brought you some coffee cake!" she calls as she unloads onto the kitchen counter, then glances around the room with her hands on her hips as if searching for a cleaning task.

Finding none, she sighs a little and sips her coffee. I smirk and take the second cup she offers. The one I made earlier is sitting cold and untouched on the counter.

"Where's Dad?"

She waves a hand and paces to the windows to peek outside. "On-site today. They're working on electrical stuff. You know I always like to skip that part. I see you haven't gotten any more furniture out there yet."

"In the two days since you last suggested it? No, I haven't."

She squints at me and lowers her voice as she asks, "How have you been sleeping?"

"Fine. I'm fine." I look away so she can't see the bags under my eyes, and find Charlie leaned against the island, staring at me like he can see into my soul. "So what's the deal with the dog?"

"Charlie," she corrects me.

"What's the deal with *Charlie*?"

She lifts her chin indignantly. "Are you saying I'm too old to try something new?"

"I—" I sputter and shake my head. *This woman.* "Are you telling me you adopted him?" I saw her less than twenty-four hours ago and there was no mention of a dog. What could have possibly changed since then?

She shrugs and digs around in the paper bag for the coffee cake that was supposedly for me. "We're fostering him."

I can't help but laugh. "What? I scarred you so badly that you can't do kids anymore and had to move on to animals?"

She gives me an unamused smile. "He's a sweetheart, and he needed a home. What was I supposed to do? Say no? You haven't even said hi to him properly."

Sighing, I squat to get on his level. I swear the beast doesn't blink. I think he has a lazy eye.

"Hi, Charlie. I'm Fletcher. I was the first stray they took in. Guess that makes us kindred spirits or something. Nice to meet you."

Charlie cocks his head like he's taking this all in.

Mom scoffs as I scratch Charlie between the ears. "Fletcher Conway."

I grin, rise back to my feet, and plant a kiss on her cheek before stealing what remains of the coffee cake. "You gonna put me to work or what?"

The corners of her lips turn down in a *now that you mention it* way as she turns to peer out the windows again. "I hope you're still good with a shovel."

Chapter Five
CHRISTINE

Casey and I stay in the hotel even once I get the keys to the new house. I don't want to show it to him, not yet. Not until it's full of furniture and all of his things. Not until I can make it look like a fun, cozy new adventure instead of a bare, pathetic downgrade.

Thankfully, Julian agreed to transfer most of the furniture from Casey's old bedroom since he'll be with me most of the time. The rest of the house though...it didn't really dawn on me how little I have until I was standing in the empty foyer.

I barely had anything to my name when I met Julian. The moment he asked me to move in with him, it was clear none of my belongings were up to par, so I let them go, thinking the time for cheap furniture was in my past.

It would be all too easy to blow through my money filling this place with nice things.

But one of the first things I did after we came to an agreement was sit down with a calculator and crunch the numbers every which way. I don't plan to sit around and do nothing for the rest of my life, but ideally, I'd like to find work that I enjoy, and the money coming in can be a bonus, not something I'm relying on.

The child support for Casey will be incredibly helpful with his school, clothes, food, childcare, a college fund, and the rest in a savings account for him for later. I want to make sure every penny goes toward making sure he never finds himself in the position I was in.

So the rest of it...I could coast along on about a hundred grand a year for the next fifty years. And that's without investing any of it.

I have no idea if that'll be enough—what habits I've grown so used to that will need to be scaled back. I'm afraid in the last seven years with Julian, I've forgotten how to budget. I've never felt less like an adult in my life.

But I'm guessing that means the five-thousand-dollar couch I was eye-fucking is out of the question.

"Mommy, are we homeless?"

My head whips to the side where Casey is sitting on the fluffy white hotel bed. He's staring hard into his room service ice cream sundae, ignoring the animated movie playing on the television across the room.

"Where would you get an idea like that?"

"That's what Nolan said," he mumbles and shoves his spoon in his mouth, smearing chocolate sauce on his lips.

I roll my eyes up to the ceiling. Nolan Bartlett. I know I shouldn't blame a child—I really shouldn't—but there is no way that kid isn't going to turn out exactly like his insufferable mother.

"He said no one lives in hotels," Casey continues.

"Well, that means it's pretty special, right? And we've had fun here, haven't we?"

He nods, still not looking at me.

"I told you, we're just here for a little vacation. It's not forever."

"Does...does Daddy not want us in the house anymore?"

Now I'm glad he isn't looking at me because I feel the color drain from my face. I swallow hard, and it takes me a few attempts before I manage to speak. "Of course that's not true. Dad always wants you there. But you know how busy he gets. It's just a very busy time right now."

Casey narrows his eyes and licks his lips. "You said he wants me there."

"Right! He does!"

"Not us."

I freeze, wide-eyed as my seven-year-old turns to me with one eyebrow raised like a fucking lawyer trapped in his tiny body.

"Well...it's complicated. It's not that he doesn't *want* us there, we're just not going to...live there...anymore. But this isn't your dad's fault, Casey. This is something he and I both agreed on."

Casey scrunches his face together as he thinks, and I jump up from the bed before he can continue his interrogation, pillow in hand.

"I think you owe me a rematch, remember?"

Reluctantly, a slow smile spreads on his chubby cheeks, and he discards the sundae on the nightstand in favor of the biggest pillow he can get his hands on.

"I'm gonna *dominate!*"

I stop by the new house the next day when Casey's at camp, trying to picture it once everything comes together. The movers already brought Casey's bedroom things upstairs, and the guy from the security system company keeps rattling the front door handle as he installs it.

The idea of furnishing this place all at once makes me feel like I need a nap, so I make a mental list as I pace through the rooms of the most important things to start with. A kitchen table, a bed and dresser for my room, a couch—

There's a knock on the front door. I stop pacing and roll my eyes. Locking himself out really isn't instilling a lot of confidence—

The door swings open before I can answer it.

But it isn't the security guy standing in my new foyer.

It's my ex-husband.

Julian Brooks walks into the house like he owns it, the same way he walks into any place. He casually slides his hands into the pockets of his trousers as he glances around with the kind of confidence I used to admire.

Now I see it for what it really is: arrogance.

"What are you doing here?" I demand.

"This is nice. I like it." He inspects the fireplace before finally letting his eyes wander to me. "I came to speak with you."

Always so goddamn formal.

"About?"

He spreads his hands as if the answer is obvious. "We might be divorced, but I'm not a monster, Christine. I care about how you're doing. I know your life has been much more uprooted than mine from this. Yours and Casey's. I wanted to see if there was anything I could do to help." He looks around the empty house again. "I know a guy—we could have this place furnished by the end of tomorrow."

I grind my teeth, loathing myself for considering it, even for a moment. It would make my life so much easier.

But I don't want to take anything else from him.

As if he can see it in my eyes, he adds, "You picked out a lot of the furniture in our home. At least take a few of the pieces that you like."

I cross my arms over my chest. "I appreciate the offer, but we're fine."

I don't need a reminder of him and our time together every time I walk in here. This is supposed to be a fresh start, a clean slate.

At least, as much of one as I'm going to get in this town.

He sighs like I'm being a difficult child, the way he did a million times over the course of our marriage.

It took me a while to figure out exactly what had been my breaking point, but it was this. These little things, little moments.

Being looked at like a fly, like a nuisance, in your own house, it eats away at you. At first, I thought maybe I wouldn't mind. You can't grow up with my mother and not get used to going without attention and affection. But another part of me, some small, young piece still lingering in the back of my mind, thought if I could figure out what he wanted, if I could master whatever role he wanted me to play, then I could earn some respect. Maybe even love.

So I overcompensated. For years. Always happy, always helpful, always supportive.

Until one day I just...couldn't do it anymore.

When I filed for divorce, he'd acted blindsided, absolutely bewildered.

Because for him, nothing had changed. Our relationship was the way it always had been. The only part of the equation that was different was me, now with a fully developed prefrontal cortex and a desperation for there to be *more* for my life.

To anyone else, it might look like he's being nice now. But

I've had a front-row seat to the way he operates for the past eight years. This is how he handles everything, how he smooths things over. Throw enough money at a problem and you're excused from any responsibility.

"Well, the offer stands if you ever change your mind. I also wanted to come by and let you know I'll be heading out of town tomorrow—"

"That's your day with Casey."

"Right. Well." He puts his hands in his pockets again. "He's still welcome to come to the house if you need the weekend off. I can keep the nanny around. Tell him we'll have to plan for next weekend instead."

"That's *my* weekend with him."

"What difference does it make?" He screws up his face in a way that's eerily similar to when Casey does it.

"The difference is you didn't *ask* me to switch weekends with you. You came over here, burst through my door, and *told* me that's what's happening. Then tried to disguise this visit as you wanting to help."

"The trip can't be moved. It's unavoidable, and I'm meeting with some very important investors. What is your reason you need next weekend instead of this one?"

I clamp my teeth together so hard a flash of pain shoots up my jaw. "None. Because my life isn't as important as yours. My schedule, my plans, they'll never measure up to what you deem important. The *reason* is we made a schedule so Casey knows what to expect. The *reason* is consistency for *him*. He's been looking forward to spending time with you all week."

He doesn't even flinch. "As I said, these plans can't be changed. It'll have to be next weekend."

I squeeze my hands into fists at my sides and let out a slow breath through my nose. "You could at least pretend to give a fuck."

His eye twitches—the only crack in his perfect demeanor. He always hated when I swore, said the vulgarity is *unbecoming*. Not *ladylike*. "This conversation is no longer productive."

"It never is."

He calmly turns on his heel and exits the house, and for a moment, I wish I *had* taken some things from his mansion, because at least then I'd have something in here to throw.

Chapter Six
FLETCHER

A week passes, but I don't see Christine again. I thought it was fate running into her like that a second time, but it's probably not statistically significant given the tiny population around here. It's not that I expected her to show up at the High Dive, but after several shifts of constantly checking the door and turning my head at any flash of blond hair in my peripheral vision, I realized I'd hoped.

I shake the water out of my hair as I carry my board to shore. The sun is fully up now, but the beach is relatively empty other than our class and their parents. Despite the waves being disappointing this morning, a few other surfers linger in the water. I'm just thankful the water is warm enough to ditch the wetsuit.

"*Great* first day in the water, everyone!" calls Harry, my co-instructor.

The eight kids in our camp gather round, huddled beneath towels now. The girl who had been riding on my board with me—Erin—stays close to my side as I join the circle.

"You did great out there," I tell her as I crouch to help

unclip her life vest. "I think you even could've managed your own board."

She quickly shakes her head, and I smile.

"Erin, by the end of this week, *you're* going to be kicking me out of your way."

She gives me a slow smile back. She's seven, the youngest this camp allows, and most of the other kids are at least two years older than her. Despite how shy she's been around this group, she was *not* shy in that water. She wants to use me as a security blanket for the week? Fine. But she stopped needing me after that first wave.

"We'll see you all tomorrow, same time!" calls Harry.

"Sweetie, you did so good! Did you have fun?" Erin's mom leans down and scoops her into a hug. Erin buries her face in her mom's neck as she nods, then peeks at me over her shoulder.

I grin at her then meet her mom's eyes. "Think you've got a budding pro athlete there."

"Thank you so much for staying with her all day," her mom says quietly.

We usually do the first few rides with the kids as they build their confidence—not the entire class—but it's easy to tell whether pushing a kid out of their comfort zone on the first day is going to help or hurt.

"Happy to do it. We had fun today, didn't we?" I hold up my hand for a high-five, and she gives me that same shy smile as she smacks her little hand against mine. "See you guys tomorrow!"

They both wave as they head to the parking lot, and I linger around to answer the other parents' questions until it's just me and Harry left.

"You did good today, kid," he says as he starts loading the boards into the storage trailer.

I roll my eyes. He's the only one who can get away with calling me that. Honestly, I'm surprised he's still teaching this camp. He started it back when I would've been young enough to be a student and brought me on as his assistant a few years ago. I actually have no idea how old he is. He could be fifty or seventy—he's got that look to him where it's impossible to tell.

"You too, old man."

He grins. "Still better looking than you."

"No doubt about that. Must be the real reason this class is always sold out. All the moms are here to see you."

"See, now you're getting it. Go on, go on." He waves me off as I try to help with the boards. "Don't pay you enough for that. Go get a life."

"You sure?"

"Don't be late tomorrow," he grunts.

"Harry, I have never once been late."

He glares as I heft up my board. "And you better not start now."

The bar is absolutely dead tonight. Uncharacteristically so. After a few hours with both Anna and me behind the bar, and less than a dozen patrons, they finally make the call and cut me. Anna's a few years younger and saving up for her next semester of school, so I don't mind. She needs the money more.

"Lucky bastard," Anna mutters under her breath with a smile.

"Is that your way of saying you'll miss me?" I bat my eyelashes as I untie my apron, but freeze as the front door slides open.

And in walks a wildly out-of-place blonde.

"Anna, grab me a beer and a glass of Riesling."

She stares at me like I've started speaking German.

"Please?"

She shakes her head as she turns away for a cup. "You're going to waste your freedom and *stay?*"

Christine slides onto one of the last stools tucked in the corner, one that's mostly hidden from the front door by the bar. I don't think she's seen me yet.

But she's about to.

Anna slides me the drinks and shakes her head again as she follows my gaze.

I rip the apron the rest of the way off, step around the bar, and head that way.

Christine frowns like she's about to tell me to leave her the hell alone, but she pauses with her mouth open, her eyes softening when she takes in my face.

"Oh. Hi."

I give her a half smile and gesture to the seat beside her. "Do you mind?"

She hesitates and chews on the inside of her cheek as she looks from me to the drinks to the stool. But then, finally, she nods.

I slide the glass to her. "Hope I didn't get it wrong."

A nearly invisible smile brushes her lips as she takes a sip. "You're not making them tonight?"

I gesture around us. "No need for two of us back there, it seems. Speaking of, what the hell are you doing here?"

She shrugs. "Maybe I like it here."

"Not even our regulars like it here."

She laughs, but that tension in her face doesn't relent. She takes another long drink of her wine, and her jaw works as she sets the glass on the bar.

Gone is the heavy sadness from the first time I saw her.

No, tonight she's *angry*.

She keeps her hand wrapped around her glass, and that gigantic ring is nowhere to be found.

"What the hell are *you* still doing here if you don't have to work?" she asks.

I hold her gaze, my smile involuntary. "Was on my way out, actually. But something caught my eye."

She stares at me like I'm a puzzle she's trying to solve, her eyes darting between mine then tracing over the rest of my face. She does it blatantly, completely unashamed. And I'm perfectly happy to sit here and let her if it means I get to do the same to her.

There's just something so interesting about her eyes. Something *more* behind them, something I've never seen in anyone else. I can practically see the waves of thoughts churning beyond the surface, and I want to pluck them out one by one until I've untangled them all.

It's hard to breathe when she looks at me this intensely, hard not to drift closer until my knee brushes hers.

But she doesn't pull away.

She leans in closer too, turning on her stool until we're facing each other and her legs fit between mine. She shifts, her leg pressing into my inner thigh, and I inhale sharply.

Her little smirk says she knows exactly what she's doing.

I sip my beer. She sips her wine.

We say nothing at all, but neither of us breaks the eye contact.

"This bar does kind of suck," she finally says, then tilts her glass back and finishes her wine in one gulp. "The one at my hotel is much nicer. Have you seen it?"

I shake my head.

"Would you like to?"

Chapter Seven
CHRISTINE

We don't go to the bar. Barely even spare it a glance.

Fletcher drove us here in my car so I wouldn't have to go back for it, and from the moment he opens my door for me to when we step into the elevator, he doesn't take his hand off my lower back.

I always hated when Julian would do it. Something about it felt like he was claiming me, steering me around parties like a tool to be used and shown off.

Fletcher's touch doesn't feel anything like that. If anything it feels…protective.

I hadn't planned on stopping in the High Dive tonight. But since it's *finally* Julian's weekend with Casey—the first time he's spent with him since we finalized everything nearly a month ago—I thought I'd treat myself to a sunset yoga class.

The studio down the street has beautiful floor-to-ceiling windows that face west—which is why their sunset class is always fully booked for a month in advance. Scoring a spot felt like a small miracle.

But there was not an ounce of zen to be found in that room.

From the moment I arrived until the end of class, I could *feel* the daggers being glared at me.

Even the instructor pretended not to see me as I walked in, and she never came over to compliment my form the way she used to.

No one talked to me. No one looked me in the eyes.

No one was outwardly *hostile*, but that's what made it so much worse.

The silence.

No one was even willing to put their mat next to mine.

It felt like being the only person not chosen in elementary gym class all over again.

That paired with getting booted from book club, the gossipy, self-important moms at Casey's summer camp drop-offs, and Julian's smug little face in my fresh-start house—I could've fucking screamed in the middle of downward facing dog.

So then I was driving home, and I passed the High Dive, and before I knew it, I was pulling into the lot.

I told myself it was for a drink. To blow off some steam.

But once I felt the overwhelming relief when I saw Fletcher...I couldn't lie to myself anymore.

This is what I walked into that bar for.

I don't wait for him to make a move—the moment we step into my hotel room, I shove him against the wall, fist my hands in his shirt, and crush my lips to his.

If he's surprised by this, he doesn't show it at all. He kisses me back just as fiercely, like he has something he wants to drown out too. One hand comes up to protect the back of my head as he steps forward and presses us against the opposite wall.

A challenge then. He's not going to give up control here easily.

His body cages me in as he kisses me in a way that has me gasping for air. His teeth, his tongue, his lips—*fuck* does he know how to use them.

He spreads my legs with his knee, and when I slide my hands up his chest, he seizes my wrists before I can get far and pins them over my head.

"This is purely a one-night thing," I breathe.

He pulls back just enough to meet my eyes and smiles like he doesn't believe that for a second.

I wish I could blame it on being drunk. But one glass of wine in? I'm barely even buzzed.

No, the fact of the matter is, I haven't been able to stop thinking about him since that first night at the bar.

I don't know what someone his age is doing spending time with me, and I don't care. My ego has taken a few too many blows this week, and I just need to get this out of my system.

That's all.

I arch my back to let my breasts brush his chest, but I don't get far before his hips pin me to the wall. He smirks against my lips. "You think you're in charge here?"

"You think you are?"

He bites my bottom lip, hard, then sweeps his hands around my ass and hefts me into his arms before I have the chance to catch my breath.

Instead of the bed I'm expecting, he sets me on the dresser and stands between my legs.

The stubborn part of me wants to keep fighting back, but as his tongue sweeps into my mouth and he deepens the kiss, I can't help it. I melt into him. And I think, for once in my life, I'd let someone tell me what to do.

Think I might even like it.

"Hold on to the back of the dresser."

I do it without hesitation, and he lowers to his knees. He

holds my gaze as his hands slide up the sides of my thighs beneath my dress, then hook around the waistband of my panties.

My chest heaves in anticipation, and he kisses the inside of my knee, then a little higher, higher. I hold my breath, but instead of continuing his path, he starts over on the other side.

I swallow hard, my fingers digging into the wood behind me.

"Chris?" he asks, his expression suddenly serious. "Are you sure?"

The sight of him on his knees and looking up at me through his lashes like that has me fighting the urge to press my thighs together.

"I'm sure."

His answering smile is full of wicked promises as he pushes my dress up to my hips, baring me to him. "Are you holding on?"

I nod.

He hooks his arms under my knees, yanks me to the edge of the dresser, then lowers his mouth to me.

I gasp at the sure sweep of his tongue, and he tightens his arms around my hips, holding me still and bracing my legs over his shoulders.

There is nothing uncertain or shy about his movements. The way he uses his tongue is downright depraved. Sounds I've never heard come out of me before fill the room—whimpers, gasps, moans, and strange combinations of all three.

He eases off as he slides a finger inside, stroking me in all the right places like he already knows my body like the back of his hand.

I let out a startled gasp as his mouth crashes against mine, his tongue claiming my mouth as thoroughly as it claimed my pussy. But just as his fingers start to push me to the edge, he eases back, and I let out a frustrated groan.

"Not yet," he whispers against my mouth with a smile. "See, I have some questions. And I have a feeling you might need a little extra motivation. If you want to come, answer me."

I stare into his eyes, breathless. "What questions?"

He kisses my jaw, my throat, the side of my neck. "I want to know every single thing you like. Even the ones you've never dared to admit out loud. The things you think about when you get yourself off."

He thrusts his fingers in deeper, harder, and my head falls back with a moan.

He hums and slides the strap of my dress off my shoulder, exposing one of my breasts. "I'll start off easy." He flicks my nipple with his tongue, and I shiver. "I think you like having me in control right now. Is that right?"

I whimper as he grinds the heel of his hand against my clit.

I nod.

"Out loud."

"Yes," I gasp.

He slowly trails his mouth across my chest until he slides the strap off my other shoulder.

"And I don't think you want me to be gentle with you tonight. Is that right?"

"Yes."

He takes my other nipple in his mouth and pulls lightly with his teeth.

I'm trembling against him, and I know he can feel it. Knows I will tell him anything he wants right now.

"And if I do this...?" He winds his fist around my hair and tugs gently.

I moan low in my throat. "Yes."

"And this..." He trails his fingers down my neck, then slowly wraps them around my throat.

"Yes."

He runs his nose along the side of my throat as his fingers hit that spot inside of me in a perfect rhythm. I lock my teeth together, so fucking close to the edge I feel it in the soles of my feet, the base of my spine.

"If I spank you?" he asks lowly in my ear.

I gulp, fighting to pull breath into my lungs. "Yes."

"Only your ass?"

I shake my head. "Anywhere but my...face." My legs shake around him, and I dig my nails into the wood so hard I'll probably leave marks. "Fuck, please...*please* don't stop."

"Am I missing anything?" He presses his forehead to mine, forcing me to look at him. "Tell me the truth. Tell me what you want, Chris."

"I want..." My eyes roll back with a groan. The heat inside me burns and blazes as it spreads, drowning out every other sensation. I can't—

"Tell me or I stop."

"...you to keep talking," I gasp.

He seals his mouth over mine as his fingers finally push me over the edge. The release is dizzying, devastating. It's all-consuming enough that I forget where I am. I forget *who* I am. He eagerly swallows each moan in a tangle of tongues and teeth.

"You like that?" he murmurs against my lips, and I can *feel* him smiling. "You like me talking to you?"

I moan as his thumb slowly works my clit to help me back down.

One arm wraps around my waist, holding me to him as I go limp. I release the dresser, and my fingers ache from holding on so tightly.

"Put your arms around my neck," he says.

I slide my hands over his shoulders, and then he's carrying me to the bed. He kisses me again, slower, softer this time, and a corner of his mouth lifts.

"I'll let you choose this one. How do you want me, Chris?"

He sets me on my feet, and I turn, then look up at him over my shoulder. "My zipper?"

He sifts through the dress bunched around my waist. It pools to my feet, and I smile in satisfaction when I hear his breath hitch.

Slowly, I crawl onto the bed, giving him a good, long look before keeping my knees firmly planted, then sliding my arms forward until my face meets the bed.

He lets out a curse under his breath, followed by the sound of him shoving his zipper down and discarding his pants. I press my cheek into the mattress to look at him, the word *condom* on the tip of my tongue, but he already has the packet in his hands.

My mouth goes dry at the sight of him. He's standing at the edge of the bed as he rips the foil open, now as naked as I am, and very visibly as hard as I am wet. And the *muscles* on him. His abs, his chest, his arms. I could tell how well defined they were from touching him, but seeing it is an entirely different story.

Maybe I want a different position after all. One with a better view...

But then he's on his knees behind me, and my eyes flutter shut as he runs the hard length of him along my pussy, pressing harder as he reaches my clit. He groans low in his chest as he lines himself up with my entrance and presses in an inch, then another.

"You're going to fucking ruin me," he rasps, then shoves the rest of the way in.

Chapter Eight
FLETCHER

Nothing has ever felt better than this. Nothing has ever *looked* better than Christine on her hands and knees for me. I repeatedly have to pause and look up at the ceiling to keep it together.

This is purely a one-night thing?

I'm going to fuck those words right out of her mouth.

And the sounds she makes as I grip her hips and thrust into her with a punishing kind of force?

Addicting. Intoxicating.

I tried easing off at first, worried it was too rough, and she immediately gasped, "Harder."

This girl is going to kill me.

I grab her hair at the roots and pull her head up from the pillow. She gasps and braces her hands beneath her.

She moans, and I lean down until my lips brush her ear. "Do you have any idea how gorgeous you look taking my dick like this? How fucking wet you are for me?"

I shove her head down to the pillow before she can

respond, and she whimpers and wiggles her hips. I release her hair in favor of strumming her clit and am rewarded with a sharp intake of breath and her pussy clenching so fucking tight around me that I have to pause.

"More," she breathes. *"More."*

I grip her hips, angling them farther up, and sink as deep into her as I can. I give her ass a tentative slap, testing how hard she likes it. She wiggles her hips again like an invitation. I do the other side—once, twice, until her perfect skin turns a pretty red for me—and she moans.

She's so goddamn responsive, so clear about what she likes. Seeing her come once, feeling it around my fingers, hearing the small, desperate sounds she made, it wasn't anywhere close to enough.

I brace my arms on either side of her face as I lean over her, driving in with a deep, slow pace. Her hands scramble for purchase along the mattress, and I take them both in mine, intertwining our fingers and pinning them to the pillow.

"You feel so good, Chris," I rasp. "So fucking good."

She turns her head, those ocean-blue eyes locking with mine, and it makes my stomach flip. The heat is still there, the lust, but there's a vulnerability that hadn't been there before. I lean closer until my nose brushes hers. I kiss her cheek, her jaw, before landing on her mouth. Our breath mingles together as I pick up the pace, just slightly.

I can tell she's close by the shaking in her legs, the way her breaths are growing ragged and fast. I don't pull back, keeping our faces less than an inch away, and tighten my hands around hers.

She squeezes back.

It starts with a small choked sound in the back of her throat, and then she's unraveling, her pussy clenching so tightly around me I hiss out a breath through my teeth. She buries her face in the pillow as she comes.

I give her a moment to catch her breath, but only a moment.

When I flip her onto her back, she lets out a gasping laugh.

"You need to tap out?"

She shakes her head, already reaching for me as I lean over her and brace my hands on either side of her face. She starts with my chest, slowly winding her fingers across my skin lower, lower.

My breath hitches as she closes her fist around my dick. She bites her lip as she slowly—fucking agonizingly slowly—strokes her hand up and down.

I let out a breathless laugh. I knew she gave up control a little too easily earlier. "You've been humoring me."

Her smile widens, and she twists her hand in a way that would make me fall to my knees if I wasn't already there.

"You planning on torturing me all night?" I force out through my teeth.

"Maybe I have some questions of my own."

I groan as she tightens her grip and quickens her pace. She has no fucking idea how close she has me. Or maybe she does. I have a feeling she knows exactly what she's doing.

"Ask me," I grit out.

She pushes herself up until our lips brush. "Do you need me to submit to you for you to get off?" she whispers.

"No."

She hums, her hand slowing to her original pace. "But you like it."

"Yes."

She hums again. "And if you could have me any way you wanted to right now, how would that be?"

"I can show you better than I can tell you."

Before she can respond, I grab her hips and pull her farther down the bed. She gasps in surprise as she lands, and I prop one of her legs on my shoulder. Her head rolls back with a moan as I repeatedly glide my dick along her pussy and over her clit.

We groan at the same time as I push inside until she takes every last inch of me. She grabs on to my arms as I slowly pull all the way out, then thrust in with as much force as I can muster.

I don't think either of us will last long this way, but I tangle one of my fists in her hair and lean close until we share the same breath, forcing her eyes to stay on mine. She stares right back, even as her breaths turn to pants, to whimpers.

Feeling her come again shoves me over the edge too, but I keep giving her everything I have until I physically can't go anymore.

I slump onto her but catch myself before letting her feel the full extent of my weight. My heart is pounding—*sprinting*—in my chest, and I roll onto my side. She's still breathless and trembling as I wrap my arms around her, and I can't help but notice how perfectly she fits against me.

The silence falls comfortably around us, and I trace my fingers along the back of her hand. After a moment, she sighs, leans back, and unleashes those eyes on me. No matter how much she does it, I find myself catching my breath every time.

"So…" She bites her lip and smiles. "How long until you can do that again?"

I throw my head back with a laugh. Letting me take over tonight was definitely her humoring me. But I like a girl who keeps me on my toes.

Might have to run down and see if that shop in the lobby

has more condoms then. Hell, this place looks fancy enough to deliver them to the room if you call.

Cradling the back of her head with my hand, I kiss her, slow and deep. A low hum escapes my throat as her lips part for me and her tongue sweeps into my mouth.

"Do you need more?" I murmur against her lips. "I'm more than happy to get back to work."

She nips playfully at my bottom lip and pulls back with a smirk and a shake of her head. "That was really…"

I raise my eyebrows as she trails off. *Mind-blowing? Awful? Underwhelming?* Too many directions that sentence could go.

"I just hope you enjoyed that as much as I did," she finishes.

I can't help the unintelligible noise that gets caught in the back of my throat. She's worried *I* didn't enjoy myself?

I laugh and cup her cheek, hoping she can see how much I mean it in my eyes. "I hope *you* enjoyed that as much as I did."

She pushes me onto my back, throws a leg over my hips, and climbs on top of me. I immediately regret not insisting on this position tonight. *Good God.*

There aren't words to describe her. *Perfect* feels too mundane, too overused. She's exquisite in a striking, demanding way. The kind of woman who inspires myths about creatures so beautiful they could lure men to their deaths with just one glance.

I run my hands up and down her legs, and her skin is so goddamn soft. She traces my chest with her fingertips, a small wrinkle forming between her eyebrows like she's thinking hard about something.

And it hits me how much I don't want to leave yet. Not now. Not in an hour. Not in the middle of the night once she falls asleep.

"Chris?"

Her eyes flick up to mine.

I squeeze her thighs. "You said this was a one-night thing. That means the whole night, right?"

She hums like she's considering it.

I sit up and wrap my arms around her waist, pulling her close until our faces are an inch away.

She narrows her eyes, and a slow smile tugs at her lips. "Okay. You can have the whole night."

Chapter Nine
CHRISTINE

I throw my head back with a shameless moan, then lick my lips for good measure. "This is the best veggie burger I've ever tasted."

"Let me see." Fletcher leans over and takes a bite out of the opposite side. "Mm." He bobs his head as he swallows, and I swat him away.

"You have your own food!" I point to his pizza that he's taken only a few bites of.

He smiles and takes one of my fries too.

I grab my plate to move to the other side of the bed, but he grabs my legs before I can get very far, drapes them across his lap, and pins them there.

"Careful." He tilts my plate before the ketchup can run off and splatter all over my robe. The very nice, very expensive white robe I'd definitely have to pay for if I ruined it.

Some movie neither of us has been paying attention to plays on the TV in the background, and I eye the remaining plates on the tray by the foot of the bed. That chocolate cake looks divine. And the bottle of white wine with it? I could *die*.

There's also a handful of condoms beside it—who would've thought you could have those delivered?—as well as a credit card on top of a receipt.

I narrow my eyes. That is not my card. I'd gone to the bathroom to freshen up while he ordered, but I figured it would automatically get charged to the room. When did he...?

"Can I ask you a personal question?"

I turn back to him, and he's watching me with his head leaning against the wall, the same ease in his expression firmly in place despite the abrupt subject change.

I shrug and pick at my fries. "Guess that depends on what it is."

"Tell me about your family."

I grimace internally, and my fingers still on my plate. *Of all questions.* Not that it's not a perfectly normal thing to ask someone, but it feels like I just stepped into a minefield. "Not much to say, really."

That's not true, but it's also not exactly a light conversation. And it's not something I talk about.

But then again, no one's ever really asked me.

No one who wanted the truthful answer.

The first person who comes to mind with the word *family* is Casey, but I'm not going to sit here and talk about my son with a one-night stand. Not that Fletcher doesn't already know I have a kid, but *knowing* and *talking* about it while we're still naked are two different things.

Silence falls between us, and when I glance at him, a small crease has formed between his eyebrows.

"You don't have to talk about it if you don't want to. I just want to know more about you."

I give him a humorless smile. "It's not...it's just a lot."

His eyes flick between mine. "Tell me anyway."

I don't know what makes me say it—maybe knowing this is

only for one night lowers the stakes. Or maybe there's something about him that makes this easier to say.

"Well, my parents met in high school. My mom got pregnant with me when she was seventeen, and they got married." I roll a fry between my fingers until it turns to mush. "My dad took off before I turned one. We never heard from him again. My mom's parents kicked her out when she found out she was pregnant, so then it was just me and her."

The words come out hollow, unemotional. As if I'm talking about someone else. And in a lot of ways, that's what it feels like. That part of my life, that version of me, sometimes I push her so far into the corners of my mind that I forget she's lurking back there.

Fletcher takes a deep breath, and he lays his hand gently on my leg. He says nothing, but I have his full attention.

"We did okay...sometimes. DV shelters let us stay for a few months here and there. She managed to get an apartment for a few years. Sometimes we lived out of the car, on food stamps, you name it. Almost ended up in the system a few times—I honestly don't know how I didn't. Eventually, she started dating again, and when she realized we could move in with whatever guy she was seeing, that started to be the new normal."

I don't know why my heart is racing just talking about it, like I can *feel* the adrenaline flooding my veins. I take a deep breath and shake my head a little. There's a lot that happened that I haven't let myself think about in a long time.

Back into the corner. Just push it back into the corner.

Fletcher squeezes my knee.

"I left when I was sixteen." I run my tongue along the inside of my teeth and shrug. "So that's my sob story."

There's no pity in his eyes, just a softness. "Do you still talk to your mom?"

"Not since the day I left."

He rubs his thumb back and forth on my leg. "Which I know probably sounds awful—"

"It doesn't," he says immediately.

"I have a lot of empathy for her. Especially now being a mom. But on the other hand...now being a mom..." I take a deep breath and shake my head. "There's a lot I can't forgive her for."

"Yeah," he says softly. "It's hard knowing they did the best they could, but you also deserved better."

That really is what it comes down to. And then the guilt that comes with thinking it wasn't good enough even when they were trying their best.

I clear my throat. "Did you grow up around here?"

He presses his lips together and gives me a smile I don't quite understand. It's not sad, exactly. But it's like I'm seeing a piece of myself reflected back.

"Uh, no. My biological parents were from PA." His eyes flick from mine to his hands on my legs. "They both died of an overdose when I was two."

I go still. "Were you—were you there?"

He nods once. "Not that I remember it, but yeah. They think it took at least twelve hours until someone called it in and the police found me."

My stomach drops, and I cover my mouth with my hand without thinking. I can't help it. I picture Casey at that age being alone for that long...*seeing* his parents like that, not being able to get them to respond...

"Ended up in the foster system. Bounced around about a dozen different families until I was thirteen." He gives me a small smirk. "Also ran away from home—but with a few other kids. Ended up with a new family here about a year later. They're great. They, uh, they actually legally adopted me when

I was seventeen." The tension in his face smooths out into a small smile, and he shrugs. "I consider them my parents. We're still very close."

"The home here—were there any other kids there with you?"

A strange shadow passes over his eyes, but then it's gone just as quickly. "Just me. So that's *my* sob story."

"So what you're saying is we're both thoroughly fucked-up."

He grins, wraps an arm around me, and pulls me closer. "Oh, definitely."

I lean against his chest, and he rests his chin on the top of my head. It feels so natural, so normal.

So…not what a one-night stand should be.

"Hey, Chris?" says Fletcher, his voice light and carefree again.

"Hm?"

"I'm dying to break into that cake."

"Oh, thank God." I all but lunge for the plate.

I don't know what time we go to sleep. Well after midnight. We make good use out of every last one of those condoms, and afterward, we just…talk. And laugh. And eat. And lie together and watch whatever comes up on the TV.

And it's like we've done this a thousand times before.

I inhale sharply and startle awake.

"Sorry, sorry," Fletcher whispers and smooths his hand over my hair.

I try to blink the blurriness out of my eyes, but the room is dark.

"What's going on—?"

"You can go back to sleep. I just have to get to work, and I didn't want to leave without saying goodbye."

Finally, his face swims into focus. "What…time is it?"

"About 4:30."

I groan and bury my face in the pillow. "Do you…? I can drive you to your car…?"

He chuckles. "No, no. I've got it."

"Are you sure?"

"Yeah, it's just a few blocks." He runs his hand over my hair again as I peer up at him. He smiles softly. "I had a really, really nice time."

I smile back. "Me too."

He hesitates like he wants to say more, but in the end, he stands and collects his wallet and keys from the dresser.

I roll over and watch as he leaves, a knot tightening in my stomach.

But he pauses before opening the door and meets my eyes. "I know this was just for the night, but if you change your mind, you have my number. I just want to be clear from my end…the door's open."

I don't know how to respond, and he doesn't wait for me to.

But as the door closes behind him, I find myself smiling.

Chapter Ten
FLETCHER

"Fletcher! Fletcher, please," a small voice wails somewhere near my ear.

I blink my eyes open, and they immediately start to burn. At first I think my vision is blurry from sleep, but no matter how much I rub my eyes, they don't clear.

I cough again, and once I start, it's hard to stop. Is that smoke?

"Fletch!" A hand tugs on mine, and I look down to see two wide brown eyes staring up at me.

"Jacks?" She's still in her matching purple butterfly PJs, her hair in the messy braids I tried to do for her before bed.

She tugs urgently on my sleeve. "Fire. Fire."

Fire?

That finally banishes the lingering sleep from my brain. I shove myself out of bed, keeping one hand in hers, and hurry toward the door.

"Did you wake the others?" I ask.

Jacks coughs and shakes her head. "You first."

I hunch low as I drag the two of us through the hall. Smoke sits in the air, and sweat breaks out along every inch of exposed skin. I go to

Joan and Bob's room first, but their bed is empty. Did they even come home last night? I thought I'd heard them drunkenly stumbling through the door around midnight.

...which means they're probably passed out on the couches downstairs. Shit.

Jacks starts to cry behind me, and I tighten my hand around hers. "Come on. Let's find Henry and Lucy. Penny's at a sleepover, right?"

"I think so."

We turn for the opposite end of the hall where the youngest kids share a room. It feels like it's getting hotter in here by the second. "We need to call 911. Can you find the phone?"

She digs her fingers into my arm, and I turn to her. Her eyes are wide, panicked. She might be the second oldest in the house, but she's still only eight. I can't ask her to split up. We'll have to hope a neighbor notices and calls.

"Okay, okay." I tighten my hand around hers to show I'm not letting go, then pull up the collar of my shirt to cover my nose and mouth and gesture for her to do the same.

I have no idea where the fire is coming from, but if I had to guess, it's downstairs. Shouldn't a smoke detector be going off at this point or something? The idiots probably disabled them so they'd stop going off while they smoked in here.

I shoulder the kids' door open but freeze at the sight of more empty beds. Where the hell—

"Fletcher!" Lucy's voice. She and Henry are huddled together beneath one of the beds.

"Come on, come on." I wave urgently for them to join us, and they stumble out. Jacks takes Henry's hand, but Lucy is crying so hard now that she's going to be impossible to reason with. There's no way she'll move on her own.

"Okay, okay." I gather her in my arms, and she tucks her face against my neck.

I try to stay low as we all head for the stairs to get beneath the smoke, but my lungs are still protesting every breath. We need to get out. And soon.

I glance over the side of the banister and stifle a curse. Flames are jumping from curtain to curtain in the TV room. And sitting in the center of it all is a stockpile of Bob's Scotch bottles. He's passed out on the recliner, his wife across from him on the sofa, a bottle of vodka in her hand. Cigarettes are discarded on the floor all around them. I don't think I could wake them up now if I tried.

I push Jacks and Henry onto the stairs in front of me. "Go! Front door. Now!"

Even as I say it, the fire spreads, the flames eating up everything in their path.

"Mr. Teddy!" Lucy wails and struggles against my arms.

Jesus Christ, we are not going back for the bear.

Henry's head pops up, eyes round. Oh God, this is going to be a domino effect. I throw my other arm around his waist before he can make a run for it and yank him up as he screams for his blanket.

"Jacks!" I yell. "Door!"

Both kids are screaming and thrashing against me now. Jacks takes the stairs two at a time and makes it to the door first.

"Use your shirt! Don't touch the handle!"

She wraps her sleeve around her hand before yanking on the door, but it doesn't open.

I set Lucy down. Just for a second. Just to help with the lock.

But it's long enough.

She turns and darts back up the stairs.

Chapter Eleven
CHRISTINE

"Lady, you gonna pay or what?"

I snap back to the man standing on the sidewalk in front of me—squat, balding, and wearing a shirt far too small to cover his bulging stomach.

Definitely *not* the twenty-three-year-old who's taken up permanent residence in my thoughts for the past week. It's entirely involuntary. I'll just be going on with my day when a flash of that night will appear—something small. A moment. A groan. A whisper.

Or, today, as chance would have it, his hand slapping my ass.

I clear my throat and shake my head, my brain not at all liking connecting the sensation with the man standing in front of me.

"Here." I thrust the stack of bills toward him, thinking that'll be the end of it, but then he licks a finger and slowly starts to count. "It's all there," I say, utterly failing at keeping the impatience from my voice.

He pauses halfway through the stack, shakes his head, then starts again from the beginning.

I turn away, inspecting the bungee cords securing the couch to the bed of the truck. Not that I'd be able to tell if there was something wrong. His son—who slipped back into their house the moment they finished strapping the couch in—seemed to know what he was doing though.

"All right," grunts the man behind me. "All here."

Like I said.

"Pleasure doing business with you."

I say nothing back because I am not a liar. I'm just glad the couch looks like the picture online. When I pulled up and saw him...well, I'll admit I had my doubts.

It's not like this is my first rodeo. Once I graduated from living out of my car at eighteen, my first place was furnished almost exclusively with secondhand marketplace finds and more than one piece of furniture I picked up off the side of the road.

But a near decade of living on the other side of the tracks has a funny way of making you forget.

At least Liam loaned me his truck for the day, otherwise there's no way I'd be able to get this thing home. I leave the couch in the truck after I pull in the driveway since Liam offered to help carry it in when he swings by to swap our cars out.

I was never particularly close with Julian's other children, seeing as they were all mostly adults and moved out before he and I even met. So the complete radio silence from them after the divorce wasn't unexpected.

But Liam sticking around was.

He wasn't rude, but I knew he never warmed up to me. But despite being twenty years older than Casey, he's always been the best with him, so whether *he* liked *me* or not, I've had a soft spot for him.

Maybe I also see a little of myself in him. Someone else who never *quite* belonged in that house. The difference, of course, being I spent the last eight years doing everything in my power to earn my way in, and he did everything in his power to fight his way out.

I carry the bags from my earlier errands inside and dump them on the kitchen counter. I forgot how much *stuff* you need in a house—plates, utensils, trash cans, scissors, first aid kit, laundry baskets, extra sheets, towels. I went to the store to grab a few things…then realized I didn't have *anything* and started throwing things into my cart at random.

I'm down to unpacking the last bag when the doorbell rings. I barely have the door open before Casey cries out, "Mom, can-I-take-Liam's-skate-camp?"

I blink, his voice blending into one long word.

Liam uncrosses his arms and ruffles Casey's hair with a smirk. "A friend and I are doing a skating camp for the next three weeks. Ages seven to ten."

"Which means I'm old enough now!" cries Casey.

"We have one spot left," adds Liam. "It starts next week."

"So can I do it? Art camp ends this week!"

My eyes ping-pong between the two of them as I try not to let my immediate reaction show on my face. As much as I like Liam, I don't necessarily want Casey following in his footsteps, at least where the dozens of tattoos and flipping around on a flimsy little board are concerned.

"Why don't you go on inside, buddy?" says Liam.

Casey's head pops up as if something brilliant occurred to him. "Mom, did you get the fruit snacks?"

I chuckle a little. "Left a pack on the table for you."

"Yes!"

He darts inside without another word, and my eyes roll back to meet Liam's.

"I promise it's age appropriate and safe. They all wear helmets and a million pads, and we don't do any fancy tricks." He lifts his hands. "Up to you." He jabs a thumb over his shoulder. "Want help bringing it in now? I'll do the heavy lifting, but I'll need you to balance out the other side."

"You think it'll fit through the door okay?"

He tilts his head to inspect it, then shrugs. "Hopefully."

I snort and follow him out to the truck. "Thanks again, Liam."

He waves me off as he unfastens the bungee cords. "It's no problem."

"Where's Gracie today?"

The same goofy smile he always gets when someone says her name appears. I don't think he realizes he does it. "She's in the city today and tomorrow. I'm driving up this weekend, then she'll come back with me for the week."

I remember hearing something about the two of them getting an apartment together in Philly last month, though Liam kept his apartment around here too so they could split their time. "Complicated little schedule you've got going on."

He shrugs, that smile still in place. "We make it work. Furniture search seems to be going well."

"It's never-ending."

Once we manage to get the couch down, he heads backward toward the house and I shuffle along after him.

"In the room with the fireplace?" he calls.

"Yes!"

It makes it through the door—thank God—and I can't help but grin as we set it down, and I take a few steps back to get a good look. Just like I thought, it's the perfect size for the room.

It's just a love seat—and ideally, I'd like to get something bigger in here eventually—but this is more than enough for me and Casey. That paired with the coffee table I picked up three days ago and the TV we got last week—it almost looks like someone lives here.

Casey skips around the corner, puppy dog eyes in tow. "So…"

I sigh dramatically. "Well, I don't know… I didn't get my hello hug, and now I can't think straight…"

Casey charges in and throws his arms around my middle. "*Please*, Mom. Pretty please. I promise to never forget to make my bed again."

Liam and I share an amused smirk, and if I didn't know any better, I'd swear he was giving me a bit of the puppy dog eyes too. Sharing only one parent, they don't have that many features in common. But in this moment, I don't know if they've ever looked more related.

Admittedly, the camps have been good for Casey. They keep him busy, give him a chance to meet friends. And I'd hate to discourage the one sibling who actually makes an effort to spend time with him.

Casey must know it the moment he's won because he starts excitedly jumping up and down before I even manage to get the words out.

"What time does it start?"

Chapter Twelve
FLETCHER

"Can you start unloading everything?" I call as I tape a big *Sign In Here* sign to one of the picnic tables beside the skate park.

Liam sighs dramatically but jogs to the parking lot without complaint. Gear is included in the cost of the camp, which means my car is one kneepad or child-sized skateboard away from exploding.

I leaf through the binder I've been using to keep all of the forms straight, making sure every kid is accounted for and I have all of the signatures. Since Liam and I are the only ones running this, we capped the camp at eight, the same number from the surfing classes I've been assisting.

It felt very…full circle to host it here, at this skate park. The same skate park where Liam and I met shortly after I'd gotten to Sweetspire. Those first few weeks I camped out here instead of going straight home after school, not sure what to make of my new parents' enthusiasm and kindness. Not sure if I should trust it. They tried to give me my space at the beginning, but it still felt like I always had eyes on me in that house.

After seeing me here a few days in a row—with no board,

and clearly no friends—Liam took me under his wing, even though I was only fourteen and he was seventeen. And knowing Liam now, that is *not* something he does, so I must have looked a terrible kind of pitiful back then.

Then it was only a matter of time until Leo came into the picture. He and Liam have been best friends all their lives, and with anyone else, it could've been a weird situation, trying to integrate myself into an already inseparable friendship. But once I came along, Leo acted as if I'd always been there. The way he welcomed me in was simple and seamless—no over-the-top trying to make me feel welcome—there was just an ease to it as if I'd known him for years. No weirdness about me being the same age as his younger sister either. It was the kind of friendship I hadn't known I needed—hadn't known *existed*.

A car door slams in the distance. I'm expecting Liam, but instead, a blur of bright pink and purple rushes toward me. I grin as Erin reaches the picnic table, a little out of breath, and her mom hurries to catch up.

"Hi, Mr. Fletcher!" She smiles, exposing a new missing tooth.

"Erin! Hey, Mrs. Clarke, how are you?" I shake her hand, then give Erin a fist bump.

"Good, good. We're excited." She wraps an arm around her daughter's shoulders. "She's been talking about this since the moment your surf camp ended."

Erin bounces on the balls of her feet and glances around the skate park, no trace left of the shy, unsure girl she'd been the first day of surf camp a few weeks ago.

"You guys are the first ones here. If you could sign in here…" I turn the binder around and flip to the first page.

"Would it…would it be all right if I stuck around…" Mrs. Clarke looks from me to Erin, her teeth sunk into her bottom lip.

"Of course. I'm sure some of the other parents will want to do the same. Feel free to hang out over here at the tables."

"Mr. Fletcher?"

"Yes, Erin?"

She chews on her lip the same way her mom does. "Am I gonna be the only girl here?"

"Absolutely not!" Liam appears with a grin and a bag slung over each shoulder. "We're split exactly half and half, actually."

Erin's eyes light up.

Liam grunts as he sets the two bags at his feet—one with the elbow and knee pads, one with the boards, which means there's one bag left in the car.

"I'll grab the last one," I say and pat Liam on the back as a few more cars pull into the parking lot.

He salutes me, slides into the picnic table, and waves at the next batch of students rolling in.

I peer at the sky as I head for my car, namely, the dark storm clouds threatening. Hopefully we won't get rained out on the first day. I heft the final bag over my shoulder, shut the trunk, and lock it. I barely make it a step away from the car before I hear someone calling my name.

"Fletcher! Fletcher!" I turn as Casey lunges in for a hug.

"Hey, Case!" I drop the bag and lean down to hug him back. "So glad you could—"

My next words shrivel and die in my mouth as I glance up at the woman waiting behind him. Blond hair, shoes far too nice for this part of town, and blue eyes that I haven't been able to get out of my head.

She stares at me, her expression growing more distraught by the second.

"Oh, this is my mom!" Casey pulls back, grins, and takes Christine's hand.

Casey's mom.

Is Christine.

Liam's half brother's mom.

Is Christine.

Mr. Candyman Brooks's ex-wife and Liam's former stepmom is…Christine.

I feel like I need to lie down.

I blink and clear my throat. "Um, go on, Case. Some of the other kids are already here. Liam's signing everyone in at the table."

Casey takes off at a run, but my eyes never leave Christine, not even for a moment. And hers don't leave mine.

The moment Casey's gone, the shock on her face hardens, and anger tightens the lines around her mouth.

"I swear, I had no idea," I say.

"This is your camp," she says slowly.

I nod.

"You're Liam's friend."

Another nod.

She covers her eyes with her hand and turns away.

"Chris—"

She whips around, her eyes steely and her voice sharp as ice. "Don't." But as fast as the anger had come, it's gone again, replaced by…I'm not sure what. Worry? Embarrassment? Her eyebrows pull together as she glances from me to Liam.

"I won't say anything."

Her eyes snap back to me.

"Mom!" calls Casey.

Christine takes a step in that direction. "No one can know about this," she says, her voice barely above a whisper.

"I swear. You don't have anything to worry about."

Even after she's gone, I don't move, not for several moments.

I've spent more time than I care to admit in the past two

weeks thinking about her, wondering if she'd use that number I gave her, hoping for it. Hoping I'd run into her again.

But *this* definitely isn't what I'd been imagining.

Now it feels like every scenario I pictured is turning to ash at my feet. She's sure as fuck never going to see me now. And God, my stomach feels so hollow at the thought.

How did I not put the pieces together before now? If she married Liam's dad seven years ago, I would've been about sixteen. Liam had already graduated by then, and he was still with his ex, who made him drop off the map for a few years. We weren't as close back then. And not running into the other Brookses has never been unusual, seeing as their circle is far above my tax bracket.

Of course I'd known Liam's dad remarried. And I've spent plenty of time with Casey the past few years with how often he's with Liam, but there's no way I could've run into Christine before.

Because I would've remembered *her*.

I scrub a hand over my face, ordering myself to get it together.

By the time I make it back to the sign-in table with the helmets, it looks like everyone else is here, and the parents are helping their kids into their pads. I'm about to step around the table to help when Liam hooks his arm around my elbow and yanks me a few paces away.

"What?"

Liam cocks his head toward Chris, who is currently tightening Casey's kneepads. Her hair looks lighter in the sun. *She* seems lighter now as she talks with Casey, her smiles coming easily. She certainly hadn't given them that freely with me. But I think I liked that. How hard-won it felt when I managed to coax one out.

"You tell me. You guys were having quite the chat in the parking lot."

I snap back to Liam and shake my head. "It was nothing. She just had a few questions about the camp."

The words sound lame, even to me.

"Don't bullshit me. There's a weird vibe. Anyone can see it. What's going on?"

I bristle under the intensity of his stare. I've never been good at keeping things from him, just like he can't keep anything from me. I glance up to find Christine already looking our way, and she quickly turns back to Casey when she catches my eye.

Lowly, I say, "You have to swear not to say anything."

Liam's eyebrows skyrocket.

I sigh. "The day she finalized the divorce, she ended up at the High Dive. Sat there pretty much all day, was really upset. And I listened to her talk. She asked me not to say anything. I'm assuming she's embarrassed and didn't think she'd ever run into me again. And I didn't put it together that she's Casey's mom until now."

It's not a lie. It's leaving out some choice details, sure, but it's not a lie.

Finally, the suspicion on his face eases. "Yeah, all right, I won't say anything."

I pat him on the shoulder and force as carefree of a smile as I can muster. "So, should we get started or what?"

Chapter Thirteen

CHRISTINE

When I got the house a few weeks ago, it felt like it would never come together. It was such a daunting task, starting over from scratch.

Turns out, when you have no life, it goes by pretty fast.

I've spent the most time on Casey's room, despite the likelihood of his interests changing before the end of the year, but I guess that's the fun part. It's the one room in the house in a constant state of change. A blank canvas to play with over and over.

For now, the walls are covered in dinosaurs and shelves upon shelves of his monster trucks. And no matter how many times I tweak the organization, the hands on the clock have barely budged.

I could go to yoga and listen to whispers behind my back for an hour. Or I could sit in a coffee shop while the surrounding tables blatantly stare. Or I could do something monumentally stupid like get drunk in a dive bar in the middle of the afternoon, then somehow find myself in bed with a friend of my former stepson.

I'm already the laughingstock of the town. At that point they'd probably print me in the newspaper—*Local Gold-Digging Whore Turned Cougar*.

Maybe the worst thing about all of my so-called friends falling off the map is…it's not at all surprising. I've seen them turn on other women in town for less.

I was never under the illusion that those relationships were anything more than convenience. Our kids go to the same schools, we frequent the same yoga studio, our husbands golf together, we're members of the same country club. We were bound to run into each other, so we might as well band together.

But it was never deeper than that. And maybe I liked it that way. It's what I'm used to, at least.

In high school, no one wanted to be friends with the girl who barely showered. My mom scared off my childhood friends—or their parents, at least—early on. And after I ran away from home, I didn't stay in one place long enough to form any meaningful relationships.

People come and go. That's just the way life is.

After the tenth time rearranging the trucks, I force myself out of Casey's room with a huff. I can't keep hiding away in this house with nothing to do for days on end. I already feel like I'm losing my damn mind.

When the time to pick up Casey from skate camp rolls around, I hesitate in my car in the parking lot, watching as the other parents collect their kids. A few come and go with little fanfare—just a wave goodbye and straight to the car. Most hang around, high-fiving their kids, watching as they show off their new skills, and talking to the two camp teachers.

The ones I can't stop staring at.

Casey is grinning ear to ear beside a small brunette girl as Liam crouches down to talk to them.

Fletcher smiles along as parents pull him this way and that with a kind of ease that leads me to believe he's done this tons of times before. None of the kids—not a single one—leaves without saying goodbye to him in one way or another. A hug, a high five, a secret handshake. Half the parents practically have to drag their kids away.

He's so...in his element.

I climb out of the car before they can notice me staring and realize Liam's girlfriend, Gracie, is here too. She hangs back a few feet as she gathers the elbow and knee pads and stuffs them in a bag. She looks adorable with her curly blond space buns and overalls. Standing next to Liam—dressed in all black and tattooed from head to toe—the two of them are perfect opposites that somehow make complete sense.

"Mom!" Casey jumps up and down and waves his board around. "Can I show you my new trick? Oh, and this is my new friend Erin." He points at the girl beside him.

"I'd love to see it. Hi, Erin. It's very nice to meet you."

She shrinks away from the attention but smiles. I brace myself as I meet the eyes of the woman I'm assuming is her mother, but she smiles warmly, no trace of the judgment I've grown accustomed to these past few weeks.

"He was the first in the class to get it today, actually."

A jolt of electricity runs through me at Fletcher's voice. Finally, I force myself to meet his eyes. He smiles, everything about it light, casual. Like he hasn't been inside of me. Like he hasn't been dreading this moment all day the way I have, and he probably hasn't. *He* has nothing to feel uncomfortable about. I'm the one who got myself in this weird fucking situation.

Casey runs along and hops on his board. I clench my hands into fists and fight the urge to cover my eyes. He's covered head to toe in pads, but that's still concrete under him and—

He skates along for a few moments, and once his board has basically lost momentum by itself, he pops one side up to brake.

He looks at me over his shoulder with a proud grin.

"Wow!" I beam and crouch down as he comes running over.

"See you tomorrow, Casey!" calls Erin as she and her mom turn for the parking lot.

Casey waves with more enthusiasm than I've ever seen from him when it comes to other kids.

"She seems nice," I say lightly.

"She's really cool! She did a surfing camp with Fletcher too. I want to do that one next!"

"Oh, did she?" I try not to let the absolute horror show on my face. First the death-on-wheels on concrete, now the ocean? This kid is going to give me a heart attack. Whatever happened to the crayons and googly eyes at art camp?

I can't help it. I glance at Fletcher. He teaches surf camp too? I know for a fact Liam doesn't surf, so it sounds like Liam's the one who got roped into this skating camp, not the other way around like I'd thought, for some reason.

How many of these kinds of things does he do?

"I'm so glad to see you!" says Gracie, a little out of breath as she finishes tying off the huge equipment bags. "I'm planning this party for a friend of mine, and that was kind of your thing, right? I just remember how great a job you did at my parents' Thanksgiving last year, and then the whole Smart Sweets event... Anyway, any chance you'd want to help out? It's for next weekend. I totally get if that's too last minute, and you probably have so much going on—!"

Liam lays a hand on her arm, his lips quivering like he's fighting a smile. "Let her answer," he says under his breath.

Gracie folds her lips together and smiles.

"I—yeah. I'd love to help."

Party planning sounds like the first *fun* thing that's come up in…well, I don't know how long. And it's not like I don't have plenty of time to kill these days.

Gracie beams. "Oh my God, that would be amazing. Are you free tomorrow? Maybe we could grab a coffee?"

"Yeah, okay."

"You're a party planner?" Fletcher asks.

"Oh." I wave a hand in front of my face. "Not officially or anything."

Liam turns the corners of his mouth down as he hefts one of the bags over his shoulder. "Wouldn't be a bad idea. Gracie's right. You always do a good job with them. See you tomorrow, Christine. Bye, Case."

"Bye, Liam! Bye, Gracie!"

Gracie offers Casey a little wave before going for the other equipment bag. Liam shoos her away before she can try to lift it and throws it over his other shoulder.

Then somehow it's just me, Casey, and Fletcher left.

I clear my throat and extend my hand toward Casey. "All right, buddy. We should get going."

Casey takes my hand with a reluctant sigh. "Will you stay and watch me tomorrow? Lots of the moms stay."

"Oh, yeah?"

I bite my lip. I've seen the moms he's talking about hanging out in the nearby picnic tables. And I know I shouldn't let them be the reason I don't show up for my kid. I don't know what would be worse, sitting with them, or giving them something else to talk about by sitting alone.

Casey stares up at me expectantly.

"Shh." Fletcher bends down to Casey's level and puts one finger to his lips. "If she sees how much everyone falls while they're practicing, she might get scared and not let you come back."

Casey whips toward me. "I never fall, Mom. Never."

I meet Fletcher's eyes over his head. He's trying to give me an out. He must think I just don't want to be here because of him.

Casey sighs and tugs my hand toward the car, his little shoulders deflated in a way that makes my heart drop. "Never mind."

"No, Casey! I want to come. I might not be able to stay for the whole time, but I'll definitely come early to pick you up and sit and watch for a while first, okay?"

"End's the best part to be here for anyway," offers Fletcher. "It's when we practice all the new things we learned, right, Case?"

He perks back up. "You promise?"

I squeeze his fingers, my eyes somehow still on Fletcher's. "Promise."

Chapter Fourteen
CHRISTINE

Gracie jumps up from the leather armchair in the back corner of the coffee shop as I step through the door. She already has various notebooks and pens spread out on the table. "Thank you again so much for meeting with me!"

It's cute in here. I don't know why I've never been inside, especially since it's right next door to Liam's tattoo shop.

And my ex-husband doesn't own it. So that's always a plus.

Gracie keeps smiling and restlessly shifting her weight, even once we both have our coffees and are sitting across from each other.

"So, this party..." I offer.

"Right!" She perks up and flips pages in one of her notebooks. "So a friend of mine got cast in this movie, and production ended up getting paused indefinitely, but it looks like they're going to finally be picking up again next month. So I wanted to throw her basically a *congrats your movie is actually getting made after all* kind of party..." She grimaces. "Just obviously not in those words."

I laugh a little. "We can work on it. Does she live here then?"

If it's even possible, Gracie perks up further. "No! They're actually going to be filming nearby, at least for some of it. The movie's based off a book, and the author is from Sweetspire. The town it's set in is fictional, but she says she largely drew on her experience growing up here."

Huh. Filming a movie out here? That'll be the talk of the town for, well, years. Maybe if I'm lucky, I'll turn into old news faster than I thought.

"Anyway, Marti and a few of the other actors will be in town next weekend for some preproduction stuff. I wasn't thinking anything big, just like a *welcome to town* kind of thing, you know? Do you think that's too fast of a turnaround?"

I flick my wrist and shake my head. I've pulled bigger things together with less. "If you give me your preferences for venue, theme, budget, and guest list size, I can make it happen."

She smiles. "I *knew* you'd be the perfect person to ask for this. Thank you so much for agreeing to help. I'd love to pay you for your time too."

"Oh, you don't have to—"

"I want to," she insists. "Really. In fact, I was thinking about what Liam said at the park yesterday. And. Well." She fishes around in her purse then sets a business card on the table between us. "No pressure, obviously. But if you ever *did* want to turn this into a business, I'd love to help. I've been specializing in helping small businesses gain traction. Not that you'd probably need my help with your contacts, but..." She trails off and shrugs. "Just in case."

I pick up the card and turn it over in my hands. Of all the ways I could start making my own money now...this is the first thing I've considered that I might actually be *good* at. I've been doing it for free for so long, I guess it hadn't occurred to me it could become something more.

I've seen my fair share of running businesses through my marriage with Julian, considering he has about a hundred of them. Then there's Liam with his shop, and Gracie... I guess I never really considered it for myself though.

Don't be stupid. You could never pull something like that off. You're just not smart enough, sweetie.

I grit my teeth. Even after all these years away, somehow the memory of my mother's voice is perfectly intact.

Back in the corner. Just shove it back in the corner.

I wave the card between two fingers before slipping it into my purse. "Thanks, Gracie. You've given me a lot to think about."

She beams, and I pull a notebook and pen out of my purse next, then lean my elbows onto my knees. "Now, tell me more about this guest list."

Chapter Fifteen
FLETCHER

"*Don't* put that there. Are you crazy?" Mom hurries toward me with her arms outstretched as if ready to take the stone from me. As if it doesn't weigh a million pounds and wouldn't send her straight to the ground.

I grunt and shift my weight, my hold starting to slip. "Then where does it go?"

She points to the opposite side of the yard as if the answer's obvious. Maybe she did already tell me that. I stumble that way —to a patch of grass with absolutely nothing else around it— then meet her eyes and lift my eyebrows in question. She nods confidently.

I finally release the damn thing, nearly out of breath. At this point, I'm not convinced she has a plan. She could very well just be enjoying watching me move heavy things back and forth.

"Trust the process!" she calls, and I wipe off the sweat from my forehead along with whatever look I had on my face. "What's got you so distracted today?"

I frown and shake my head. "I'm not distracted."

She narrows her eyes in that scary way she does that makes me feel like she has X-ray vision, so I pretend to be very interested in the new bags of mulch scattered through the yard.

I haven't given any thought at all to the prospect of Christine hanging around the camp longer than usual today. Didn't spend any extra time doing my hair, or put on a second coat of deodorant, or overthink what to wear. I usually opt for athletic wear for the camps—something easy to move around in. Something easy to wrangle the kids in.

But today it was like I was seeing everything in my closet with fresh eyes, wondering how obviously twenty-three my choices paint me in a way I never have before.

My phone rings in my pocket, mercifully cutting off whatever she was going to say. I shoot her an apologetic smile as I bring it to my ear and turn away.

"Hey, Liam."

He sighs. "We've got a problem. Are you free?"

I hold up a finger to Mom before heading for the house and slipping into the kitchen. "What's up?"

"I'm tied up with a client for the next few hours, otherwise I'd do it myself. It's Asher."

My stomach drops. I was starting to think we were in the clear with him. It's been almost a year since the last time one of us had to peel him off the floor. "How bad is it?"

Of Liam's siblings, Asher's always been one of the wilder ones, but things seemed to calm down once he stopped hanging out with his douche of a best friend last year.

And for someone like Mr. Candyman Brooks, image is everything. Having one kid defect like Liam was bad enough, but *two*? And on top of his divorce? He's been threatening to ship Asher off for years—not that any of his previous stints in rehab made a difference.

"I don't know. Bad enough for whatever girl he's with to

call the first number she could find in his phone. She just left this frantic voicemail that I should get there as soon as I could, and now she's not picking up."

I close my eyes. "Shit."

"Look, I can cancel if—"

"No, no. I've got him. Do you know where he is?"

Liam sighs. "Home, I think. And you know if my dad sees—"

"He won't. I'm heading over right now." I gesture through the window at Mom, hold up my keys, then point to the garage. She frowns but nods and waves me off.

The line crackles as I dip into the garage. "Send me an update when you can?"

"Of course."

I rub my eyes as I pull onto the road and head in the direction of the Brooks mansion. It sits squarely between Sweetspire and the next town over. It's quiet as I loop up the winding drive. The mansion is as gaudy and foreboding as ever, but something about it feels more ominous now.

Not that I've frequented the place. Liam and I have spent most of our time together over the years, well, just about anywhere else. Half the time when he called, I figured he was looking for an excuse to get the hell out of here.

Maybe it's knowing Christine that has it feeling different.

Despite the Brooks grandeur being a better match for her than someplace like the High Dive, I have trouble picturing her here. Picturing her with *him*. She's so full of life, and Liam's dad has always felt like a vampire to me.

I frown at the time on my phone as I head for the front door. It's not even noon. Why the hell is Asher fucked-up first thing in the morning? And since their sister, Makayla, started a new branch of the business last year and brought him on as an employee, for the first time in his life, Asher has a job he's supposed to be reporting to.

The front door's unlocked, and the house is quiet as I step inside. Judging by the other cars out front, their cleaning crew is here somewhere.

I try calling Ash's phone, but it goes straight to voicemail.

No matter how many times I've been in Liam's house, I still get lost. I follow one of the curved staircases—because of course there needs to be *two*—to the second floor, and peek in each room I pass. Asher used to have a room on the third floor when we were teenagers, but I'm pretty sure he moved into Liam's old room after he moved out. It's bigger and has a little balcony overlooking the pool.

But Liam's old room is empty. I check the bathroom, the hall, hell, even the closets, but he's nowhere to be found.

I was hoping to do this quietly, but…

"Ash?" I call.

There's a thump directly over my head, then footsteps pound somewhere off to the left—if I'm remembering correctly, the stairs to the third floor are over there. Just as I reach the bottom, a flash of dark hair appears at the top.

I blink and shake my head. "Carson?"

Other than seeing her around with Gracie here and there, I've barely run into her since we graduated high school, and I still haven't gotten used to her new look. It's the polar opposite of how I remember her. She swapped out the blond hair and tomboy outfits for silver chains, ripped black jeans, and a dark bob.

I also don't think I've ever seen her and Asher in the same room. So then why is she…?

We don't have time for this.

Her eyes are wide, and she waves an impatient hand for me

to join her. She leads me to Asher's old room—now a guest room, I think—

Where Asher is currently passed out shirtless in the middle of the floor.

"Fuck." I kneel beside him, checking for a pulse, then for signs of breathing. "How long has he been like this?"

She lingers in the door, her arms crossed tightly over her chest. "About half an hour."

"What did he take?"

She chews on her lip and shakes her head. "I don't know."

"Carson, you have to tell me—"

"I really don't know! We weren't—I wasn't doing that with him. I don't do that stuff."

I check the floor around him, then his pockets, but come up with nothing.

"Asher." I shake his shoulders, then peel back his eyelids to get a look at his pupillary response.

"What are you doing?" asks Carson, her voice edged with panic.

"Asher." I take his face between my hands and gently slap his cheeks. "Asher, wake up."

"I didn't know if I needed to call an ambulance," Carson continues. "But he was breathing, so…"

"Asher, come on, buddy." I shake him harder. Between the three of us—Liam, Leo, and me—we've been in this situation with him at least half a dozen times before, and only once did he end up needing to go to the hospital. And that…didn't go well. But if I can't wake him up…

"Help me get him to the bathroom," I decide.

Carson, to her credit, doesn't hesitate. We each take an arm over our shoulders and shuffle him to the en suite.

"You might want to look away for this part," I mutter as we position him over the toilet and I force his jaw open.

She cringes but shakes her head and tightens her hold to keep him upright.

At least there's a toothbrush on the counter I can use instead of my fingers. Not that I haven't done that before too. He gags as I push it to the back of his throat, but nothing comes out.

"Come on, Ash." I cringe as I fish around with it.

"He's gonna be okay, right?" Carson gasps. Is she *crying*?

Finally, *finally*, he retches into the toilet. I have no idea how long ago he ingested whatever he took, so I make sure he throws up a few more times for good measure.

His eyes open with the third one, and he catches himself against the toilet with shaky hands.

"Ash? You good?"

He grabs some toilet paper to wipe his mouth and gives me a weak smile. "Oh, hey, Fletch. Fancy seeing you here."

Carson disappears into the room as we flush the toilet, and Ash rests his back against the bathtub.

"What the hell, man?" I ask gently.

Carson returns with a glass of water, and Asher gives her a grateful smile before pushing himself to his feet to rinse out his mouth at the sink. Carson and I follow closely behind, but he manages to maneuver himself into the room and sit on the foot of the bed.

He meets Carson's eyes first. "I'm sorry."

Now that he seems okay, she puts as much distance between them as possible and rests her back against the opposite wall, her arms crossed over her chest. "You scared the shit out of me."

He grimaces and looks at his hands in his lap.

"You feeling okay?" I ask.

He nods. "I'll just sleep it off."

"Ash, what's going on? It's not even eleven yet. And you have work—"

"I know," he snaps, all the usual cheerfulness gone from his voice.

It's surprising enough that I stumble back a step.

He winces and rubs his eyes with both hands. "I'm sorry. Can you just—can we not tell Liam about this?"

"He already knows. That's why I'm here."

He groans and flops onto his back.

I sigh and glance at the time on my phone.

"I can take it from here if you need to get going," Carson offers.

"You sure?"

She nods, though her glare doesn't waver from Asher's prone form on the bed. The last thing I hear as I head down the stairs is "What the *fuck* were you thinking?"

The nerves from this morning about seeing Christine prove to be unfounded, because today, Casey arrives with Liam instead. I offer him a brief recount of the Asher situation before camp starts, but other than a shadow passing over his expression, he doesn't comment on it, so we let it drop.

I have a feeling Asher will not be given the same luxury.

As the minutes tick by and we get closer to the end of camp, I catch myself repeatedly checking the parking lot. But then we're fifteen minutes until the cut-off time, then ten, five.

Then parents are arriving, and one by one, the kids head out for the day, leaving just me, Liam, and Casey waiting a good ten minutes afterward.

Liam frowns down at his phone after trying to call her. "No answer. Just rang a million times."

Something gnaws at the pit of my stomach. This doesn't feel right. I could tell she didn't love the idea of hanging around here, but I also believed her when she promised Casey she'd show.

Granted, I might not know her too well, but this doesn't seem like her.

"Do you think she forgot?" Casey asks, his wide, sad puppy dog eyes staring up at me.

"Something must have come up," I assure him. "Something she couldn't avoid. She'd be here if she could."

Liam curses under his breath and checks his phone again. "I've got a client coming in fifteen—"

I wave him off. "Go on."

He looks from me to Casey with a furrowed brow. "You sure?"

"Yeah. We'll hang out for a few more minutes, and if she still doesn't show, I'll drive him home and check in to make sure everything's okay."

He shoots one last apologetic look at Casey before turning and jogging to his truck. The moment he's gone, Casey edges closer to me, his hand twitching toward mine like he wants to take it but isn't sure. I offer mine, and his tiny fingers grab it immediately.

"Do you think Mommy's okay?"

I squeeze his hand. "Oh, I'm sure she is, bud."

I frown as I say it, my eyes locked on the entrance to the parking lot, willing that gaudy SUV to appear, but the road remains empty.

I glance from Casey to my car—the last one in the lot.

"I'm hungry," laments Casey.

"Come on." I tug him toward my car, the address I snagged from his parent sheet already in the GPS on my phone. Fuck, I don't have a booster seat for him. A seat belt in my back seat and driving five under the speed limit will have to suffice.

Casey bobs along to the radio as we drive, apparently unconcerned now, but I can't help the anxiety thrumming in my veins and drum my fingers against the steering wheel. That pit in my stomach only grows wider when we pull up to his house and Christine's car is sitting in the driveway.

"Oh, Mom *is* home," says Casey.

I punch in the phone number she listed on the sheet then help Casey out of the car.

It rings and rings as we walk toward the front door, and I pause, cocking my head as we reach the front step. Slowly, I lower the phone from my ear, but I can still hear the ringing.

I squint through the window beside the door as I knock. All the lights are on, but there's no movement. It sounds like the phone is near the back of the house.

No answer.

"We keep a key here!" Casey announces as he snatches a painted rock off to the side of the door.

"Good thinking, buddy." I take the key from him, but the moment I open the door, a security alarm beeps in warning.

"My birthday!" cries Casey, pointing at the pad on the wall. "It's my birthday!"

I wince, trying to remember. I know it's in the summer.

Casey huffs. "May 29."

"I knew that."

I punch in the numbers, and the alarm shuts off abruptly, casting the house into a hollow kind of silence.

"I'm home!" Casey calls.

"Casey?"

Christine's voice is thin, high, and far away. And sounds… panicked?

I hit the stairs at a run. "Chris?"

"I'm up here!" she shrieks, her voice definitely edged with panic now.

I reach the top floor, and the ladder to the attic is lowered in the middle of the hall. Something groans and creaks up there. I grab the rungs but hesitate when I realize Casey followed me up here.

"Stay right here, okay, buddy?"

He looks from me to the hole in the ceiling, his little face screwed up with worry.

"Casey," I say, my voice firm.

"Okay!"

I make short work of the ladder and duck into the cramped space. It's lit by a single battery-powered lantern discarded beside the opening, and Christine is in the center of the room.

Namely, hanging on for dear life because the floor caved in. Splintered floorboards surround her, the breaks jagged and uneven. Her chest is pressed against the rim, arms braced on what remains of the floor in front of her, the rest of her disappearing into the hole.

"Shit," I mutter as I scramble into the room.

"Careful!" she gasps. "I don't know how much more of it's unstable."

The surrounding wood is discolored, and the scent of rot and mildew is heavy in the air. I cough against the dust swirling around us as it catches the weak light filtering through the attic windows.

I test my weight and inch forward. The floorboards groan but seem like they'll hold.

"How long have you been hanging here?"

"Please don't make me answer that."

I drop to my knees in front of her and wedge my hands under her arms to pull her up, but her nails are still dug into the floorboards.

"You have to let go."

She looks up at me with wide, panicked eyes.

"You're all right. I've got you," I say softly.

She swallows hard and squeezes her eyes shut before releasing her hold. I start pulling her through before she can feel a drop, and she lets out a breathy little sob as she collapses against me. I can *feel* how fast her heart is beating through her chest, and her hands tremble as she curls her fingers tightly around the fabric of my shirt.

"Shit," I breathe, taking in the rest of her. The undersides of her arms are all scraped up. I have a million questions, like what the hell she's doing up here in the first place, or why she didn't just drop down the few feet into Casey's room, but I settle on "You hurt anywhere else?"

She glances down at herself like she's not sure.

"No, no," she says, her voice several octaves too high. "I'm fine. Sorry." She waves a shaky hand in front of her face. "Thanks for the hand." She gestures the way I came. "And Casey—God, you drove him here? What time is it? I didn't—I was—I probably should've just let go, but I—I'm not the best with h-heights, and if I moved, it felt like more was going to b-break—" She hiccups around the last word.

Jesus Christ, she's scared to death.

"Hey." I pull her in against my chest before I can think better of it and cradle the back of her head with my hand. "You're all right. Take a deep breath."

"Mommy! There's a *hole* in my ceiling!" calls Casey.

"Oh God, I was going to pick up Casey early to watch him skate," she whispers and covers her face with her hands.

I rub my thumb along her arm. "As far as alibis go, I think you've got a good one."

"Mom! Did you hear me? I said there's a *hole* in the ceiling!"

"Come on. Let's get you down." I climb to my feet first and

hold her hand to help her up. She still has that shell-shocked look in her eyes, but she lets me.

Casey gasps when we hit the bottom of the ladder, his eyes going round at the blood on Christine's arms. "You're hurt."

"Oh, Casey, sweetie, it's nothing. I'm fine."

"You have a first aid kit?" I ask.

She nods as she shoots a look inside Casey's bedroom. The debris is scattered all over his floor—dust and bits of plaster and plywood. Poor Casey's bed is covered in it.

"Kitchen," she murmurs.

"Hey, Case, weren't you telling me your favorite show comes on right after camp?"

He perks up. "It does! Mom usually records it so I can watch it later."

I extend my hand toward him. "Can you show me how to turn it on?"

He grins as he links his little fingers through mine. I meet Christine's eyes before heading down the stairs. "You. Kitchen table."

She blinks at me as if stunned.

Once I have Casey happily occupied on the couch, I dig through the cabinets in the kitchen until I find the first aid kit Christine was talking about.

She shuffles into the room and sinks into a chair at the table. "I can take it from here," she says, though her voice doesn't hold much conviction.

"You could," I say lightly as I take the seat across from her and gesture for her arm.

Luckily, under the light, they're not as bad as I originally thought. The undersides of her arms must have scraped against the edges of the floor as she caught herself, but nothing looks too deep.

She hisses through her teeth as I start cleaning them.

"Sorry. I know it stings."

She says nothing, her face screwed up in an expression I've seen on Casey a dozen times as I secure a bandage over the first arm and move to the second.

"So, heights, huh?" I say lightly as the peroxide hits her skin.

Her eyes snap to mine, but she winces less this time, so the distraction worked for something.

"It's not funny."

I shrug and fish around in the kit for another bandage. "I don't hear anyone laughing."

Neither of us says anything else as I finish up. Music from the TV and Casey's laughter filter through the doorway.

"What were you doing in the attic?" I ask.

She sighs and rubs her eyes. "Casey's dad had a bunch of stuff sent over—photo albums, Casey's baby clothes, that kind of thing. I was just looking for a good place to store them. Now I get to fix a *hole* in my ceiling."

"Oh, I can do that."

She peers up at me, her eyebrows drawn together in utter confusion, and I laugh.

"My parents flip houses for a living. I've been helping since I was a teenager. I'm pretty handy with that kind of stuff."

Her eyes narrow. "Bartending, kids' camps, flipping houses…am I missing anything else?"

"That about sums me up." I smirk. "I like to keep busy."

She clears her throat, rises from the table, and grabs the first aid kit. "Which is exactly why you don't have time for this. And it's not your problem. I can find someone to hire."

I follow her deeper into the kitchen as she puts the box away. "Hire me."

"Fletcher." Her voice is a small, exasperated exhale.

"I want to help."

"It's not a good idea."

"Why not? I have the skills. I already have the materials I'd need leftover from a build. I'd want to inspect the surrounding area to make sure you won't have any more problems first, but I could have it done in a few days—"

Finally, she turns to face me, those striking blue eyes meeting mine in a way that makes my breath catch. "You *know* why not," she whispers.

I swear I don't imagine it. For a moment—just a moment, but long enough—her gaze flicks to my mouth. And I recognize that look in her eyes, even though this is the first time I've seen it since that night.

I can't help it. I smile. Because the moment I found out who she was, I thought I was dead in the water.

But I might have a fighting chance here after all.

But that's not what this is about, and I don't want her to think that's what this is about. She really does need that ceiling fixed, and not from some semicompetent handyman who will charge her too much and cut too many corners. Especially not when it's something I can do in my sleep.

And it's clear whoever did the inspection prior to her buying this place did a shit job. She might even have a case here if she wants to sue. No one should have missed that level of damage. Pointing that out right now will probably just make her feel worse.

Luckily, the attic only runs over the end of the hall and Casey's room, so the rest of the house should be safe until it's fixed.

"I can be perfectly professional. I'll even charge you my premium rate. Five bucks an hour. It'll need a more thorough inspection, but the good news is the damage seems pretty localized."

That, finally, gets a small smile out of her, even if it's accompanied by an eye roll.

"Thank you for the help earlier. And bringing Casey home. I'm not usually a professional damsel in distress."

I tilt my head to the side. Is that what this is about? She feels like she's hit her quota for accepting other people's help? Or is it *my* help that's the problem?

"Tell you what, I'm off this Saturday from the bar, so if you don't find someone else to fix it by then, you can give me a call. And if I don't hear from you, I won't bring it up again. But I am going to inspect it before I leave to make sure it's at least safe enough for you guys to stay until then, all right?"

Slowly, she nods.

Considering it's already Thursday, I like my odds.

Chapter Sixteen

CHRISTINE

Casey sleeps in my bed the next night. Even after I clean up all the debris that landed in his room, he's still too afraid to go in there, convinced monsters in the attic can see him through the hole. He sends me in to rescue his favorite toys too so they won't be scared of the monsters either.

As it turns out, Sweetspire does not come with a ton of handyman options. Of the available ones, no one can get out here sooner than Saturday, and despite my minimal knowledge of the subject, their quotes seem outrageous. Sure, it's a big hole, but *several* thousand dollars?

A quick rabbit hole of internet videos later and I confirm what I already knew—I definitely cannot do it myself.

On Friday, Casey heads over to his new friend Erin's house for a playdate after camp. I put in a few hours of work compiling some party venue and catering options for Gracie—though DIY workarounds might be the way to go for most things to stay in budget. But if we can get creative with the venue to keep costs down, that'll give us more wiggle room.

Once I get started brainstorming ideas…it's hard to stop.

By the time I glance at the clock, several hours have passed and I've gained a new kink in my neck.

But God, I am *buzzing*.

I know she wanted to keep this casual, simple. But there are so many directions we could take it. The theme options alone are endless. On one side, we could base it off Sweetspire, keep it beachy and light, or in the complete opposite direction, we could lean into the book-slash-movie's vibe. I mean, zombies! I've never gotten to do a zombie party before.

After all the luncheons and dinner parties I helped Julian with...I try to picture his face if I'd offered up *that* as a theme idea, and nearly snort my seltzer out my nose.

The rest of the day is spent cleaning the backlog of dishes and laundry. Every time I pass Casey's room, I wince as I catch sight of that hole. I desperately try to come up with a solution other than calling Fletcher. I don't know what my resistance to it is, exactly. Something about it feels like opening a door I won't be able to close. A door that needs to stay closed.

And all the reasons why are a lot easier to remember when he's not right in front of me.

Because when he is, I have these moments where I'm in that hotel room with him again, and I forget. I forget about Liam and the age difference and the divorce and being the town pariah. I forget about how this could blow back on Casey.

Because when he is...

I don't let myself finish the thought.

I'm elbow-deep in hot, soapy water when my phone starts ringing on the other side of the kitchen.

"Shit." I try to shut the sink off with my elbow.

But the entire faucet pops off instead.

Water shoots straight up in the air. The spray attachment goes wild too, flipping this way and that around me. "*Shit!*" I fumble for it, getting soaked in the process, but it keeps building momentum and spinning faster until it slams against the backsplash hard enough to crack the tile.

Once I get ahold of the faucet head, I try to shove it back into place where the water is exploding from, to no avail. I scramble down to the cabinet beneath it. How the hell do you turn the water off? Is there some kind of switch?

I turn the first valve I can find, and mercifully, the water stops.

I hang my head between my shoulders, breathing hard. I am now dripping head to toe, and so is the rest of the kitchen.

I know I'm out of practice with all this domestic shit from years at the Brooks mansion, but seriously? How can I possibly be this bad at *everything*?

"For fuck's sake," I mutter under my breath as I climb to my feet. Upon closer inspection, the faucet is an old, flimsy thing, and the hole it detached from is all cracked and musty looking. I grimace as I take in the broken backsplash. Luckily, it's only one tile. I poke at it gingerly, and it gives way…exposing dark, splotchy stains.

"Ugh!" I jump back, covering my mouth with the inside of my elbow. Is that *mold*? And if it's behind this tile, I'm willing to bet it's plenty of other places too.

I rip off my rubber gloves and toss them in the sink. First my car, then the ceiling, the kitchen… Is this some overdue karma or something? Seriously, can anything else possibly go wrong? I wince and knock on the wooden table as soon as the thought pops into my head.

This money will last me for the next fifty years, my ass. This house is going to eat every last cent at this rate, and I'm going to end up right back where I started from.

I know it's unreasonable with how much is sitting in the bank to feel the need to hold on to as much as possible, that once it's gone, it's gone. But it's a hard habit to break.

Maybe it was stupid buying this place, stupid thinking I could do this on my own. I don't know what I'm doing.

We could've rented somewhere. Maybe leaving in the first place was the mistake. I could've suffered through it, I think. Swallowed my pride, my dignity. Maybe Casey would've been better off.

I squeeze my eyes shut and try to pretend I can't hear my mother's voice in the back of my mind. Telling me how stupid I am. How worthless. How I'll never do anything right. That one day I'll have a kid just like me as punishment.

Hot, frustrated tears sting my eyes, and I ball my hands into fists, forcing them down along with a few deep breaths.

Back into the corner. Just shove it back into the corner.

I can deal with this. I can.

The phone has stopped ringing by now, and I sigh as I wipe the water from my face and grab it off the table. Some unsaved number. And they didn't leave a message.

I hesitate with the phone in my hand. The hole in the ceiling was one thing, but the mold? What if it's not safe for Casey to be breathing in here? I can't put this off, and my pride doesn't matter right now. I scroll through my contacts until I find the right one, then close my eyes as I force myself to hit call.

Chapter Seventeen
FLETCHER

The bar is pretty dead when I show up Friday afternoon. Anna waves from where she's polishing the beer glasses as I punch in and grab an apron to tie around my waist.

"How's the camp going?" she asks.

"It's great. We got a good group of kids this round. And the parents seem less likely to have a heart attack now that we've gotten through the first week."

She snorts. "I don't know how you do it with them all sitting there watching you like that. Sounds fucking terrifying."

I smirk and wipe down the bar top. It can feel a bit like performing, but I guess I've gotten used to it by now.

"How are the summer classes?"

She shrugs. "The credits will be nice. Hoping it'll let me wrap things up a semester early. *So*," she adds, her voice an entirely different tone now. One that tells me I'm not going to like whatever she says next. "How are things with that blonde from the other week?"

I cut my eyes to her as a group of three women walks through the door. With how slow business has been lately, it's become rare for us both to be on shift, and we haven't worked together since that night. I'm surprised management wanted both of us here today. "Don't know what you're talking about."

She smirks and lifts her eyebrows but turns her attention to the glass in her hands. "So I *didn't* see you leave with her?"

"Anna," I warn.

She narrows her eyes and turns to me. Shit, I shouldn't have reacted at all. Now I've caught her interest. At least if she's referring to Christine as *that blonde*, it sounds like she doesn't know who she is.

Not that I'd mind if she did, but I know Christine would.

I jerk my head to the side as the women slide onto seats at the end of the bar and head that way.

The one in the middle, a brunette with fancy sunglasses on top of her head and giant diamonds in her ears, layers her hands on the bar. From a cursory glance, I can tell the others are just as decked out. What the hell are they doing here?

"What can I get you?"

"We will take three of your delicious bottomless mimosas," she says.

I feel a single eyebrow creep up my face of its own accord. I don't know if anyone has ever described something here as delicious. We also have certainly never had bottomless mimosas. I say as much.

The woman's jaw drops open in theatrical shock. "Since when?"

I glance at Anna out of the corner of my eye. "At least in the two years I've been working here."

"Well, last time we were here, the other bartender did it for us," pipes up the blonde on her left.

"Who?" I point at Anna down the bar. "Her?"

The blonde shakes her head and waves a hand. "A different one."

I give her a thin smile. "Anna and I are the only two bartenders here. But I'm happy to get you some mimosas. Is orange juice okay? We also have—"

"Is your manager here?" asks the third woman, the one who is so deeply tanned her skin looks like leather.

I sigh inwardly but keep a smile on my face as I nod my head to the side. "That would be Anna."

It is not, in fact, Anna, but they don't know that. The real manager, Bridget, would most definitely approve though if it means not bothering her.

Leave it to the richest people in here to fight me on a drink that's already discounted to six dollars.

"So what'll it be? Orange juice, grapefruit, or cranberry?"

I expect them to fight me on it some more, but thankfully, they each ask for orange and let me walk away.

"Sorry," Anna says out of the corner of her mouth as I pull a bottle of champagne from the fridge. "Should've warned you about them."

"They've been here before?" I ask as I pop the cork.

She nods and grabs the orange juice for me. "Once last week. Got so drunk I thought I'd have to kick them out. Seemed like they were looking for someone."

I pause and glance at them over my shoulder, my eyebrows pulling together. My mind jumps to Christine. I don't know if that's because I haven't been able to get her off my mind in general, or because she's the only other person I've seen in here that's as out of place. I can't see her being friends with them though. Maybe it's presumptuous to think I know her that well, but from what I've seen of her personality, I can't imagine her *liking* them.

I gather the drinks and can't help but overhear their conversation as I walk over.

"...well *I* always thought it was especially callous of her, given the timing," says the woman in the middle. "He was devastated after Lily's death. Vulnerable. And she swooped right in."

"Then managed to get herself pregnant to seal the deal," agrees the tan one.

"Here you are." I slide the drinks in front of them, but none of them acknowledge me.

"The nerve for her to stick around town too?" The third woman laughs, and the sound is ugly and hard. "Should've gone back to whatever backwater town she came from."

I walk away before I have to hear any more. Unfortunately for me, the bar is quiet, and their voices carry.

"…and now poor Casey. That kid doesn't stand a chance. He'll probably turn out just like her…"

I freeze a few paces from Anna. Her eyes shoot to my face, and I stare back at her, the blood in my veins running hot. She cocks her head, a question in her eyes, and whatever she sees on my face is enough to spur her forward. She grabs my forearm and pulls me to the other side of the bar.

"Take a deep breath," she murmurs.

I do. Then another.

It doesn't help.

One of the women's laughs cuts through the room again, and my jaw ticks.

Anna's eyes flick between mine. "You know who they're talking about."

It isn't a question.

She sighs when I don't respond. "I can take over. Go take a break."

I shake my head.

"Fletcher—"

I know she's right. There is no good scenario here if I stay. What I really want to do is kick them the fuck out, but they're the type to cause a big scene, threaten lawyers, and who knows what else. If I say anything, they'll love it. *Why is this random bartender jumping to her defense?* It'll give them a slew of new material to gossip about, and in the long run, that only hurts Christine more. I clench my hands into fists at my sides.

My phone buzzes in my apron pocket, and Anna nudges me toward the break room.

"Go. Take that. I'll handle them. Please, Fletch. I'll even spit in one of their drinks."

She smirks as I meet her eyes, and I sigh. "Fine," I grumble, then fish my phone out as I walk. I only make it a few paces before I pause at the sight of the name on the screen.

Chapter Eighteen
CHRISTINE

"Oh no. What happened to you?" Fletcher covers his mouth with his hand as I swing the door open, but there's no mistaking the amusement in his eyes.

I must look even worse than I feel. Defeated, I shuffle to the side to let him through, then lead him to the kitchen. He steps around me as he takes in the chaos—the broken sink, the tile falling off the wall, the remaining water dripping from the ceiling. I tried to clean up most of what I could reach. He frowns as he gets closer to inspect the sink and winces as he notices the mold.

"I'm sorry. I didn't know who else to call. Maybe I should've just texted you a picture. I hope you weren't busy—"

He turns to me, looking utterly bewildered. "I'm glad you called, Chris. Are you all right?"

I cross my arms over my chest. I changed into some dry clothes after calling him, but I can still feel how wet my hair is, and my makeup has seen better days. "Just mortified."

There's a strange softness in his eyes that I don't know

what to do with. But then he turns away, sets his hands on his hips, and sighs.

"The sink I could fix, no problem. The mold...I *could* do it, but I think we're better safe than sorry. I can contact some guys I've worked with in the past. We're gonna have to see how far it's spread. You'll probably want to find somewhere else to stay while they deal with it. I'd guess at least a week."

I collapse onto one of the kitchen chairs, brace my elbows on the table, and rest my head in my hands.

"Good news is, I could do the ceiling in that same window, so when you guys get back, everything will be taken care of."

"Until the next thing breaks," I mutter under my breath.

"I know this is overwhelming, but it's all fixable."

The chair next to me scratches back against the floor, and Fletcher gives me a small, tired smile as he sits.

"Thank you for getting over here so fast. Wait—are you not working at the bar today?"

A weird look crosses his face. "I was. Didn't really need two of us bartending. They let me off. How are your arms?"

"Oh." I glance down. I took the bandages off this morning and all but forgot about them. "They're fine. Just scratches."

I startle as his fingers gently bracelet my wrist. He lifts my arm a few inches to inspect the wounds. I take the opportunity to get a better look at his face. Up close, the signs of exhaustion are a lot clearer. The bags under his eyes are dark.

"Are you all right?" I ask quietly.

His eyes flick up to mine, surprised. "Fine," he says in the immediate way people always do when they don't mean it. He smiles like he can tell I don't believe him. "If you and Casey need someplace to stay, I have a guest room—"

I open my mouth to protest.

"—which I know you won't accept, but I needed to offer.

This is already going to be an...expense. I don't want you to have to pay for a hotel on top of it."

"I'm almost afraid to ask, but how expensive are you thinking it'll be?"

He twists his mouth to the side. "It'll depend on a few things—like how far it's spread. Then you'll have to put the whole kitchen back together." He sighs and scratches the back of his neck. "I'd guess a few thousand. The sink and the ceiling I can do for free though."

"No."

"Chris—"

"*No.* You can do it, but I'm paying you for it."

He sighs and rubs his eyes. "I'm not just saying that because I like you. I'd offer the same to anyone in my life. People can just help each other, you know. It doesn't have to be a transaction."

I stare at him, and when he lowers his hand, he laughs.

"Oh, don't look so surprised. You *know* I like you. I respect your reasons for wanting boundaries here, but that doesn't change how I feel about you."

How I feel about you.

That is not at all the *it was one night, it didn't mean anything* that I need. This goes beyond some mild awkwardness because we've seen each other naked. *How I feel.* In present tense. As in, it is currently ongoing.

I push up from the table. Then take a step back when there's still not enough distance between us. This was a bad, bad idea.

"Right. So. If you would pass along the contact info for the company or whatever, I'd appreciate it, then I can take it from here."

"Chris," he sighs, and now I can't look at him because I can still remember *exactly* how good he looked naked.

I remember exactly how it felt to kiss him. To have his hands on me. Inside of me.

I remember the way he whimpered and groaned in a way most men try so hard not to let you hear, and I have no idea why, because even just the memory of it has me breathing faster.

I remember the way he had me trembling, begging, *out of my fucking mind* with how good it felt.

I remember talking with him after. Sometimes about nothing at all, sometimes about things I've never shared with anyone because for some reason it was easier with him.

It was easy to laugh. To smile.

To let him hold me until we fell asleep.

It was all just…easy.

Until. *Until.*

"Chris," he repeats, and his voice sounds different now. Like a question. A hope.

I hear him get up from the table, hear him come closer. I *feel* it. I can feel when he's close. Feel when he's looking. Feel him even when he's across the room.

And when he's not, I look for him. I wonder where he is.

And this is *not* the *it was one night, it didn't mean anything* that I need.

My hands are shaking and I don't know why. The room feels too small. I can smell his skin, even from here.

I turn around, and he's standing close. Too, too close. His eyes burn as they meet mine. That mix of green and brown that has me staring into them, trying to find where one color stops and the other begins.

"This cannot happen," I grit out through my teeth, but the words sound so small, so weak, that even I don't believe myself.

He takes my face between his hands and kisses me.

I want to resist. I want to push him away. I want to tell him to stop.

But I fist my hand in his hair and pull him closer.

He backs me up until I press against the wall, his lips never breaking from mine. He groans into my mouth, or maybe I do.

I want more, *more*.

But he doesn't touch me. His hands don't leave my face, and I can feel how much he's holding himself back. He frames my jaw with his thumbs to angle my face up to his, his fingers curling around the back of my neck as he kisses me slowly, deeply, in a way that's almost tender.

In a way that I know means he's about to let me go.

A whimper escapes me, and he pulls back an inch. He brushes my hair behind my ears and holds my face like it's something delicate.

"This cannot happen," I repeat, even though the words are small and hold no conviction.

"Okay," he murmurs.

I search his eyes. "That's it? Just okay?"

"I'm not going to talk you into this. I think I've made it clear where I stand. I want you. And I think you want me too."

I should lie. But even if I did, I think he'd be able to tell. I'm pretty sure it's written all over my face.

The lines around his eyes soften, and his thumb runs across my cheek. "I want you in whatever way I can have you. If you need to hide me to make that happen, I wouldn't take it personally. Just let me be here. Let me be here for you."

I squeeze my eyes closed. "Fletcher—"

"And outside of this house, I'll act however you want me to. Pretend I don't know you, if that's what you need."

My heart drops. "You deserve better than that." I lower his hands from my face and pull in a deep breath as I lean my head against the wall. How the hell did we end up here?

"Tell me you don't think about me," he says. "Tell me you don't think about that night. Because I can't stop thinking about it. All I do these days is think about you."

I don't say anything—I can't. Because of course I've thought about it. No matter how hard I've tried, I haven't been able to stop. I haven't had a moment of peace since it happened. Even when I'm not actively thinking about it, I can *feel* it somewhere deep down, the shift.

I'd thought maybe it was because it had been so long. Julian and my sex life deteriorated long before the marriage. The last time I had a one-night stand would've been over ten years ago.

And it definitely hadn't gone the same way.

But if it wasn't about that, if it wasn't just the sex…I haven't let myself think about that. I *can't*.

"You're too young for me, Fletcher," I whisper.

"See, I'm not buying that."

"You are a *decade* younger than me. That's a big deal."

He doesn't respond at first, and when I look to him, a small, playful smile tugs at the corners of his mouth.

"Don't men have shorter life expectancies on average? I think it's six years. And you're nine years older. So that pretty much evens us out. That leaves a three-year gap, if you're being stingy. And three years is perfectly acceptable."

I fight the urge to smile. He's clearly thought about this before. "Your mental gymnastics are truly impressive." Quietly, I add, "People would think I'm taking advantage of you."

"If I was eighteen, I could see that. But I'm not some naive kid. But if you see me that way, then yeah, I'd say we have a problem."

"Of course I don't see you that way."

"So that's it then? You're just worried about what other people would think?"

"No." It's not nearly as simple as that, but I don't know how else to explain. "You know that I was twenty-three when I met Julian?"

Granted, that age difference was a lot more than nine years. At the time, I thought I knew exactly what I was getting into. Thought I knew what I wanted. Thought the playing field was even. And as much as I don't want to, when I look at Fletcher, a part of me can't help but see a past version of myself.

Fletcher is quiet for what feels like a very long time, his expression unreadable, but his eyes are locked on my face like he's searching for something.

Finally, he says, "You are nothing like him. And this is nothing like that. This is something. You can't tell me it's not."

He's so close I can smell his cologne, feel the heat radiating from his skin.

"This might come across as insensitive, but things are bad already, aren't they? People with their stupid fucking gossip—would it be so much worse if you add me to it? The way I see it, give them something to talk about. You're giving them too much power, Chris. And they don't matter."

If that's all there was to it, maybe I would.

"It's not about..." I shake my head, a tear escaping from the corner of my eye.

"Then what—"

"It's Casey," I all but sob.

I know I'm not a perfect mom. I might not even be a good one. But I'll be damned if I don't at least try to be better than mine was for me.

And if there's one thing she never, ever did for me, it was put me first.

Even *having* me. She made it all too clear she never wanted to. But at the time, she thought it would secure my dad, keep him from breaking up with her after they graduated high school like he'd been threatening to do.

And it worked. For a few years.
Until he left anyway.
Then all she had left was me.
Fletcher's face falls.

"I can't—I can't do that to him—" I pull in a shuddering breath. "I can't hurt him like this. I know you'd never hurt him. But the other kids at school? The people in this town? The way they'd look at him, the things they'd say? What about when he's old enough to truly understand and is embarrassed of me? Resents me? I can't do that to him. You want to know if I want this, but what I want doesn't matter because I have to—for him —" I hiccup, every word coming out more breathless than the last.

He folds me into his arms and tucks my head beneath his chin. The floodgate breaks, and the tears I've been holding back all day, all month, for the past eight years, maybe even longer than that, run free.

"I'm sorry," I whisper.

"No. Don't be. That's all you had to say." He strokes the back of my head. "I know you're going through hell right now. Not just with the divorce, but I've seen the way people in town... You don't deserve it. And I wish more than anything that I could fix this for you. But you don't have to do this alone. Let me be here for you, even if it's only when no one can see."

Being on my own is nothing new. Even before I left home— even when I was married to Julian—I knew at the end of the day, the only person I could count on was myself.

But being used to it doesn't make it any less exhausting.

And it wouldn't be forever. Not long enough that I'd get so used to leaning on him that my own legs wouldn't be able to hold me up anymore once he leaves, but just for now...just until the worst of this blows over...

"I know you think that's unfair to me," he continues. "But let me be the one to make that call. I'm asking you, just for a moment, to set it all aside. It's just you and me standing here. And I want you to tell me how it feels. Because I feel like I don't ever want to let go."

All the fight left in me deflates. "And I feel like I don't want you to."

Slowly, I pull away and peel my eyes up to his. The way he gazes back, like the light of the sun itself is on fire behind his eyes—I know for certain no one else has ever looked at me like that. An emotion I can't quite read weighs down his features. He almost seems...sad?

"You never called. After that night. Even before you knew who I was." His voice is so raw, vulnerable. It makes my heart twist.

I swallow hard. "I wanted to."

It's embarrassing, actually, the number of times I had to talk myself out of it.

"I need you to be perfectly clear with me. What are we doing here, Chris?"

I lay my hand against the side of his face. "I want you. And not just...like this." I smile a little and shrug. "I want you around. I *like* having you around. But I don't want to confuse Casey, and I don't want to make things worse for him."

"So we keep this between you and me for now."

I chew on my lip. "Is that okay?"

He rubs his nose along mine and nods.

"Are you sure?" I whisper. "Do you promise that's okay?"

He takes my face between his hands, kisses me, and smiles. "I promise."

Chapter Nineteen

FLETCHER

I set Lucy down. Just for a second. Just to help with the lock.
But it's long enough.
She turns and darts back up the stairs.
"Lucy!" I scream, and the effort tears at my throat.
Once the door is open, I shove Henry and Jacks onto the porch. "Go! Get away from the house. Wait across the street."
"What about you?" Jacks cries.
"I'll be right there," I promise. And I hope I'm not lying.
I grab two shoes waiting by the door and throw one at each of our foster parents. "Wake up!" I yell, but I don't stick around to see if it worked. I'm not going to feel bad about it, and I'm sure as hell not going to help them over Lucy. I race up the stairs, my limbs starting to feel sluggish and heavy, and cover my mouth with my shirt.

My chest seizes with each cough, and my eyes are burning so much I can barely see in front of me.

As soon as I hit the upstairs hallway, the house makes a terrible groan, and part of the ceiling collapses, blocking off the stairs. I flinch and throw an arm over my head instinctively. Sparks fly through the black smoke billowing up in the air.

"Lu-cy," I try to yell, but I can't get the word past the tightening in my throat. I crawl to her room on my hands and knees.

She's passed out in the middle of the floor, one hand reaching for Mr. Teddy under her bed.

This fucking bear.

It's the ugliest, rattiest bear I've ever seen with a missing eye and stuffing spilling out of its arms. I grab its paw and yank it toward me.

More smoke is pouring into the room by the second. I cross to the window, shove it open, and knock out the screen with my elbow. I stick my head through the window and look down. There's nothing below to catch our fall other than the dead bushes along the side of the house.

"Help!" I try to yell into the night, but nothing comes out.

I pull Lucy and Mr. Teddy closer to the window, then pause and double back for Henry's blanket on the opposite bed. Lucy won't wake no matter how much I shake her, so I do the only thing I can think of.

I doubt they'll help, but I toss out all of the pillows in the room. Then I strip the sheets off both beds and tie them together, my hands shaking. Black spots crowd in on my vision, and I feel myself on the last edge of consciousness.

The fire roars in the distance, and I hear something crash, like more of the ceiling collapsed downstairs.

I squeeze my eyes closed and can picture the photograph sitting on my nightstand. The only picture I have of my birth parents. I can't go back for it. I can't.

I don't have time I don't have time I don't have time.

I use the sheets to secure Lucy to my chest instead, and with Mr. Teddy and the blanket in hand, I jump.

Chapter Twenty
CHRISTINE

Casey wails and kicks as hard as he can against the back of my seat. "Please don't make me go. *Please.*"

My hands ache from how tightly I'm gripping the steering wheel even though we're parked. Tears stream down my cheeks, but I hope he can't see them past my sunglasses.

I stare up at the mansion I called home for seven years with a mountain of dread sitting in the pit of my stomach.

"Casey," I start, my voice gentle, but that just makes him cry harder.

"I want to stay with you!"

A very small, very petty version of myself finds a bit of satisfaction in that, but I shove her down. Especially knowing *why* Casey isn't champing at the bit to see his dad the way he used to. According to the nanny, there was an…incident last time. One that resorted in Julian snapping and screaming in Casey's face—to "shut the hell up" I believe were his exact words—which, of course, left Casey sobbing, inconsolable, and then he hid somewhere no one could find him for over an hour. All because Julian had an oh-so-important work call.

I unbuckle my seat belt and climb out of the car. Even once outside, his screams are plain as day. I suck in a deep breath before opening his door. His face is bright red from all the screaming, and tears cover his chubby little cheeks.

"Casey," I try again, my voice firmer. "Sweetheart, it's just for the weekend."

"No!" He resumes his kicking.

"Your dad even said he'd take you up to a Phillies game—"

"*I. Don't. Want. To!*"

I sigh and look around helplessly. The fact of the matter is, *I* don't want to leave him here with Julian any more than he wants to go. But the custody agreement is what it is. And the last thing I want to do is piss off Julian enough for him to retaliate and do something crazy—like try to get *full* custody to spite me.

Justified or not, I know without a doubt he'd succeed. He has every person in this town, and probably even farther than that, in his pocket.

We wouldn't stand a chance.

My stomach roils at the thought of it.

"He hired Nanny Dina back, remember? She's fun to play with, isn't she? And I'm sure she'll let you call me every day. And the pool is open! Don't you miss the pool?"

He looks up at me with round, pitiful eyes, and my heart feels like it's splitting clean down the middle.

But he's not screaming anymore.

The timing, admittedly, is beneficial with the mold scare. At least this gets Casey out of the house, and since Liam and Gracie are in the city this weekend, they offered to let me take their apartment for the next few days. If the cleanup ends up taking longer than that, I guess we'll have to ride it out in a hotel again.

Because as tempting as it is to take Fletcher up on his guest room offer...I can't. I *shouldn't*.

This—whatever *this* is—is so new. Talk about getting too comfortable leaning on him. And that feels like...well, that feels like the type of offer my mother would jump on.

I don't know if Casey is coming around to the idea or if he's just worn himself out, but I lean into the car to grab his overnight bag.

When he climbs out of the car, he crosses his arms over his chest and won't look at me. I offer my hand, but he ignores it and takes off toward the front door.

I pinch my lips together to keep them from wobbling, throw the bag over my shoulder, and follow after him.

My phone buzzes as I climb back into the car.

A picture of Casey's room appears. I zoom in on the ceiling, but you can't even tell there had been a hole.

That, at least, is one fewer disaster in my life.

Fletcher: good as new

Christine: Thank you. Really.

Fletcher: Good news on the mold too. Sounds like they'll be able to wrap it up before the end of the weekend. You guys should be good to come back on Monday!

Fletcher: ...how'd the drop-off go with Casey?

My shoulders slump as the tears start up again.

Christine: He hates me for making him go. And his dad's not even here. I had to leave him with the nanny.

Fletcher: Let me buy you a drink

I frown and tap my fingers against the side of the phone. It's one thing if people see me sitting at the bar while he's working...but seeing us together...

Fletcher: And by that I mean let me get a bottle and you can drink it at my place

Considering the alternative is I go to Liam's place and cry and drink by myself...

Fletcher: I have snacks too

I laugh and shake my head.

Christine: Make it a Riesling.

Fletcher: I know :)

"Okay, so, give me the tour. And I need full commentary."

Fletcher passes me a glass of wine over the generous kitchen island, which is a beautiful dark quartz. I haven't been able to stop staring at it since I walked in the door. The entire kitchen, really. The touches are understated, nothing too flashy, but it's clear everything was meticulously chosen, from the hardware to the cabinets to the light fixtures.

In the Brooks household, I always had the feeling I was in a museum. The kitchen looked like it belonged in a five-star restaurant with a full staff—everything bright and shiny and top-of-the-line.

Fletcher's is...cozy. And warm. Inviting.

"Do you have before and after pictures?" I add.

He smiles as he pours himself a glass. "I do..."

There's something bashful about the way he slides his phone to me. I pace to the spot the kitchen ends and the living room begins and hold up the phone to see them side by side.

"Oh! You took out this whole wall."

He nods.

I spin around. The space for the kitchen table is twice as big now and feeds directly into the living space. It also lets in the light from the back windows more.

The kitchen in the before picture is an assaulting, pitiful thing. Pink paint with rooster wallpaper, outdated appliances, and the laundry was right next to the stove. The lights are so warm-toned they cast an ugly yellow tint to everything. I squint from the phone to the room around me again, almost getting hit with a wave of vertigo.

"This can't be the same house," I decide.

He laughs and paces to my side. "Did consider keeping the roosters though."

"*You* did *all* of this?"

He smirks and swipes to the next picture, this one of the living room. "You sound so surprised."

I turn around to compare. The change here is less drastic—though he did swap out the light fixtures, and the paint and hardwood flooring look new.

"No, I'm…impressed." That doesn't even feel like a strong enough word. I'm in *awe*. I turn to him with a wide smile. "Show me more?"

"These look the most different. Mainly just updated everything else. Though I did knock a few other walls down so I could separate the laundry and make the primary bedroom bigger." He offers the hand not holding his wine, then guides me toward the sliding glass doors at the back of the kitchen. "The deck is new though. Everything else out here is a work in progress, obviously."

I actually gasp as we step outside. Gorgeous deep wood curves around the back of the house beneath a pergola. It's large enough for two chairs, an outdoor sofa, and fire pit to sit on one side, and there's a dining set and swing on the other.

A few steps lead down to the yard full of half-finished projects.

"I see you're doing some landscaping."

He chuckles. "Yeah, my mom's helping me out with that. It's

kind of her specialty. She's going a little overboard, but she's been so excited about it, so I don't have the heart to rein her in."

It looks like they're making a stone walkway from the deck to the opposite side of the yard.

"What's going to be over there?" I ask, pointing.

"Some kind of water feature, I think. It gets good shade from the trees over there, so probably another sitting area. Then we'll do some plants along the sides here."

"I think it's nice that you and your mom are so close." I venture to the other side of the deck and test out the couch. *Ugh*, it's even more comfortable than it looks.

The houses around here tend to be squished pretty closely together, but the amount of foliage offers a nice sense of privacy. Better than the yard at our house, by far. We have the view of the ocean going for us, but it's clear the previous owner didn't put much effort into maintaining it. And sitting out there makes me feel like a bug under a microscope on display for the neighbors. The same feeling I have everywhere I go these days, to be honest.

The kind of feeling that makes me want to hole up in the house and close all the blinds to salvage whatever peace I can get.

Fletcher's hand brushes my knee, and I blink. I hadn't realized he followed me over here.

"Where'd you go?" he murmurs.

I force a smile and shake my head. "Just thinking about how much work our yard needs in comparison."

I can tell by the look in his eye that he doesn't quite buy it, but he lets it go and turns to the fire pit. "Want this on?"

"*Please.*"

I tuck my knees into my chest and make myself comfortable on the sofa as Fletcher kneels and messes around with something on the other side of the fire pit until it ignites.

"Are you as close with your dad as you are with your mom?" I ask.

He bobs his head and slides into the seat next to me. "He's been busy with one of their flips, so he hasn't been around as much lately, but yeah. He's..." A smile rises to his face. "He's a real softy."

I try to imagine it, having not one, but *two* parents you actually liked. Who liked you back. And I just...can't. My brain goes entirely blank.

Fletcher pulls one of my legs across his lap and leaves his hand on my ankle. "You wanna talk about today?"

I twist my mouth to the side, my nose burning with the threat of tears as I remember the sound of Casey's cries in the car. Desperate, *pleading* with me not to leave him. I can't even blame him if he ends up looking at me like the bad guy in all of this.

Julian can talk a big game all he wants about spending time with his son, but I know what the reality will be. Julian will do what Julian always does—he'll go about his usual schedule, and Casey will wait around for any scrap of attention he'll throw him, wondering why he's not good enough for more than a few seconds of his time.

It was easier to shield Casey from it when I was in the house too, to distract him.

"I don't know if I'm doing the right thing," I whisper.

Fletcher strokes his thumb along my leg. "It's new. The divorce, the custody—it'll take some getting used to for everyone."

"I just don't want him to feel let down by the both of us." I sniff and swipe my hand under my nose. "You know what?

Actually, I don't want to think about this anymore. Talk to me about something else."

Fletcher's eyebrows pinch together in concern, but all he says is "Like what?"

"Like...tell me more about you."

"What do you want to know?"

"Everything."

A corner of his mouth kicks up, and he runs his hands up and down my legs. "I feel like you know a lot."

I shrug and finish off my wine. "Tell me something I don't know."

He hums and leans his head back like he's thinking hard about it. But then he gets this wide, goofy smile on his face. "My mom got a dog. His name's Charlie. He has a lazy eye and he's the size of a horse. She just showed up at my house with him one day out of nowhere."

That was the first thing that popped into his head? *He's trying to lighten the mood*, I realize. And it works. I laugh at the sheer randomness of it. "Is she always like that? Impulsive?"

He thinks about it for a second, then chuckles. "Yeah, I guess so. She just does her own thing."

"She sounds fun."

"That's a good word for her. She's just...happy. Happiest person I think I've ever met." He juts his chin at my empty wineglass. "Another?"

I smile and offer it to him.

He heads inside for the bottle, and I close my eyes, breathing in the fresh air and enjoying the gentle roar of the fire.

Once he's back and both of our glasses are refilled, he says, "Does this mean I get to ask you something now?"

I roll my head to the side to look at him. "I guess fair's fair."

He searches my face, as if debating his next words. But then something shifts behind his eyes, like he decided against whatever it was. Instead, he says, "I hear you throw a hell of a party. So when do I get to see you in action?"

I smirk. "Well, I actually *am* helping Gracie with something for next weekend. Do you want to come?"

"Would that...be okay?"

"I don't mean *with* me, obviously," I say quickly. "It's for a friend of hers who's from out of town, and Gracie wants her to get to know some people around here. A lot of people you know will be there—like Liam and Asher, and Gracie's brother. It's a pretty open guest list."

His eyes search mine. "But you'll be there?"

I nod.

His smile softens. "Then absolutely."

Hours pass like minutes as we drink and talk and soak in the last moments of the day. The sun sets, and Fletcher has to replace the propane tank to keep the fire going, but still, we don't go inside. We break out a second bottle of wine, and the later it gets, the closer I inch toward him on the couch without really meaning to. We add a blanket into the mix at some point, and he keeps my legs draped over his lap, his hands never breaking contact with me in one way or another—resting on my knee, stroking the inside of my ankle, or my shoulder, or linking with my own.

And every once in a while, he'll get this look on his face, like he's physically holding himself back from saying something, but then he'll shift the conversation to something equally light—what movies are my and Casey's favorites, what kind of music I listen to.

Once I'm several glasses of wine in, I say, "Just ask me whatever it is, Fletch."

He frowns and sips his drink. "Don't know what you mean."

I nudge him in the ribs, and he rolls his head toward me, his lips pressed together in a sheepish smile. "You don't have to answer it."

I nod.

"I...I guess I just wondered what led you here. I know you left home at sixteen, and you met your ex when you were around my age. So, what happened in between? That's a good six, seven years. And how the hell did you end up with a guy like that? Because you seem like the kind of person who wouldn't put up with his shit for even a second, let alone eight years."

My stomach dips a little, the same way it always does when memories from that time threaten to resurface. I blow out the air in my cheeks. To put it simply: a lot. A lot happened in those years.

And not much of it was good.

"I am now. I didn't used to be. I didn't used to be...a good person, Fletcher."

"I don't believe that for a second."

I don't meet his eyes. I can't.

"I know what people around here say about me. That I married him for his money. And they're not wrong," I whisper. "They're not wrong. But that also wasn't all it was."

I swallow hard and squint at the fire. The wine has me feeling barely in my body, and it loosens my tongue in a way I'll probably hate myself for in the morning. Fletcher strokes his thumb along my knee and waits.

"Things were...things were *bad* growing up. I never had clean clothes. Half of my mom's boyfriends liked looking at me more than her. Instead of helping me, it made her angry and bitter and jealous. I actually preferred the times we didn't have a roof over our heads, because at least then I was free of them. I kept thinking if I could just get out of West Virginia, then things would work out somehow. So I left. I didn't have a car—I didn't even have a bank account. But I had enough to buy a bus ticket that would get me to Richmond."

Fletcher shifts a little closer to me, and I startle out of whatever trance I'd been in as he brushes my hair behind my ear. Despite the heavy look in his eyes, it's not the same judgment and disgust I've grown used to seeing these past few months. "So you just went? All by yourself?"

I nod.

"What did you do when you got there?"

I shrug. Everything I owned could fit into a backpack and a duffel bag. The day I stepped off that bus...first, there was a moment of pure, giddy joy. I'd never seen a city that big, never been that far from home. And I'd done it. *I'd done it.*

But then reality came crashing in. And the icy, heavy *fear* that flooded my veins. I thought I'd felt fear before. Lived with it day in and day out.

But this chapter of my life was something different entirely. Not knowing where I'd sleep, when I'd eat next—that was nothing new. But doing it alone was.

I clear my throat, but the tightness there remains. "I got lucky. Really lucky. My plan was to find a job, maybe waiting tables. I'd done some of that back home. I didn't have enough money for a place to stay, but I could afford this cheap gym membership, so at least I had access to their showers. And I could put my things in their locker rooms during the day as long as I went back for them before they closed.

"I ended up finding a job as a maid at a hotel. A lot of the other workers were undocumented, so no one really asked questions. They paid me under the table in cash, and I started sleeping in the storage unit in the basement there behind the shelves, hoping no one would notice me. I figured if I could save up enough money for some cheap car—it wouldn't even need to run well—then I could go back to sleeping in there. And it worked, for a few weeks."

Fletcher lets out a deep breath, and a deep line is etched between his eyebrows now, but his gaze never leaves my face. His hand tightens around my knee.

"One of the other maids found me one morning. Her name was Irma. Until then, we'd barely exchanged a few words. She didn't speak much English. Before I could say anything, she turned around and left. I thought for sure she'd tell someone. I waited all day to hear from our boss, thinking they'd fire me… but then nothing happened. Until I went back there that night, and she was already there waiting." I smile a little and feel tears stinging the backs of my eyes. "She didn't say anything. She just offered me her hand. I don't know why I trusted her, but I did. She didn't have a car either, so we walked—it must have been at least a few miles—straight through the city until we got to this tiny house that was falling apart. It had two bedrooms and one bathroom, but about eight people were staying there. Nine now, with me."

I sniffle and clear my throat again. It doesn't help. Quietly, I add, "I don't know if I would've made it without her."

"How long did you stay with her?"

The tears I've been holding back fall.

"Chris." Fletcher closes what little distance was left between us and cups the back of my head with his hand.

"She died just a few months later. Heart attack." I blow out a breath and throw my hands up. "I—I barely knew her. We could barely communicate. I don't know why I'm—"

He pulls me against his chest and tucks my head beneath his chin. "That doesn't mean she wasn't important to you. She's someone who showed you kindness when you needed it."

"I think she's the reason I realized how bad things with my mom were. Because I only spent a few months with her, and I realized the way she tried to help me, to take care of me...my own mother had *never* done that."

Fletcher runs his hand up and down my back.

"Anyway. Staying there, it helped get me on my feet. I took on another job and saved as much as I could. Eventually managed to get my own place with some roommates. And things got uneventful for a while. When Julian came into the picture—I was up in DC. I'd never been and wanted to do some of the touristy sightseeing things. He was there on business."

I take a long, slow drink of my wine.

"I know how people see him. I know what people say. But I don't think he's a bad person. Or...I don't think he was always a bad person. He *really* loved his first wife. I knew he hadn't moved on when we met, and after eight years together, he still hasn't. I don't think he ever will. Life took the one person he ever really loved away from him, and I think he let that harden him past the point of no return. And instead of strengthening the relationships he has with their kids, it's like it was too painful. Maybe he sees too much of her in them.

"My point is, he might not have loved me, at least not like that. But when we met, we were both just...sad. And I think we were both hoping that the other would be the answer to pull us out of it. *But*, if I'm being honest, I don't think I would've pursued anything with him if not for his money too. And I know exactly how that sounds."

Fletcher doesn't say anything for what feels like a very, very long time. I peek up at his face, and the glow of the fire flickers across his profile.

"I don't think that makes you a bad person, Chris. One of the reasons people want money so much is for security. To feel safe, taken care of, so that they don't have to worry. You grew up without that. You never felt safe or secure; you never had someone really take care of you. So of course when you got older, you sought that out for yourself in the only way you knew how. That doesn't make you a bad person. I think...well, I think that makes you a survivor."

When he meets my eyes, the way he's looking at me isn't any different than how he looked at me before. And I realize I can take the comments and the jabs and the judgmental scowls from everyone in this town, but not from him. *Not from him.*

The knot in my chest loosens, and he cradles the side of my face and presses his thumb beneath my eye, catching a tear before it can fall.

"You should add psychologist to your very long list of job titles," I whisper.

He cracks a smile, and his eyes soften. "Stay."

I sigh and start to pull back, but he tightens his hold. "Stay here tonight, Chris. It's late. We've been drinking. I don't want you driving home."

"I am perfectly capable of getting myself home."

"I know you are... But can we also acknowledge that you haven't had the best luck lately? Do we really want to tempt fate here?"

I snort out a laugh. "I bet you've secretly loved it though. All those opportunities to swoop in and save the day."

"Damn right I have." We both laugh, and his thumb strokes my cheek. "Universe was throwing me a bone. Knew I needed a way in somehow."

My gaze drifts to his lips, so close to mine. I'm the one to lean in, but the second my mouth meets his, he pulls me in close and kisses me like I didn't just drop all of my dirty laundry at his feet. He weaves one hand through my hair, the other wrapping around my back as I climb into his lap and hold his face with both hands.

The way he kisses me has me drunker than the wine. My

stomach flips, and I feel like I'm on fire. Like I can't *breathe* unless he's kissing me. I whimper against his mouth, and he pulls me closer, kisses me harder, until we're both breathless.

But then abruptly, he pulls away.

I stare down at him, and his face pinches together like it's physically paining him to stop.

"I'm not having sex with you tonight," he says.

My eyebrows shoot up. "No?"

He looks from my eyes to my lips, and despite the clear longing burning beneath the surface, he says, "No. Because that's not all this is for me, and I don't ever want you to think that's all I want from you. You had a bad day, and I wanted to be here for you. And I want to be very clear that was my only intention inviting you over here."

My stomach clenches, and that fire in my veins spreads further. "You can't say things like that and then expect me not to want to sleep with you."

He chuckles breathlessly and runs his hands over my hair, then leaves them at the nape of my neck. He stares at me, and I can see the internal battle raging behind his eyes, but in the end, he sighs and says, "Come on. I'll get you something to wear and set you up in the guest room."

It becomes quickly apparent as I hold his hand and follow him to the second floor that driving home wouldn't have been an option. I sway a little on my feet and repeatedly have to brace my other hand on the railing.

He leaves me in the second bedroom with a T-shirt and a pair of his boxers on the dresser.

The room is nice, if a little plain. A queen-size bed, two nightstands, a dresser. The bathroom is across the hall, and once I've changed, I venture over there. It's nearly identical to the one of the first floor—sleek, updated, small.

The floor creaks, and Fletcher steps out of the primary bedroom, now wearing nothing but a pair of sweatpants.

And this point he's just taunting me.

I hook my hand around my opposite elbow and lean against the wall in the hallway. "You're really going to put me in your guest room?"

"Yeah, I am." He smiles and slowly crosses the distance between us. The amusement in his eyes fades as he stops in front of me, replaced by that same low burning fire I'd seen in them outside. "Chris, I'm more attracted to you than I've ever been to anyone in my life. So yeah, it would be easy to fall into bed with you every damn time we're in the same room. But I don't want that physical attraction I have for you to overshadow everything else." His brow furrows, and the intensity in his eyes pins me to the spot. "I want to get to know you. I want to spend time with you. And I need to be able to show you that with more than just my words. So yes, I'm going to put you in my guest room, and I'm going to kiss you on the cheek and say goodnight, and then I'm going to walk away."

I swallow hard as his words melt through me. Because as much as I want his self-control to slip and for him to take me against the wall here and now... I think I need what he's saying even more.

"So." He takes one final step forward and slides his hand along my face until he cups the side of my head. I take a deep breath, bracing myself for the scent of him as he leans in and presses his lips to my opposite cheek. "Goodnight," he murmurs against my skin.

I'm practically vibrating with need as he hesitates for a second, two. A shaky breath passes my lips.

But then, true to his word, he pulls back and meets my eyes one last time before turning away and walking back to his room.

Chapter Twenty-One
CHRISTINE

The plain, unassuming bed in Fletcher's guest room is *heaven*. I don't think I've ever fallen asleep faster. The blissful, dreamless sleep, however, is short-lived.

The floorboards creak outside my door, and I startle awake. I blink, my vision blurry, and watch under the crack in the door as the shadows of footsteps pass and head downstairs.

Fletcher's already up? What time is it?

I roll over and grab my phone from the nightstand. God, it's not even 4:30 AM yet.

Psychopath.

I tuck myself deeper into the blankets and promptly fall back asleep.

By the time I wake again, sunlight is streaming through the window, and something smells *divine*.

I stumble out of bed and toward the stairs like a woman possessed. After everything with Casey yesterday, I didn't have much of an appetite. My stomach is now very loudly protesting that choice.

I round the corner, and Fletcher is standing in the kitchen with his back to me, switching between several pans on the stove. From the smell of it, there's potatoes and eggs in there somewhere.

"Can I help with anything?" I ask.

He whips around, his smile immediate, and shakes his head. "Have a seat."

He's already dressed for the day. It's nothing fancy—some shorts, a gray crewneck, and a baseball cap—but my ovaries are a little too enthused at the sight. I immediately regret not looking in the mirror before coming down here. I slide onto one of the barstools and tuck my hair behind my ears.

"How do you take your coffee?" he asks.

"Anything's fine."

He opens a cabinet and pulls two mugs down. "I don't want *fine*. I want *good*. How do you like it?"

"As sugary and sweet as you can possibly make it."

He smiles wide as he juggles pouring the coffee, procuring the extra ingredients for mine, and keeping everything he's cooking on the stove in good shape.

"Are you sure I can't help?"

"Don't lift a finger." As if it's a well-practiced routine, he flips all the burners off, adds the creamer, and walks over to slide a cup in front of me. "I hope you're hungry," he says as I blow on the coffee a few times and take a sip.

"Starving," I admit, then look up at him with wide eyes. "Caramel creamer?"

He smirks, shrugs, and takes a sip of his. "So I like it sweet too." He braces his arms on the island across from me and leans forward. "You sleep okay?"

I bob my head. "That bed is insanely comfortable. Did I hear you get up at like four in the morning though?"

His smile falters, just for a second, but then he spurs back into action to put together a few plates by the stove. He shrugs with his back to me. "I've always been a morning person."

By the time he sets a plate in front of me, it's piled high with hash browns, an omelet, and berries. I shamelessly dive in and moan as I take the first bite.

He grins as he takes the seat beside me. "Good?"

"Delicious."

His grin settles into a self-satisfied little smirk as I inhale my plate.

I feel him watching me and hold up a hand to cover my mouth as I chew. "What?"

His smile is soft, and he shakes his head. "I'm just really glad you're here, Chris."

I stop chewing, but before I can respond, there's a knock on the door.

My eyes widen. "Are you expecting someone?" I whisper.

He frowns and shakes his head.

The person knocks again.

I jump up from my seat as if just now remembering where I am. What I'm *wearing*. I point down at his boxers, then to the stairs as if to say *I need to go change.*

He nods and waits until I'm halfway up the stairs before getting up.

I have one foot in the guest room when I hear him open the door and say, "Mom?"

You have got to be fucking kidding me.

I yank yesterday's clothes on, then tiptoe to the bathroom to check myself in the mirror. After dabbing a wet towel under my eyes to pick up some smeared makeup and running my hands through my hair a few times, it's not that bad.

But when I'm done, I freeze. Am I supposed to go down there? I can't hide up here forever. What if she's planning on staying for a while? I can hear the low buzz of their voices but can't make out what they're saying.

She's probably seen the two plates and coffees on the counter by now, so she knows someone else is here. At least Fletcher let me hide my car in his garage last night, so she didn't see that.

But meeting his *mother*? That's about as far from *let's have a secret drink at my place* as you can get.

Seeing no other choice, I steel myself with a breath and head downstairs. Fletcher's eyes shoot to me the moment I round the corner. He's at the head of the kitchen table, and a woman with a wide, floppy hat is sitting across from him with her back to me.

And there's a *mountain* of a dog beside her.

Fletch shoots to his feet and heads toward me, mouthing *I'm so sorry* as soon as he's out of his mom's sight range.

She turns around and beams.

Despite not being blood related, I can see so much of Fletcher in that look. Her eyes light up, like she's genuinely delighted to see me even though we've never met.

"Mom," Fletcher says slowly. "This is Christine. Christine, this is my mother, Jodie."

"So nice to meet you." She jumps up, and I smile, expecting her to go for a handshake, but then she's throwing her arms around me and pulling me into a tight hug.

"Oh. You too." I laugh a little as she pulls away. Fletcher's hand brushes my back as if to steady me, then yanks away like he thought better of it.

"And this must be Charlie," I add.

The dog stares at me, his tongue hanging out of the corner of his mouth.

Jodie stands up a little straighter, her smile broadening as she looks between me and her son. There's a glint in her eyes that makes me shift my weight uncomfortably. "So you've talked about him."

"I may have mentioned my mother lost her mind and mistook a horse for a dog," Fletcher mutters.

"I'm sorry to just show up," she says. "I saw that the weather was supposed to be not quite so hot and thought we could make some good progress in the backyard." Out of the corner of her mouth, she adds, "It's not like you usually have company. How was I supposed to know?"

"I was on my way out anyway," I say.

Fletcher turns to me, the light in his eyes dimming. Does he want me to stay? I figured me excusing myself would be the cleanest, easiest way out of this situation.

"Oh, nonsense!" says his mom. "I see you haven't even had a chance to finish your coffee yet. And besides, I could use another opinion. Come, come." She heads for the back door and waves for me to join her. "I need you to tell my son he's wrong. Maybe he'll listen to you."

Fletcher sighs. "Mom, don't rope her into this. She has—"

"Hush. No one asked you. I'm talking with Christine. Don't follow us. I want her unbiased opinion."

I pinch my lips together to hold in my laugh, especially when I see the exasperation bleeding into Fletcher's expression.

Seeing as I apparently have no choice in the matter, I slip my coffee from the counter and start to follow, but Charlie cuts in front, ambling along like his legs can barely hold his weight.

She stops in the center of the yard and gives Charlie's head a single pat as he plops down at her feet.

"So, um, what did you need another opinion on?" I ask as I step up beside her.

She waves a hand. "Oh, nothing. But stand here with me for

a bit and pretend like we're talking about it, will you? Let him sweat in there."

I bark out a laugh, and she grins at me. I have a feeling she gets her way whether she has the majority vote or not.

"It really is looking amazing back here though," I add. "Which I hear is your doing."

"Thank you. That's kind of you to say. If left to his own devices, this would be a boring, empty plot of grass. He's got an eye for the interior stuff, I'll give him that, but *here*." She spreads her hands wide as if presenting art. "This is where the magic can happen."

I sip my coffee and pretend to not notice the way she's sizing me up now.

"How's he doing?" she asks suddenly.

I blink. "Fletcher? I—I mean, well, I think?"

The corners of her lips turn down. "Has he been sleeping?"

Sleeping? My mind jumps to this morning. With how late we went to bed, he couldn't have gotten more than a few hours of sleep. And come to think of it, the only other night we spent together—at the hotel—he slipped out at an ungodly hour then too. But I'd chocked it up to his work schedule.

At my silence, she sighs. "I know he doesn't like me digging into his business. I just worry...if the nightmares are back... prolonged sleep deprivation like that is no joke. Just, if you care about him, look out for him, would you?"

Not knowing how else to respond, I nod.

Nightmares?

I don't know why she thinks we're close enough that he would've opened up to me about something like that, and I don't know why my stomach dips at the realization that he hasn't.

I poured my guts out to him last night—hell, even that first night together, he got more information out of me than anyone has in years, maybe ever.

At the time, I'd thought he'd done the same.

I glance at the windows over my shoulder even though the sun reflecting off them prevents me from seeing him on the other side.

Apparently there's still a lot about him that I don't know.

FLETCHER

Christine leaves not long after whatever conversation she had with my mother outside.

"Mom, you don't have to clean," I sigh as she starts collecting the pots off the stove. I step in and take them before she can reach the sink, because the only thing that'll stop her is if I do it immediately. "What did you say to Chris?"

Mom frowns and shakes her head like I've said something ridiculous. "Nothing. Anyway, why didn't you tell me you were dating someone? Especially someone that pretty?"

"We're just friends, Mom."

She scoffs and slides onto a barstool as I coat everything in soap. "I did *not* raise you to be afraid of commitment."

"I—I am not afraid of commitment."

She squints at me. "Then why are you playing games with her?"

I throw my hands up and laugh. "I'm not playing games!"

"You're also not her friend, so tell me the truth."

I cover my face with my hands and groan.

"What? You think you're going to find someone better?" she continues.

"Mom."

"One girl isn't enough for you? Is that it? Because I know I raised you better than *that*."

"It's not *me*," I snap, then grimace. Shouldn't have said that.

Her eyebrows nearly disappear into her hairline. "*She* doesn't want to make things official?"

I sigh and focus on rinsing the dishes. "It's complicated. Please, Mom, for once in your life, stay out of this."

She's silent for a long time, which can only mean she's analyzing me—my expression, my body language, my *aura*, which she insists she can see. I try to give nothing away, but it's useless against whatever superpowers she's got.

"So you two are dating," she finally says.

I flick the faucet off and I rub my eyes until stars burst behind my eyelids. "No, Mom. I told you. We're just friends."

She scoffs. "I could've lit a cigarette in the air around you two."

I squint a single eye open. "You don't smoke, and that's not even an expression."

"I know, I just made it up. It's called being creative."

I press the heels of my hands into my eyes again.

"She's important to you."

"I'm not talking about this anymore," I mutter.

"Well, let me tell you this, Fletcher Conway, if that girl can't see what she has right in front of her, then she—"

"*Don't* finish that sentence."

She hums. "You're protective of her." She sounds pleased.

I'm never getting out of here alive.

I drop my hands and meet her eyes. "Mom, you are welcome in my life. You know that. But this? I need you to stay out of it. I'm not kidding around."

She stares at me, hard. The way that used to make me squirm as a kid. But now, I stare right back.

And finally, *finally*, she raises her palms in a placating gesture. "Fine."

Other than Chris taking Casey to and from camp, I don't see her much for the rest of the week. And from what I hear, she spends basically every waking hour with Gracie as they finalize everything for the party the following weekend.

I show up thirty minutes after Chris said it would start in a pathetic attempt to mask my eagerness. When I first pull up, all I can do is stare. I never doubted her for a second, but *oh my God*. I don't know why I was expecting some kind of small get-together, but every sidewalk leading up to the house for several blocks is packed.

Carson offered her place for the venue to help Gracie's budget, and it's clear every saved penny got put to good use. Despite being a well-known place for a party around here, I don't think I've been to Carson's more than once or twice. It's not difficult to pick out though.

It's the only house on the block that looks like it time traveled to October in the middle of July.

Lights from the lawn drench the outside in neon purple and red, and boards are haphazardly nailed over the windows as if it's condemned. Fog from a dry ice machine seeps out of the front door, and screams intermittently pierce the air from somewhere inside.

I asked Christine to spare me the details so I could be surprised. I'd been picturing something posh and fancy—something more fitting for a Brooks. Definitely not a haunted house. I guess she did say the movie had zombies.

As I draw closer, I notice a news crew stationed in the opposite lawn. A man I don't recognize in an expensive-looking suit nods along to whatever the reporter is telling him as the camera crew sets up.

A line winds down the sidewalk, waiting to get through the front door. Judging by the strobe lights and music pouring out from the backyard, the main party is back there once you make it through the house.

Perfect timing, apparently, because Christine chooses that moment to slip out the gate. My grin when I see her is immediate. She's in a gray floor-length dress that's absolutely ripped to shreds and covered in fake blood. Her hair is twice the size it usually is and looks like she just jumped out of an airplane.

I jog across the street as she turns for the side door to the garage.

"Wish you would've given me a heads-up on the dress code," I say.

Her eyes crinkle around her smile. "You made it."

God, that smile threatens to knock the wind out of me.

She shamelessly looks me up and down before turning for the door. "And you look great. Costumes are just for the actors in the house."

I grab the door and hold it open for her. "So you're telling me I missed you jumping out and scaring people in there?"

"Oh, don't worry, I'll make my return." She gives me a slow wink over her shoulder before flipping on the garage lights, illuminating what she must have come in here for. Extra ice, drinks, and snacks are lined up along the wall.

"Are the movie people here yet?"

Her eyes go comically wide. "Yeah! Did you see that some news stations showed up to cover it? I thought it was just going to be Gracie's friend, but a few of her costars and the producer are here. And I think a PR person—I don't know.

There were a lot of names all at once. I guess they saw this as an opportunity for some free publicity."

Her words come out so fast they nearly trip over each other. She's *nervous*, I realize. Something I don't think I've ever seen from her before.

"Chris." I soften my voice. "It looks amazing."

She scoffs as she bends down for an ice bag. "You haven't even been inside yet!"

I scoop up the bag before she can. "Then lead the way."

"Oh no." She tries to take the bag from me, but I back up a step. "You're not taking the shortcut. You're going through that house."

I sigh and let her take the bag. I have a feeling she'll start wrestling me for it if I don't.

"Of course. Wouldn't want to miss the full experience."

"You can skip the line though," she says. "Security at the door has your name."

"Oh, am I on *the list*?"

"See you inside." She offers a coy smile before disappearing through the door.

The line outside erupts in whispers as I cut to the front, but no one says anything to me. Maybe they think I'm part of the movie. I can't help but feel bad about it. And if it didn't look like it would take an hour, I'd just wait my turn. My impatience to see Christine—even if I'm offered only stolen glimpses tonight—wins out.

Okay, and my curiosity. If the screams piercing the air every few seconds are any indication, she did an amazing job in there. The laughter and music drifting from the backyard is quite the contrast.

I'd mostly been joking in the garage, but when I tell my name to the burly security guard—bouncer? Did she seriously hire a bouncer?—at the front, he literally pulls out a list before grunting and letting me pass.

The moment I step inside, he tugs the door shut behind me, casting me into near darkness. Fog drifts along the floor, illuminated by the green light strips on the baseboards. I inch down the hall, and it feels unusually narrow, only a few inches wider than the set of my shoulders. It can't always be like this—

Something touches the back of my neck, and I let out a startled noise and whip around just as the hand disappears through the wall on my right.

"Jesus Christ," I mutter, then quicken my steps.

More hands shoot out on either side as I move, tugging at my clothes. Low, zombie-like groans echo from whoever the hands belong to.

When I turn into what I'm assuming used to be the living room, the lights shift to purple and the fog doubles. I can only see so much in the darkness, but the walls seem to be covered in tattered, blood-soaked wallpaper and ripped quarantine sighs. They're streaked with handprints, as if people were desperately trying to escape.

On the other side of the room, the TV is on. It flickers on and off over and over, the sound of static filling the room.

A flash of movement in my peripheral vision nearly makes me jump out of my skin. A dark figure lingers in the corner—has it been there the entire time? It's so close to the doorway to the kitchen that there's no way to continue without passing it.

I wonder if Chris has cameras in here and she's sitting somewhere laughing at me.

"I will give you five dollars to stay the hell away from me," I say.

The figure slinks away from the wall and—

—removes the hood of his cloak.

"Oh, hey, Fletch," says Asher.

I let out a breathy laugh and cross the distance between us. "Didn't know you got roped into this."

"Oh, I volunteered," he says with a grin.

Of course he did.

He slips his hood back on, letting it fall low enough to obscure his face. "Gotta stay in character. I'll catch you later?"

I pat him on the back and brace myself as I round the corner to the kitchen, but no one jumps out at me. There's a makeshift wall cutting down the middle, forcing you to snake through the laundry room before circling to the back door. Body parts are strewn throughout, dripping in fake blood. Red LED lights along the floor illuminate the way, but they're dim. That along with the fog has me squinting trying to see more than a foot in front of myself.

God, I hate haunted houses. I tug on the collar of my shirt, my chest feeling tight. *It's fog, not smoke. You can breathe just fine.*

But every time I blink, I can see the orange glow of the fire, feel the heat singeing the hairs in my nose, feel my lungs aching around each breath. A distorted laugh track echoes in the distance—

Something wraps around me from behind, and I spin, my breaths shallow and my heart in my throat.

"Fletcher?"

I blink, and it takes several moments too long for my vision to focus on Christine.

Long enough for her to release her arms around my neck and take a step away from me.

The red lights cast strange shadows over her features. I must have drifted forward without realizing, because we're in the laundry room now, a few steps away from the haunted house's exit.

I let out a shaky breath and try to disguise it as a laugh. "You scared me."

She squints like she doesn't believe me, and I smooth out whatever expression was on my face.

"So did I pay my dues or what?" I say, trying to keep my voice light. "Am I allowed at the party now?"

A chorus of screams erupts at the front of the house as a new group steps inside, and that, thankfully, ushers Chris forward. I follow her to the back door, and the moment she opens it, the music floods inside.

The backyard is smaller than mine, but Chris put every inch to good use. The DJ is on the far side, and warm string lights and lanterns crisscross overhead. There are a few bar tables along the outskirts, as well as a long table full of food and drinks, but the main attraction is the dance floor in the center.

Once I'm out of that fog, I finally feel like I can *breathe.*

Chris shoots me a quick smile before heading off into the crowd, and I force my face not to show my disappointment. But of course she can't hang around me all night. I'm sure she has a million things to juggle to keep things running smoothly, and I told her I could do this. That I could keep things under wraps when we're in public. Staring at her ass as she traipses across the lawn probably doesn't have me off to a great start.

"Hey, Fletch, you made it!" Liam claps me on the back with a wide grin. Gracie hangs off his arm, her smile warm but her eyes alert, as if scanning the party for disaster to strike at any minute.

"Congrats on the party, Gracie," I say. "It looks amazing."

Her eyes finally focus on my face, and her smile turns a little sheepish. "Thanks. It turned out even better than I could have hoped for. Christine is a miracle worker."

One corner of my mouth kicks up despite myself. I clear my throat. "Where's your friend—the guest of honor?"

"Oh, I think that's me!" A tiny brunette appears on Gracie's other side. She thrusts her hand out to shake. "I'm Martina. But everybody calls me Marti."

I offer my hand, and she shakes it firmly. "Fletcher. Congrats on the movie."

She beams so wide I can see every one of her teeth. "Thank you. I still can't quite believe it."

The side gate creaks open on my right, and two men slink through like they're trying not to be seen. One is the man I saw talking with the reporters earlier. He says something to the other before disappearing into the crowd. The second man hesitates by the gate with so much tension in his body he's practically vibrating. He's younger than the first, his suit more expensive looking. His shoulders are thrown back and his head is held high, but there's something off with his eyes. They flicker around restlessly, never focusing on one person or thing for more than a few seconds.

There's a noticeable shift in the air the moment he steps into the yard, especially with the female population. Spines straighten, whispers are exchanged, and every eye in the room seems to find its way to him, but the second he makes eye contact, people hurriedly look away.

What in the hell...

"Marti. There you are." Suit man pops in, wraps an arm around her shoulders, and starts angling her toward the gate like the rest of us aren't there. "We're going to start with a few shots by the drinks. I think laughing will be best. Make it look like you're having a good time with him." When he notices the second man didn't follow, he flaps a hand impatiently until he joins us.

"Stephen!" Marti chastises. "Rude. I was talking to people."

The man glances at us, the lift of his eyebrow distinctly unimpressed. "Apologies, but we have a little work to be done. I'll bring her back. Jared, are you ready?"

The second man just stares at him.

"Right." He hooks one arm through each of theirs and tugs them toward the food table.

Marti pushes her lower lip out and offers a mouthed *Sorry* over her shoulder.

"*So*," Liam says, drawing the word out, his attention on his girlfriend. "Have you gotten his autograph yet?"

She swats him in the chest. "Enough."

"He seems like he'd be perfectly down for a selfie," he continues.

"Who is he?" I ask.

"Jared Morgan," Gracie says on a sigh, as if that explains everything.

He must be the costar. I follow the path they carve through the crowd—which isn't difficult, since everyone gives them a wide berth. Odd. Don't people usually swarm celebrities? Jared's still glaring at Stephen—some PR person, I'd guess—as a photographer prepares to take a picture of him and Marti.

Things turn relatively uneventful after that. I spend a good amount of time looking for Christine but pretending I'm not. I catch glimpses—a flash of her hair, her profile, her laugh somewhere in the crowd. But she doesn't stop moving all night, making sure everything is perfect.

And it is *perfect*. Not that I've been to many events like this, but I've never seen one run so smoothly. All the guests seem satisfied, and at some point, Gracie even relaxes enough to join in the fun.

She'd shrugged it off that day at the skatepark like this was some passing hobby for her. But Christine is damn good at this.

In the rare moment when I manage to catch her eye across the yard, I smile, hoping she can see in my eyes how proud I am of her. I can see her cheeks redden, even from here, and it's the single best moment I have all night.

Chapter Twenty-Three
CHRISTINE

"You're gonna stay the *whole* time?" Casey demands.

I nod seriously as I hold the car door open and wait for him to climb down. At some point in the past few weeks, he decided he's absolutely too old for my help now. "Every last minute."

His feet have barely hit the pavement before he takes my hand and drags me toward the skate park with every ounce of strength he has.

"Casey—"

"Moms sit over here," he informs me as he leads the way to the picnic tables.

Fletcher looks up from the makeshift sign-in table as we approach, and a wide smile spreads across his face.

"Case! Ready to show us what you're made of today?"

Casey nods excitedly, then points at the seat he wants me to take.

I laugh a little but comply.

It's the final day of camp, which means it's basically a

performance to the parents to show everything they learned over the past three weeks.

Fletcher's eyes meet mine as Casey dives for the stockpile of skateboards to pick which one he wants. "You're sticking around today?"

I shrug and widen my eyes in mock awe. "Had to see what all the fuss was about. Casey said his teacher was like a skating god or something."

Fletch's eyes crease around his grin. "Did he now?"

I make a big show of looking around the rest of the park, which is still mostly empty. "So where is Liam anyway?"

He throws his head back in a laugh, then crosses his arms over his chest and shakes his head. "You are a mean, mean woman."

I press my lips together to hold my response back.

I can think of quite a few times he didn't seem to think I was mean.

"I'm here, I'm here. Hey, Case." Liam jogs up with a tired smile and pats Fletcher on the back. "Christine, hey, thank you again for helping with that party last week. Gracie hasn't stopped talking about it since."

I wave a hand in front of my face. "Of course."

"No, really. I know you put a lot of work into it."

"It was really something," Fletcher adds.

I squirm a little under the praise. Truthfully, the party turned out even better than I could have hoped for. If anything, I'm relieved. Especially with the way some news outlets picked it up and tied it to talk of that upcoming movie. Thank *God* it wasn't a disaster.

And with my name attached to it now...who knows. Maybe Gracie was right and this could turn into a new chapter for me.

"I was happy to do it."

As the other kids and their parents start arriving, Liam and

Fletcher get pulled this way and that, answering questions or helping the kids get into their gear.

"Oh, hi!" Gloria, Erin's mom, slides into the seat next to me as she smiles and waves at her daughter. Out of the corner of her mouth, she says, "Are you going to be covering your eyes this whole time too?"

I laugh, a weight lifting from my shoulders that I hadn't realized was there at the sight of a friendly face. The other moms aren't rude, exactly, but they congregate around a different table. "Probably."

"Erin's been asking about doing another playdate," she adds.

"Oh, I'm sure Casey would love that. I swear I heard about the fort they made for *days*."

"That's about how long it took to clean it up," says Gloria, and we both laugh.

Fletcher looks over at the sound, his eyes catching mine, and my smile grows—then I remember where I am and quickly look away.

The kids start with some of the smaller obstacles around the park—little ramps and rails. Hearing Casey describe what they were learning and watching it are two very different things. I wince and brace my shoulders each time one of them goes, even when it isn't my kid. They do the tricks one by one, with either Liam or Fletcher lingering nearby as if ready to intervene. For some of the smaller kids, they break out their own skateboards and push alongside them to help them gain some speed, then keep holding their hand throughout the duration of the trick.

When it's not Casey's turn, I can't help it. My eyes keep getting pulled back to Fletcher. He cheers the kids on and gives each of them a high five after every trick. But despite that easy smile, his eyes miss nothing. He tracks every movement, and though most of the kids land their tricks successfully, it's like he can already tell when something will go wrong, and he jumps in and throws an arm around the kid's waist, catching them before they can hit the ground.

One of the girls freezes up at the top of a ramp, chewing on her lip and looking from the concrete in front of her to the picnic tables. Fletcher inches closer, talking to her in a voice too low to hear.

She murmurs something, and he cups a hand around his ear like he can't hear her. "Why?"

"I'm brave and tough!" she calls.

He flashes his stupidly perfect toothy smile. "That's right. Now let's go."

She lowers her head, all business now, and kicks off.

It's wrong on so many levels, but I am an absolute puddle watching it. Watching *him*.

But then it comes to that monstrous hole in the ground—the bowl, I think they called it—and I feel like I'm about to be sick.

Gloria pats my leg comfortingly as Casey steps up to the edge, head held high. Fletcher hops over the side so he stands at the bottom while Casey balances his board at the top. My heart is in my throat, and I find myself rising to my feet.

Fletcher holds out his hand for Casey to grab.

I force myself not to turn away because I know how badly Casey wants me to watch, even though every cell in my body is screaming to cover my eyes.

Casey drops down into the bowl, and Fletcher keeps holding his hand until he hits the bottom, then lets him go. I hold my breath as Casey shoots across at way too fast of a speed, but instead of slamming into the other side or tumbling off, he glides halfway up, turns, and rolls back toward us with a huge grin, completely in control.

I'm jumping up and down and cheering before I realize it.

Both from relief, but also...something else. Life has felt like it came to a screeching halt the moment I decided to go through with the divorce. Like everything's been on pause. But over a year has passed now. And somewhere in there...Casey has grown up. I was so wary about this camp, thinking he was too young for it. I don't know if I'm impressed or shocked or...sad. Maybe a strange combination of all three.

Casey stops, kicks up the board, and flashes a proud grin up at me.

Since it's the last day, the camp runs late with a mini celebration. They order pizza, and the kids are presented with little finger skateboards to take home.

Gloria and Erin are deep in conversation with Liam on the other side of the park, and I linger by the pizza table as Casey runs around with a few of the other kids.

I'd like to think Gloria being the only friendly person here is all in my head, but every time I meet one of the parents' eyes and smile, they either pretend to not see, or they give me a tight, uncomfortable twitch of their lips and turn away.

I take a sip from my water bottle and focus on Casey instead. He's laughing and chasing one of the other boys around, so carefree and...happy. I don't think I've ever seen him this way around other kids.

"So. How does it feel to be the mother of the star student?" Fletcher leans against the table beside me, a slight smile on his lips as he watches the kids.

"He really was good, wasn't he?"

"It meant a lot to him to have you here. And I know...being here isn't the most comfortable for you."

At first I think he's talking about himself, but he's frowning, his gaze trained on the other moms who snubbed me a few minutes ago.

I grimace. So it's as obvious on the outside as it feels.

"You look beautiful," he murmurs.

I glance at him out of the corner of my eye. "Don't flirt with me here."

"Then where would you like me to flirt with you?"

The harder I try to fight my smile, the wider his smirk grows. I shake my head and turn back to the park...

...and see a sleek black SUV pull up to the curb on the opposite side.

And out steps my ex-husband.

Casey freezes when he sees him, and the rest of his friends go running off without him.

"Hey, bud," calls Julian.

"What the hell?" I shove away from the table.

Casey whips around with wide eyes when he sees me coming. I'd asked him a while ago if he wanted me to invite his dad too, but he'd been pretty adamant that he only wanted me to come today. Did he change his mind and somehow invite him here? But judging by his face, he's as surprised as I am.

"What are you doing here, Julian?" I ask.

"I need a reason to see my son?" When I don't bother to dignify that with a response, he sighs. "I got back early from my trip. Thought I'd pick him up, we could spend some time together—"

"You thought you'd just come pick him up?" I cut in. "Without running it by me first?"

"I think I've been very patient with you through this whole ordeal," he says in a low voice. "I don't need your permission to see my son. Come on, Casey. Get in the car."

"You're not taking him anywhere. If you hadn't noticed,

today's kind of a big deal for him. He's playing with his friends right now."

"Looks like things are pretty much done here anyway, so what's the big deal?" Julian's gaze cuts to me. "Nothing to cause a scene over."

The rage boiling inside of me threatens to reach a breaking point. *I* am not the one causing a scene. I clench my hands into fists at my sides and force myself not to yell. "You can't swoop in whenever you feel like it. You want to see him? Fine. Then you talk to me, and we plan something. You don't get to just show up and take him."

"Everything all right over here?" Fletcher steps up beside me, arms crossed over his chest and his jaw hard as he takes Julian in.

Julian barely spares him a glance. "We're fine. Come on, Casey—"

Fletcher takes another step forward. "You're not taking him anywhere."

That, finally, gets Julian to look at him. His lip curls. "And who the hell are you?" His eyes flick to me, and his lip curls further, like I'm some dogshit smeared on the bottom of his designer shoes. "Is this what you've been up to?"

"You need to leave, unless you'd like me to call the police," says Fletcher.

Julian barks out a cold, mean laugh. "I'd very much like it if you did. Go on, go on. Call them. Or better yet?" He pulls his phone out of his suit pocket. "Do you want their personal numbers? Is the deputy okay, or should I try the sheriff instead?"

Dread pools in the pit of my stomach like hot tar. I don't care what our legal documents say. If Julian wants to take him, I don't think anyone would stop him.

"See, I run this camp," says Fletcher. "And I'm legally obligated to ensure the kids only leave with the adults on their forms. Casey only has one person legally permitted to pick him up. His mom."

I turn, then freeze.

"Casey?" I ask in a small voice.

Fletcher whips around.

He was standing right behind me. He was there just a second ago.

I look around wildly, thinking maybe he got pulled back into a game with his friends, but no. They're all over on the opposite side of the park, and there's no sign of him.

Not in the bowl, not by the tables, not with the other kids.

"Casey," I mean to call, but it comes out closer to a gasp.

"Jesus Christ." Julian stomps up beside me. "Are you happy now—?"

Fletcher steps between us. "How about you get the fuck out of her face and go look for your son?"

Tears build rapidly in my eyes as I whip my head back and forth. "Casey," I gasp. "Casey."

Someone jogs over to us—I think it's Liam. He and Fletcher exchange words, but I can barely hear over the roaring in my ears. My breaths come in short and fast as I stumble through the park, desperately looking around.

"He gets upset and hides when people argue," Liam is saying. "He's probably just camped out somewhere."

"Stay with her, okay? Look around here and call the police. I'm gonna jump in the car and circle the park. Chris. Chris?" A hand finds my face, then eyes are right in front of mine. "Breathe. Take a deep breath. Breathe. Liam's going to stay right here with you, and I'm going to go find him, okay?"

"Casey," I gasp like it's the only word I can say.

Fletcher presses his lips together into a hard line, stares at me for a second longer, then releases me and takes off. "Stay with her," he calls before disappearing into the parking lot.

Chapter Twenty-Four
FLETCHER

I tried to stay calm in front of Christine, but as soon as I take off toward the parking lot, all bets are off. I call out for Casey over and over, my heart *sprinting* in my chest.

Like Liam said, he's probably just hiding somewhere.

There's no way something happened to him. There's no way someone took him. Not when I was standing right there. I was *right* there.

I blink, and for a moment, I'm back in the fire. I'm chasing Lucy up the stairs, barely able to see a foot in front of me through the smoke. I'm calling for her, but my voice strains against my throat.

I shake my head to clear it.

Casey. I have to find Casey.

I search every corner of the park on the way to the parking lot, but he's nowhere to be seen. My hands shake as I unlock my car, jump inside, and turn it on. I'm about to shift into drive when a flash of movement in my rearview mirror catches my attention. I whip around, and there it is again through the back window.

I jump out of the truck and circle to the back.

And there in the bed, tucked in the corner, is Casey.

A choked sound escapes my throat, and I nearly fall to my knees.

"Christine! Liam! Over here!" I shout before jumping into the bed and hurrying toward him.

He's curled into a ball, his arms over his head like he's shielding himself from an explosion.

"Casey," I say gently as I crouch in front of him.

He peers up at me, his cheeks stained with tears.

I take his face between my hands, inspecting every inch of him. "You all right? You okay?"

He sniffles and nods.

"Oh, thank God." I pull him against my chest and let out a shaky breath.

"I'm sorry," he hiccups.

"Oh, Casey. It's okay. It's okay. I'm just glad you're okay." I peek over the top of the car to make sure Chris and Liam heard me. Sure enough, they're both hurrying over.

"I don't want to go with him," he whispers.

I tighten my arms. "You don't have to, Casey. I promise." I pull back and look him in the eyes. "But you can't run off like that, okay? You scared your mom and me really bad."

God, he looks fucking terrified. *Of his own dad.*

I hate this for him. I hate it so goddamn much. I've always had a soft spot for him, even before Christine came into the picture. He's probably the smartest kid I've ever met, and genuinely funny. He makes me laugh so hard my stomach hurts sometimes. And he's kind. Not in a *just following what he's taught is polite* kind of way. You can tell that empathy comes naturally to him.

But I've seen what bad situations can do to kids. Seen their personalities change, their lights dim. It was all around me growing up.

Logically, I know this isn't the same. But the thought of that happening to him, I can't bear it.

His lower lip wobbles. "I'm sorry."

"I know. Come on. Let's go see your mom." I scoop him up, and he wraps his arms around my neck as I climb down from the truck.

Christine is fully sobbing by the time she reaches us, and I gently transfer Casey to her arms.

"He's fine," I say. "He's okay."

She falls to her knees and brushes Casey's hair from his face, inspecting him much like I did a second ago.

"I'm sorry," Casey cries.

"Oh, Casey. You can't run off like that, okay? Promise me."

He nods, and she pulls him into a tight hug.

I check for any sign of Julian, but Liam already beat me to the punch. The two of them stand a few yards away, arguing and gesturing wildly with their hands. But after a few moments, their dad relents and turns for his car.

I crouch on Casey's other side and run my hand over Christine's hair. Despite having Casey back now, she hasn't stopped crying, and her breathing is dangerously close to hyperventilating. I lean my forehead against hers. "He's gone. He's leaving. It's all right. You're okay. You're both okay."

Tears stream down her cheeks as she pulls in a shaky breath. Casey's face is buried against her chest, and she keeps one arm protectively wrapped around him, her other hand fisted in my shirt.

For a moment, I'm lost in her eyes as the adrenaline subsides.

But then. *But then.*

My eyes widen, and I drop my hand from her face and pull back.

Her eyebrows tug together in question before she sits up a little straighter, as if also just now remembering where we are.

That there are many, many people around.

"Chris," I breathe, hoping she can see how sorry I am in my eyes. "I didn't—I wasn't thinking—"

She shrinks into herself as she looks around, her arms tightening protectively around Casey, but then she turns back to me. Her eyes flick between mine, something I don't quite understand brewing beneath the surface, and she leans in.

"Chris," I murmur, right before she presses her lips to mine.

The way I kiss her back is immediate, instinctual.

"I don't care anymore," she whispers, and more tears fall as she meets my eyes.

The...*defeat* in her voice, I can't stand to hear it. "Chris," I breathe.

She shakes her head. "I don't care anymore. Let them—let them. I *can't* care anymore."

Hesitantly, I cup her face and stroke my thumb over her cheek. This woman who's never done anything to anyone, and she hasn't deserved even a fraction of what she's gotten.

And the way she looks at me, with so much softness, so much trust, I think I could do just about anything as long as she keeps looking at me this way.

"Let me take you both home."

She gives a shaky nod and keeps her death grip on Casey as they rise to their feet.

"We'll take your car." I leave one hand on her back as I guide them that way. When I meet Liam's eyes, his expression is blank, but he's very much staring at us now.

I strap Casey in first, then squeeze Christine's shoulder as she climbs into the passenger seat and let her know I'll be right back before bracing myself and walking over to Liam.

He says nothing as I approach, but his eyebrows are sky-high as he looks from me to Chris.

"How'd it go with your dad?" I ask.

Liam rolls his eyes. "He backed off. For now, at least."

"Look, Li—"

"So how long has *this* been going on?"

I sigh. "What I told you a few weeks ago, about her coming into the bar, that was true. But we've also…run into each other quite a bit since then."

Liam frowns and nods slowly. I can't get a good read on him. With how easygoing he is about most things, I guess I just assumed he wouldn't be upset by this. But he and I usually don't keep things from each other.

"I really didn't know who she was until that first day of camp," I hurry to add, as if that makes it any better, and run my hand along the back of my neck. "So, over a month now, I guess. And I would've told you, but I promised her I wouldn't say anything."

He blows the air out of his cheeks, but then all he says is "Huh."

I grimace. "Huh?"

He shrugs. "It's fucking weird, I'm not going to lie. But also…I don't know. I don't have anything against it, I guess."

I mean, that's more than I could've hoped for. "You're cool with this? Really?"

He shrugs again, then a slow smile that I don't at all like the look of splits his face. "But to be clear, since she technically used to be my stepmom, does that mean I should call you Dad now?"

I chuckle and shake my head. "Shut up." I jab a thumb over my shoulder. "I've gotta—"

"Yeah." I turn, but don't make it far before he calls, "Fletch?"

When I look back at him, his eyebrows are drawn low over his eyes. "Just...if anything else comes up with my dad, if you guys need anything, call me, all right?"

I nod. "Thanks, Li."

Casey is so quiet in the back seat that I think he's asleep at first. But when I glance in the rearview mirror at a red light, I see his little face scrunched up like he's thinking hard as he looks from me to his mom.

What just happened seems to truly sink in for Christine about halfway into the drive. She sits up straighter, every muscle going rigid, and turns around to look at her son.

I have no idea if me jumping in right now will make matters worse, so I keep my mouth shut and wait for her to take the lead.

"You were so great today, honey," Chris finally says. "I was *so* impressed watching you. I don't know how you do it. It looked so scary."

"It's not that scary," Casey mumbles.

Casey, who usually glows under even the smallest scrap of praise.

This is not good.

I open my mouth, close it. I don't know if Casey still views me as his friend or as Public Enemy Number One now that he saw me kissing his mom. I glance at Christine out of the corner of my eye, but she seems as lost on what to do here as I am.

We pull up to the house, and I've barely shut off the engine before Casey unbuckles his seat belt, throws open his door, and marches toward the porch. He grabs the rock that hides the extra key and lets himself inside.

Christine hurries after him, but I hesitate in the car and rub my eyes.

Stupid. What was I *thinking*? I just fucking lost my mind back there. I was barely aware of where I was. All I knew was I needed to find Casey, and I needed to make sure he and Christine were okay. No one else around us registered. No one else around us *existed.*

And now Chris will be the one to suffer for it.

I climb out of the car and hesitantly let myself into the house. The main floor is empty, and quiet voices drift from upstairs. I head that way but pause when I make it outside Casey's door.

"Well, that's okay," says Christine. "You can think about it, and we can talk again later when you're ready, okay?"

Casey's response is too quiet for me to hear, then Chris is stepping into the hall, her shoulders drooped and her eyes exhausted.

I follow her to her bedroom at the opposite end of the hall so we're out of Casey's earshot before saying, "Chris, I'm so sorry. I didn't mean to—"

She lays her hand on my arm. "Fletch."

"I panicked. I wasn't thinking—"

"Fletcher."

"God, and to spring this on Casey…"

"Fletcher." She takes my face between both hands, forcing me to look at her, then brings her lips to mine. I freeze, and the kiss is over as quickly as it started. Her blue eyes bore into mine, and she gives my face a little shake. "I'm not upset with you."

"You're not?"

She tilts her head to the side like the thought is baffling to her. "For standing up for us? For finding Casey? For making sure I was okay? No, Fletcher, of course not."

I take my first full breath since we pulled into the driveway.

She smiles sadly and drops her hands.

"How'd it go in there?" I murmur.

She sighs and shakes her head. "He doesn't want to talk about it right now. I guess I'll just give him space." She chews on her lip. "I don't know how to handle this. I'm supposed to be the parent here, but I don't know what I'm doing."

"Can I...would it be all right if I talk to him?"

She looks from me to Casey's door. After a moment, she nods. I squeeze her shoulder, and she stays put as I turn for Casey's room.

He's sitting on his bed when I step inside, holding a stuffed sea lion in his lap.

"Hey, Case," I offer and hesitate a step into the room. He doesn't respond, but he doesn't ask me to leave, so I push forward and take the seat next to him.

I try to put myself in his shoes, to imagine what would be helpful to hear right now. But seeing as I never had a bond with a parent at his age like he does with Chris, it's difficult to picture.

But maybe he doesn't need a parent right now. Maybe he just needs a friend.

"You want to go get ice cream?" I ask. "Just you and me?"

He peeks up at me.

"And we can talk about it if you want to. Or we can just eat if you don't."

He hugs the sea lion tighter to his chest and nods.

We take the ice cream to go, then I park next to the beach and let him sit in the front seat with me while we eat. He inhales the first of his two scoops without a word, but just when I've started to give up hope in this little expedition, he says, "So you and my mom are boyfriend girlfriend."

He doesn't say it like a question, but I nod anyway. Honestly, I don't know if that's true. Don't know if that's how Christine sees this, or if this is something casual that I just paraded out in the open like an idiot. I'm not about to fumble my way through explaining that to a seven-year-old though.

His face scrunches together as he processes this answer.

"We're friends, aren't we, Case?"

He peeks at me out of the corner of his eye. After a moment, he nods.

"I want you to know that being with your mom doesn't change that for me. Does that make you not want to be friends anymore?"

He frowns down at his ice cream. "I still want to be friends."

"Well, good. Because I'd be sad if you didn't." This time when he peeks up at me, he's smiling a little. "Do you have any questions you want to ask me?"

He thinks about this for a while. But finally, he says, "Are you mean to her?"

I rear my head back. That's definitely not what I was expecting. Is *that* what this is about? I could understand wanting his mom to himself, or even feeling like someone was trying to replace his dad. But he's worried about *Chris*?

"No, Casey," I say softly. "I'm never mean to her."

He nods once, his little forehead scrunched up. "My dad's mean to her."

It feels like my heart falls into my stomach. How much did he hear before Chris left? How much did he see? Of course he's worried about his mom being in another relationship if the only one he's ever seen was something bad.

I swallow hard. "I care about your mom a lot, Case. And I care about you. I would never hurt either of you. You don't ever have to worry about that. And you don't ever have to worry about me being mean to her. I'm sorry that this probably surprised you."

"Can we go home now?"

I can't read the look on his face, can't tell if this made a difference or not, but I force a smile and keep my voice light as I say, "Yeah, bud. Let's go home."

Chapter Twenty-Five
CHRISTINE

Every time I hear a car drive by, I rush to the window to see if it's Fletcher pulling in. They haven't even been gone for twenty minutes, but it feels like hours.

Maybe it was a mistake sending Casey off with him. But then again, maybe Casey will be more willing to listen to him than me right now. That's what him agreeing to talk with Fletcher in the first place suggests. And I try not to feel...*hurt* by that.

I'm his mom. But when I tried to talk to him, he just shut down.

Fletcher on the other hand...Fletcher isn't just someone he looks up to. He's someone he wants to *be*. His talented, impressive teacher. The friend of his cool older brother.

I have no idea if that's going to help or hurt right now.

My shoulders tense as Fletch rounds the corner and pulls my car into the driveway. I half expect Casey to beeline for the door, but he hops out and waits for Fletcher, then the two head for the house hand in hand.

The sight of it does weird, cruel things to my heart.

I brace myself as they step through the door—I have no idea if Casey's seeming forgiveness extends to me—but when he turns the corner and sees me in the living room, he beams.

"Mom, can we make a fort and have a movie night?"

I blink from him to Fletcher, who lingers a few steps behind. What could he have possibly said to Casey to get a full one-eighty mood switch? He widens his eyes and shrugs.

"Uh, sure," I say. "I can make some popcorn. And we have fruit snacks."

"Can Fletcher stay?"

I freeze. Fletcher freezes.

"Well," I say slowly and meet his eyes. "Fletcher might have other plans…"

"I don't." He crouches beside Casey. "If it's okay with your mom, I'd love to stay."

I stare at my son, momentarily too stunned to know what to do. While they were gone, I'd been mentally preparing myself for days of pouting, maybe weeks, maybe more. A small part of me had worried this had irreversibly altered his trust in me.

I blink tears out of my eyes as my gaze drifts to Fletcher. "Of course you can stay."

Fletcher pats Casey on the back once before rising to his feet and heading for the kitchen. "You two get started on the fort. I'll get the snacks!"

We aren't allowed to start the movie until the fort is perfect, which includes a lot of Casey barking orders and pointing at things he wants us to move. All of the kitchen chairs end up in the living room, and it takes two sets of sheets to drape on top to cover it all.

This is only the first step. The interior, apparently, is just as important. It requires the perfect combination of pillows and blankets for a comfortable seat, as well as enough pillows to lounge against.

Enough being every single pillow we have in the house, and even then, Casey insists on bringing down all of his stuffed animals too.

When all is said and done and the three of us are tucked together inside the fort, Casey lasts thirty minutes of the movie before he passes out. He's curled into a ball on his side with his head in my lap, his favorite stuffed sea lion tucked beneath his chin, and his mouth wide open as he snores. The TV offers the only light in the room now that the sun set.

I run a hand over Casey's hair, and when he doesn't stir, I sigh and murmur, "I'm gonna take him upstairs."

"I can do it," Fletcher offers, then winces, like maybe he's worried he overstepped. Truthfully, Casey's getting a little heavy for me these days, but I'm in denial about it. I smile and nod. He slides Casey into his arms—Mr. Flippers still in place—and heads for Casey's room.

I search for the remote and pause the dance battle between cartoon turtles currently happening on the screen. It doesn't occur to me until Fletcher's footsteps creak down the stairs that he left his car at the park earlier today.

"He is *out*." He smiles as he reaches the bottom of the stairs.

"You can take my car to get yourself home," I offer as I climb out of the fort.

He tilts the corners of his lips down and shakes his head. "I'm not leaving you without one here. I'll see if Li or Leo can pick me up."

"Thank you." I wave a hand around us. "For everything today. For being so good with him. I don't know what you said to get through to him, but thank you."

He drifts closer and shrugs. "Just told him the truth. That I care about you, and I care about him."

He stops less than a pace away. Close enough for me to smell his cologne, to have to crane my neck to see his face. His forehead creases.

"Chris, I just—I just want you to know that however you want to handle things after today, I understand. Between us, I mean. If this is still something you don't want out in the open, I can...I don't know. Keep my distance for a while? People will get tired of talking if there's nothing new for them to gossip about. And—"

"No."

His eyes snap to mine, and for a moment, I'm lost in them. What he's saying...he's right. Things would be bad for a few days—weeks maybe—but if we stopped giving them new material, the gossip would get old and they'd move on to something shinier and new.

But something feels different today. Something's changed.

Maybe it was seeing Fletcher give comfort to my son in a way I couldn't, or maybe it was the comfort he brought to *me*, the kind I haven't known in a long time—if I've ever felt it at all, really.

And letting this town take that away from me to save face, well, that feels more like letting them win than anything else.

"I'm tired of the secrets," I whisper. "I'm tired of the hiding and pretending and feeling like I'm the one doing something wrong."

Slowly, he lifts his hand and lightly traces his fingertips over my cheek. My eyes flutter shut as a million thoughts war in my mind. Because as much as I want to let it all go, the one thought that trips me up time and time again is...Casey. Tonight—the three of us spending time together—may have been a very, very bad idea.

"I'm just worried if Casey gets attached, that when you leave, it'll just hurt him more," I whisper.

He stares at me, the look on his face almost *offended*. "When? Why are you assuming I will?"

Did I say when? I hadn't meant to...but I guess that is what I meant. I shrug helplessly. "Because everyone always does."

His face falls. After a deep breath, he takes one of my hands in his and props the other beneath my chin. The intensity in his eyes pins me to the spot. "Not this time, Chris."

I lay a hand over his and bring it down from my face. "Look, Fletcher, I'm complicated. I have enough baggage for a lifetime. And you're young—"

He tightens his fingers around mine before I can let go of his hand. "Don't do that."

"Just let me say this. You're young, Fletcher. I don't mean that in any bad way, and it's never something I think about when we're together, but it's still true. And I wouldn't hold it against you if you weren't ready for everything that being with me—*really* being with me—entails."

He's quiet, and I search his eyes, pleading with him to understand.

But then he murmurs, "Don't push me away because you think I'm going to leave. Because I'm right here. And I'm not leaving. There is nothing about you or your past that scares me. I have known what I was getting into from the start, and I never would've wasted your time if I didn't think I could handle it." My eyes burn, and I scrunch my nose as I fight back tears. He frames my face with his hands and angles it up, forcing me to meet his eyes. "I am all in, Chris. But I need to know if you're all in with me too."

I don't know if I've ever been all in on something in my life. Keeping one foot out the door is what keeps you safe. Keeps you ready for when disaster inevitably strikes. It doesn't protect you from the pain altogether, but I imagine it would be ten times worse without it.

"I don't know if I know how to be," I admit.

He gives me a soft, sad smile. "I know that feeling. I had it when my parents first took me in. But they helped me through it. Now all I'm asking is for you to let me help you."

What he's saying—it sets off every fight or flight alarm bell in my head. My mother's voice is blended in there somewhere. *You can't trust him. He says that now, but what about in ten years when it's time to trade you in for a newer model? You're too broken by now. There's no fixing you anymore.*

"I feel like this is worth taking a leap of faith for," he adds. "Do you?"

It doesn't just feel like a leap. It feels like a drop. Out of an airplane. Flying over a deep and endless ocean when I don't know how to swim.

But that fear tightening my chest, that instinctual urge to *run*, when I look into Fletcher's eyes, it quiets in a way I don't know it ever has before.

"I do too," I whisper.

Chapter Twenty-Six
FLETCHER

It's dark by the time Liam drops me off at the skate park. Unsurprisingly, my car is the last one in the lot. As I start the engine and my eyes flick to the rearview mirror, a flash from earlier in the day makes my stomach clench. Casey cowering in the corner, covering his head like he was bracing for impact. I let out a slow breath through my nose and force my jaw to unclench.

It doesn't hit how tired I am until I pull into my garage. I climb out of the car, eyes barely open, and shuffle toward the door—

—the door that's already sitting open.

I freeze. There's no way I left it like that. And if I had, it's directly in front of my windshield, so I would've noticed it once I got in the car.

I grab the baseball bat sitting beside the door, then ease it open.

The house is quiet, dark.

Maybe I'm overreacting. Maybe I *did* leave the door—

A floorboard creaks upstairs. My head snaps up at the

sound, but I wait, straining my ear to hear more. It sounded like the guest room, maybe the bathroom up there. Not far enough back for my room.

It occurs to me staying quiet is fairly pointless considering they heard me open the garage and pull in. They know I'm here.

"I have a gun, and I've already called the police," I call.

The words seem to echo in the silence.

My palms sweat as I tighten my hands around the bat and head toward the stairs. Probably would be smarter to call the cops, but...

More footsteps overhead, coming this way. I sidestep into the kitchen where I can see the foot of the stairs but they can't see me. I raise the bat as the footsteps thud closer.

I don't know what someone would be doing in here in the first place. It's not like there's much to steal, and there are much bigger, nicer, more expensive houses in the neighborhood. Maybe because I'm late on the train of those fancy security systems.

"Don't shoot!"

A girl appears at the bottom of the stairs, hands in the air and facing away from me. I can't pick out much in the dark—just her short and slim build, and it looks like she has long hair. But that voice...something about it...

Who the hell...

I hit the switch on the wall, and she flinches and squints as the harsh kitchen lights wash over us. She turns, her brown eyes finding me.

My heart stutters in my chest.

The bat slips through my fingers and clatters against the ground.

She lowers her hands, an amused smile pulling at her lips as she takes in my face. "Miss me?"

Chapter Twenty-Seven
CHRISTINE

It's almost physically painful letting Casey go to his playdate at Erin's house the next day after everything that went down the day before, but I don't want to let my urge to cling to him to feel like a punishment. So I put on a smile and hide my teary eyes behind my sunglasses as I drop him off and wave to Gloria.

My phone is currently littered with notifications from Julian's assistant with invites to his calendar. I guess I should be grateful he took the altercation at the skate park to heart enough to schedule ahead. Something about his assistant—not even him—penciling in his son like some afternoon meeting will always rub me the wrong way.

But what's really weighing on me is the notifications that *aren't* there. I texted Fletcher last night to make sure he made it home okay and to let him know he left his wallet behind, then again to thank him for the help, but he didn't respond. At first I thought he went straight to bed—I know I passed out the moment I lay down last night—but even today, still, nothing.

I know he's working at the bar, so he's probably busy.

Maybe forgot to charge his phone. I feel like I can't text him again without coming off as clingy.

That logic does nothing to stop me from checking my phone a hundred times.

I huff out a breath and toss the phone onto my passenger seat. The entire thing is absurd. I'm thirty-two fucking years old, not some starry-eyed teenager. And I have no interest in playing games.

The High Dive opened a few hours ago, so he should already be there.

The parking lot is mostly empty when I pull up, and Fletcher's car is noticeably absent. But with how much he uses his skateboard to get around, that's not saying much.

The bar is just as empty, with only a few people occupying one of the booths in the back. The other bartender—Anna, I think her name is—looks up as I step inside with his wallet in hand.

"Is Fletcher here?" I ask.

She sets down the glass she'd been drying and blows the air out of her cheeks. "He *should* be."

I stop short.

She shrugs and moves on to another glass. "They called me in when he didn't show. No one's been able to get a hold of him."

That doesn't sound like him at all.

Anna frowns as she takes in my face. "Is everything all right?"

"Yeah." I wave her off, already turning for the door. "Thank you."

My mind spins through a million different scenarios as I climb into my car, none of them good. What if something happened last night? If he got into an accident on his way home? And I hate that I even consider it—that it's remotely a possibility—but I saw the way Julian looked at him yesterday. There's no way he'd...

I hit the main road going fifteen over the speed limit and tighten my fists around the steering wheel. I try calling him, but it goes straight to voicemail.

What the hell is going on?

By the time I reach his house, my doomsday thoughts have hit their peak, and my hands shake as I hurry toward the front door. I know I'm probably overreacting, that I'm still just shaken up from yesterday.

I force down a deep breath as I ring the doorbell. He's going to come to the door, perfectly fine and unharmed, and with a reasonable explanation for falling off the face of the earth and—

The door swings open.

And staring back at me is a...girl.

Her dirty blond hair is piled into a messy bun on the top of her head, and she's in matching oversize sweats, ones that are way too big for her.

Ones that look like they probably belong to...

My stomach drops, no, *plummets*.

The longer I stare at her, the younger she seems to become. Her features are round, soft, her skin untouched by age. She lifts a single eyebrow and pops a hip out to the side.

"Can I help you?"

I hold up the wallet lamely. "I was looking for Fletcher."

"Chris." Fletch appears behind the girl, a little out of breath. His eyes widen as he looks from me to her.

"You forgot your wallet." My voice comes out harder this time, and all of those worries and fears and anxieties that had been building in my chest the entire drive sharpen into something else. I hold it out, just desperately wanting to get out of here now.

"This is Jacks," Fletcher rushes to say. "My old foster sister."

I freeze, my eyes snapping to his.

"Jacks, can you give us a minute?" he murmurs.

She smacks her gum, shrugs, and heads back into the house. Fletch steps onto the porch, closes the door behind him, and takes the wallet from me with a rueful smile. "Thanks."

"Your foster sister," I repeat. In all the hours upon hours we've talked about our pasts…he's never mentioned her. Or any other kids he grew up with, for that matter.

"She showed up last night. I haven't seen her in…" He trails off and shakes his head. "Nine years? But she came to me for help, and I couldn't turn her away."

My gaze trails over his shoulder, though I can't see her through the windows anymore. "How old is she?"

"Seventeen—er, eighteen. She just turned eighteen yesterday."

Now I truly feel like an idiot for automatically assuming the worst.

"I'm sorry to show up like this. But I hadn't heard from you, and the bar said you didn't show up for work today…"

"Shit." He pats down his pockets. "I must've left my phone in the car last night. Things have been…" He sighs and runs a hand through his hair. His eyes soften as they fall on me, as if it's just now registering that I'm standing here. "Do you want to come in? To be honest, I—I could use your help here. I'm a bit in over my head." He blinks, taking in the sidewalk and car behind me. "Where's Casey?"

I don't think I've ever seen him this…manic.

"Casey's at a friend's house." I lay my hand on his arm. "Whatever you need. Just tell me how I can help."

His shoulders slump with his exhale, like the exhaustion is catching up to him all at once. "She ran away from her foster home. Apparently she's been bounced around a lot—been stuck in a lot of bad places. Says she's dropping out of school. She's refusing to go back. I don't—I don't know what to do. I won't leave her out on the street, and I don't blame her for not having any faith in the system after the placements they've given her. And she's eighteen now, so..." He meets my eyes, and his are wide, pleading. "What am I supposed to do?"

It's such a stark contrast to the calm, confident way he handled everything yesterday.

It's more than fair if it's my turn to return the favor. I take his hand in mine and squeeze. "You take it one thing at a time. Would it be all right if I come in and try to talk to her?"

The relief in his eyes is immediate, and he steps aside to let me pass.

Chapter Twenty-Eight
FLETCHER

"So." Jacks sizes Chris up from across the kitchen table, folds her hands together on the surface, and leans forward. "You a social worker?"

Chris's eyebrows pull together. "No."

Jacks doesn't blink. "Shrink?"

Chris turns to me.

"Jacks," I sigh.

She throws her hands up. "Well, I know you roped her into this somehow, so you might as well just tell me."

"She's not—" I rub my eyes.

This all has been one never-ending day. We stayed up most of the night talking—catching up, me trying to convince her dropping out of school is a bad idea—and I barely got a few hours of sleep. It's not that I'm not glad to see her. Of course I am. Of all the foster siblings I've had in my life, she's the one I was closest to. The one I've wondered about the most. The one I've worried about. But seeing her after all this time...it's stirring up a lot that I've kept carefully buried for years.

A headache pulses behind my eye sockets. "Christine is my..." I meet her eyes. "Girlfriend."

I gauge her reaction to the term, but she doesn't seem opposed to it. We pretty much agreed to as much, just without the label. After keeping us a secret, it still feels like I'm doing something I'm not supposed to by saying it though.

But I *like* it.

In fact, I'd like to say it again.

Jacks throws her head back and laughs. No, *cackles*. "How long have you been into cougars?"

My attention snaps to her. "Jacks!"

"What? No offense, obviously you're hot. But how old are you?" When Christine doesn't answer right away, Jacks sighs and pushes on. "Don't tell me you're one of those chicks that thinks it's rude to talk about age. Laaaame. It's not rude to ask girls that until, what? After twenty-one? That's just perpetuating the stupid idea that women can't age."

I put my face in my hands. I feel like I've been running—*sprinting*—trying to catch up with Jacks since the moment she got here. She was always free-spirited growing up. But it was nothing like this. Or maybe it was. Maybe this is what the eighteen-year-old version of that looks like.

Christine laughs softly beside me. Thankfully, she doesn't seem offended. If anything, that smile she's giving Jacks looks approving.

"You know, you're right," she says. "I hadn't really thought about when women start to think that way. To answer your question, I'm about nine years older than your brother."

Jacks leans back in her chair and crosses her arms.

"So Fletcher tells me you don't want to go back to school."

Jacks's eyes narrow to slits as she turns to me. "And let me guess," she deadpans. "You're going to try to talk me out of it too."

"Well, no."

Jacks and I both whip toward her in surprise.

Christine shrugs. "Have you thought about getting your GED? That's what I did after I dropped out at sixteen. Then at least you'll have more options available to you moving forward, just in case you want them."

I don't know why it hadn't occurred to me until now that Christine is probably the *perfect* person to talk to about this stuff considering her own history.

Jacks uncrosses her arms and starts picking at her black nail polish. "You dropped out at sixteen?"

Chris nods. "And ran away from home."

Jacks's fingers pause.

"So all I'm trying to say is, I'm not here to talk you out of anything. I know you had your reasons. But maybe Fletcher and I can help you figure out what to do *now* to set you up for something better."

She actually seems to be listening to Chris, something she definitely was not doing with me, so I stay quiet.

"Have you thought about taking the GED?" Chris asks.

Jacks shakes her head.

Chris shrugs. "Well, I'd be happy to help you study if you decide you want to."

"Why would you do that?" asks Jacks. She sounds utterly perplexed, as if no one's ever offered to do something nice for her before.

The guilt that's settled into the pit of my stomach since the moment I realized it was her grows heavier and heavier.

She gave me the gist of what happened to her after I left, but I could tell it barely scratched the surface. It's not that I haven't thought about her, wondered about her. It's not like leaving her behind was easy. But even if I'd stayed, we would've been split up as they sent us off to new houses anyway. At least, that's part of how I justified it to myself at the time.

After the fire...I felt like I needed to put all of that behind me. To cut all ties. I was barely keeping my head above water back then. And with the crowd I left town with, taking Jacks with me wasn't an option.

They were older, all sixteen to eighteen, and stoned or drunk half the time. Between the breaking and entering, vandalism, and the armed robbery that finally made me split ways with them...there was no way I was bringing an eight-year-old into that.

But at the time, it looked like my only way out, so I took it.

Chris doesn't seem taken aback. If anything, she smiles like the question is exactly what she'd expect. "Because you're clearly important to Fletcher, and Fletcher is important to me. And when I was your age, someone who didn't know me helped me, and it probably saved my life. Call it paying it forward."

It's selfish and small because this is not at all about me, but I can't help from smiling all the same. *Fletcher is important to me.*

Jacks goes back to picking at her nail polish, and her forehead wrinkles like she's thinking hard about something. I think this is the first time she's been this quiet since she got here. I can't tell if it's because Chris is getting through to her in a way I couldn't, or if she's shutting down because she feels ganged up on.

"Is Jacks short for something?" Chris offers.

"Jacklyn," she mutters.

Chris's phone vibrates against the table, and she doesn't even glance at the screen before silencing it.

I curse under my breath as what she said on the porch finally sinks in. *Work.* They both turn to me as I push to my feet. "I'll be right back." I pat my pockets as if my phone will have magically reappeared there. Hopefully I'm right and it'll be sitting in the car waiting for me. "I need to call the bar."

I lock eyes with Christine again, and she nods as if to say *Go on, we're good here.*

Jacks, at least, no longer has that calculating glint in her eye. Despite how different she seems now, I recognized that look immediately. The one that, back in the day, told me I'd probably have one of the kids come running and crying into my room later to tell me all about what she'd done. The pranks were usually harmless—taking the laces out of their shoes, hiding their stuffed animals—just enough to make sure they *knew* she was upset with them.

Jacks rolls her eyes when she notices my hesitation. "Leave so I can tell her embarrassing stories about you."

"You could at least pretend to be grateful," I mumble as I head for the garage.

"It's not real gratitude if you have to beg for it!" she calls.

I snort as the door closes behind me.

"You're really showing your age here with this."

I sigh as my car falls off the cliff—*again*—just as hers crosses the finish line. In my defense, I haven't touched this game in probably five years.

This is also her first time ever playing, and she's still kicking my ass, so maybe I just suck.

Video games have never interested me much, but this game was one of the first things my parents bought when they took me in—I guess they figured, what fourteen-year-old boy wouldn't be excited about an Xbox? Other than the occasional night with Leo and Liam, it usually collects dust in my closet.

I don't know why it was the first thing to pop into my head

after Chris left earlier. It was just *something* for us to do together that got her to stop staring at me. She's always had that piercing gaze—even as kids—the kind that makes you feel like she can read your mind.

Barely a few seconds into the next game, my car plummets off the cliff again.

Jacks cackles and peers at my controller. "Are you even hitting the right buttons?"

I pull it closer to my chest so she can't see—but I do double-check that I am, in fact, using the right ones. "Maybe I'm letting you win. Trying to make you feel welcome and everything."

"Just remind me to never get in a car with you in real life."

I scoff. "I am an excellent driver."

Her eyebrows inch up as my car takes another dive. "I really see no evidence of that."

We play another few rounds in silence, but I catch her smirks in my periphery every time I nosedive off another cliff.

I bite my lip to hold back from asking what she thinks about all the GED stuff she and Christine were talking about. She said she'd think about it, and I have a feeling if I keep asking, I'll push her in the opposite direction.

"You could've called," I say quietly.

"So could you," she says, her voice clipped.

My eyes close for a second. I could've reached out after I left. Not knowing where she was placed after Joan and Bob was the excuse I'd told myself, but the truth is, I never looked back, never tried to find her. Not that it would've been easy—maybe even impossible—to track her down, but I'd never even *tried*.

I clear my throat. "I meant before coming all this way. What if the address you'd found was wrong? Or—"

"I figured it'd be harder to tell me to get lost if you had to look me in the eye first."

I set the controller on the couch between us. "I never would've told you to get lost."

She stays focused on the screen as her car passes the finish line.

"I'm sorry," I say, my voice coming out rough. "That I left. That I never checked back in."

Her jaw hardens, and she nods.

"But I would really, *really* like to make it up to you now."

That, finally, gets her to look over at me. "If what you actually want is for me to leave, I'd rather you tell me that than pretend."

I shake my head and scoot closer to her on the couch. "I'm not pretending."

"I know it's weird," she says as she turns back to the screen. "Me showing up here. I just..." Her shoulders slump on her exhale. "I didn't know where else to go."

"Weird?" I lean back and kick my feet up on the coffee table. I cast her a sideways smile, hoping to defuse the tension. "I would've been *insulted* if you'd gone anywhere else."

She rolls her eyes, but smirks as she hands me my controller. "Come on. I'll give you some pointers."

Chapter Twenty-Nine
CHRISTINE

"Mommy, it's on *fire!*" Casey shrieks and points at the stove.

I spin on my heel. The pancakes are, in fact, very smokey and undoubtedly burnt, but thankfully it's not an actual fire. I quickly flip off the stove, remove the pan from the heat, and shove open the window over the sink.

That was my *third* attempt, and the last of the batter.

We've been at this for thirty minutes, and poor Casey is still waiting patiently at the table with his—now empty—cup of juice.

"I didn't really want pancakes anyway," Casey offers.

I close my eyes and let out a breathy laugh. One of these days I'll master something other than cereal.

Despite the many years I have under my belt of fending for myself, I didn't have access to a kitchen for the majority of that time, leaving my cooking skills rather lacking. And when I moved in with Julian, he always insisted his private chefs do everything.

Sandwiches, I can do. Snack trays, no problem. Anything requiring electricity...well, it usually turns out like this.

Sometimes I feel like a teenage boy who just went off to college with no life skills.

I slide a bowl of Casey's backup cereal in front of him and shuffle to the coffee maker for a second cup. I'm probably more upset about it than he is. Pancakes sounded really good.

I glance at my phone on the counter as I stir in some coffee creamer. No response from Fletcher yet. Jacks and I are supposed to have our first study session, but we never agreed on a time or place. It'll be a nice distraction for me since Julian's taking Casey today. I chew on my lip and peek at Casey shoveling cereal into his mouth, remembering how our last transfer to Julian went. But he seems pretty calm about it today. Maybe he's forgiven and forgotten the earlier incidents with Julian.

Maybe he just misses him.

Julian hasn't pulled any other stunts since the skate park, at least. I didn't get an apology, of course, and I had to coordinate today with his assistant, not him, but I think that's as good as we're going to get.

The thought of doing this for the rest of Casey's childhood makes me want to crawl into bed.

Casey has barely finished his breakfast when there's a knock on the door. "I've got it!" he calls, jumping to his feet.

I trail behind as he sprints to the door, swings it open, and reveals Dina, his nanny.

I can see his face fall even from here.

"Hi, Case!" She beams and squats down for a hug. He slumps into her unenthusiastically and pulls back just as fast.

"Where's my dad?" he asks.

Dina meets my eyes over his head, an apologetic expression flashing over her face. "His meetings ran longer than expected, so he's not back in town yet—"

"He's not even here?" Casey's voice shoots up in a high whine that always precedes a full meltdown.

"He should be back tonight," Dina rushes to say, as if also recognizing what's about to happen. And with how much time she spends with him, she must.

I consider myself pretty freaking lucky on the kid front. Casey is as close to an angel as they come, but he's still just a kid. A kid whose entire life has been flipped inside out this past year. The tantrums are few and far between, but when they hit, you can tell he's been bottling things up for a good long while.

My chest twinges. Maybe that's my fault. I've always thought he and I had a great relationship, that we talk. But maybe I should've found someone else he could talk to a long time ago.

I've never tried therapy myself, never really saw the point of rehashing all of my issues, as if I'm not already painfully aware of them. But with Casey, maybe it's worth a try.

"He said he wants to take you out for dinner!" continues Dina. "Anywhere you want."

"I. Don't. Want. Dinner!" Casey turns away and bolts up the stairs.

Dina sighs and points after him. "Should I...?"

I wave her off and open the door wider. "Why don't you come in? Let's give him a minute. Do you want some coffee?"

"I—yes, that would be great. Thank you."

I rub my eyes as she follows me to the kitchen. "Did he actually say he'd be back for dinner?"

Her hesitation is answer enough.

I sigh as I pour her a mug.

This entire situation is infuriating. I would've taken sole custody in a heartbeat. *He's* the one who fought for this. And clearly not so he could spend time with Casey. It was about saving face. *What would this town say about him if he just abandoned his child?* He wants to look like the loving, involved father without ever having to play the actual part. And if it's this bad at the beginning, I don't have much hope that things will improve.

My phone lights up on the counter with a notification from Fletcher, but I don't reach for it.

"I don't want to derail your day," Dina says. "I can watch him here for a bit, if you'd like, until I can convince him to go. I saw his overnight bag by the door. Is there anything else I should make sure to bring?"

"No, it's all in there." I offer her a tired smile, tighten my fist around my coffee, and head upstairs to try to console my son for the millionth time on why his father can't be bothered to see him.

Since Jacks is still new to town and getting to know all the local shops, I let her pick our study location. After driving to the shore and parking, we walk up the main street. She lingers a little too long near the Brooks smoothie place for comfort, but we end up winding our way to the coffee shop beside Liam's tattoo studio, Milano's.

"What's your drink of choice?" I ask, my voice painfully chipper as we step through the door.

She was silent the entire drive here, no matter my lame attempts at small talk—*so how are you settling in? I heard you're having dinner with Fletcher and his parents tonight—so fun!*—and as the adult in this situation, I feel like it's my job to make this not awkward.

She stares blankly at the menu overhead.

Maybe she doesn't have a lot of experience with ordering at

coffee shops. I can count on one hand my experiences before the age of eighteen, and even then, it was rare I was able to afford it.

"I love their iced lattes," I offer. "They have a lot of flavors too—the lavender honey is my favorite. But they also have iced teas and hot chocolate if you don't want caffeine!"

She glances at me sideways, then back to the menu. "Just… whatever you're having."

"Okay!" I beam. "Go ahead and pick out a table. I'll meet you there."

The second she walks away, I cringe at myself, but I can't seem to turn the *pep mode* off. It's a defense mechanism, I think. Slipping into the role I played in the Brooks household for the last eight years. Cheery and happy and *there is most definitely nothing wrong with my life!!*

I let the smile drop as I order the coffees, suddenly exhausted. By the time I meet Jacks at the corner table by the fireplace, she's already spread out the books we picked up from the library and is currently flipping through one.

I hand her the latte and brace myself as she takes a sip. To my relief, she turns the corners of her mouth down in an appreciative way and nods. I twist my head to see which book she was looking at.

"So, you like science?"

"It's one of the few things I don't suck at," she mutters, her eyes flicking up to meet mine.

"That was always my best too," I say quietly, a million things I haven't thought about in a long time rushing to the surface as if they've been waiting *years* for this opportunity.

I swallow hard, hoping it doesn't show on my face.

Back when I was preparing for the test, I had the most ridiculous plans. Biology major in college. Med school. Not that I particularly liked science—or even thought I'd like being a doctor. Pretty sure I plucked the idea out of thin air. Just something to prove to my mom that she was wrong about me.

But it always came back to money. I didn't have enough for a college application fee, let alone tuition—let alone *med school*. And besides, by then, I'd met Julian.

And if you don't try, you can't fail.

So I guess she was right about me after all.

The doctor thing never would have worked out anyway. Being fueled by spite only would've lasted me so long. Maybe I didn't make something of myself the way I thought I would... but I got Casey. And I wouldn't change a single thing that led me here for that alone.

"What do I need to score to pass this anyway?" asks Jacks, pulling me out of my thoughts.

"You need at least a 145 in each subject. There are 800 possible points, so—"

"I need a C, basically."

I smirk. "Sounds like you're pretty decent at math too." I pull a notebook from my bag and flip to the page labeled GED. "They offer the test pretty often, so you could really take it just about whenever you want, but I think we should nail down a date so you have something specific to work toward. You can take each subject on a different day, or do it all at once, but if you do that, that's nearly eight hours of straight testing. There's also not a ton of pressure since you can retake the test twice if you need to. And if you need *more* retakes after that, you'd just have to wait sixty days first."

I glance up to find her staring at me with wide eyes.

I wince and click my pen. "Too much information?"

"I'm just...surprised. That you know so much."

"I like to be prepared."

I don't bother adding how much free time I have these days,

and the moment I had a task that felt *meaningful*, I couldn't help but spring on it like a feral animal.

Most of the details of the test seem the same from when I took it—the main differences being the rules in Virginia versus New Jersey.

Her eyebrows lift as she nods slowly.

"So. We can circle back on picking a date after we lay some groundwork to see how much time you want for studying. Do you want to start with one of your stronger subjects then, or get your least favorite out of the way first?"

"The social studies one is probably going to kick my ass." She winces. "I always skipped that class."

The bell above the door rings as someone enters the building. I don't turn, but an ice-cold chill travels down my spine as the woman orders her coffee.

I recognize her voice immediately, and my shoulders tense up to my ears. Two others chime in their orders, then the clack of high heels against the hard floor fills the store as they take the table on the opposite side of the shop.

I press my lips together and let out a slow breath through my nose. *It doesn't matter. I will not let this matter.*

"I think we should start with social studies then," I say, forcing enthusiasm back into my voice. "At least get a baseline for where you're at so we have an idea of what we're working with."

Jacks nods her agreement and fishes that book out of the stack.

"I think Thursday is a *much* better choice for book club night," trills Lola Bartlett. Her voice carries through the store like Styrofoam rubbing together. "That way it doesn't clash with tennis on Wednesday anymore."

"I told Mimi she could join us," says Francine. "Since we have that open spot now."

My eye twitches as I take the book from Jacks. Seriously, are we thirteen years old?

"Do you have a way you learn best?" I ask, and it comes out through my teeth. "Flash cards, maybe?"

"Oh my gosh!" gasps Brooklyn. "It *just* occurred to me we'll need to find a new place for the getaway trip. You know, since we can't use"—she lowers her voice, though it's still perfectly audible—"Julian's cabin anymore."

My fist tightens around my coffee.

Honestly, I don't care that I got kicked out of book club. I don't care if I ever see any one of them again. I don't even really care about the pathetically transparent way they're trying to rub my nose in it right now. I just want one fucking day of peace in this town.

And maybe, I realize, Jacks has something to do with it. Maybe it's wishful thinking that she hasn't heard the gossip yet—that there's one person around here who can get to know me for me, without all the baggage—but I should've known that wouldn't last for long.

Their conversation dips too low for me to hear their next few sentences, but I catch bits and phrases.

"...did you *see*..."

"...I mean, how *young* is he?"

"Is that even legal?"

"...maybe he cheated on her, and this is some kind of revenge..."

"...well, *I* heard..."

I refuse to look over and give them the satisfaction, but Jacks glances from me to their table. Slowly, a single eyebrow arches, then plenty loud for them to hear, she says, "You know they're talking about you, right?"

The conversation comes to an abrupt halt. They at least have the decency to look a little embarrassed. Francine's blush has spread all the way to the roots of her poorly bleached hair.

"It's sad, isn't it?" Jacks continues. "How much hearing they must have lost in their old age if they can't tell how much their voices are carrying."

Now they're all red, but I don't think it's from embarrassment. Jacks has no idea how much of a sore spot she just hit—or maybe she does. I was always the youngest of the group—a point of contention that was never voiced, but I always felt. Maybe under different circumstances I'd have some sympathy for how pressured they felt for all of the Botox and hair dye and surgeries.

Maybe.

Their chairs all shove back at once, and the bell above the door rings as they leave.

When I meet Jacks's eyes again, her mouth is curled into a smug little grin, and I find myself smiling back.

Chapter Thirty

FLETCHER

"Stop fidgeting."

Jacks scowls at me, and a brief, dizzying moment of vertigo washes through me as I flash back to the many times she gave me that look as kids. Despite the way her features have matured, that look hasn't changed.

She faces the large glass door, eyes flicking to the doorbell like she wants to ring it again. "I'm not fidgeting."

She continues to pick away at her nail polish.

"They're good people," I say softly. "And they're excited to meet you. They're going to love you."

"They love *you*," she mutters under her breath. "Because you're all shiny and normal."

Normal.

It makes sense that she'd see it that way. I was given more of a fair shot at it than she was—whatever normal means anyway. But I wasn't that much younger than she is now when they took me in. Those first fourteen years don't automatically get scrubbed clean.

"Oh, so I'm normal now? Guess I'll take that over weird."

She snorts, but she's finally left her nails alone. "You're still weird."

Mom takes that moment to appear. Knowing her, she was hanging back and getting a good look at us through the windows first.

She swings the door open and smiles wide, an apron layered over her polka-dot dress. "Hi, honey. You're just in time. Dinner's almost ready. And you must be Jacks."

Jacks freezes, but Mom springs forward anyway and wraps her into a hug. "We're *so* happy to meet you. Come in! Come in!" She squeezes Jacks for another moment before opening the door wider, revealing Charlie waiting for her a pace away.

"Oh!" Jacks lets out a surprised gasp, and Charlie lazily rolls his head in her direction, his tongue hanging out the side of his mouth.

"That's Charlie," I mutter.

"Good boy," Mom croons as she heads to the kitchen at the back of the house, and Charlie dutifully peels himself off the floor and lumbers after her.

Jacks eyes the pile of slobber left behind with disgust, but follows me wordlessly into the house.

It already smells amazing in here. Mom didn't tell me what she planned on making, only insisted we join them for dinner the second I told her about Jacks showing up. Something with garlic.

"Where's Dad?" I ask.

Mom bends down to check whatever's in the oven. "He'll be back in a minute. Sent him to pick up something for dessert. Hope you don't mind store-bought."

Jacks turns to me with wide eyes. I'm not sure why it makes the tips of my ears burn.

I can count on one hand the number of homemade meals I had before coming here. At the house where Jacks and I met, it was a constant cycle of ramen noodles and whatever microwave dinners were on clearance.

I know Mom's just trying to make her feel welcome, but now it feels more like bragging.

Look what I got after I got out.

"You really didn't have to do all this," I mumble.

"Nonsense! Go ahead and have a seat. Fletcher, will you grab some drinks?"

Jacks hesitantly pulls out a chair at the kitchen table where all the places are already set. She keeps her hands folded tightly in her lap like she's afraid to touch anything.

"So, Jacks!" calls Mom as I set a few waters on the table. "You and Fletcher lived together for four years, is that right?"

Jacks rubs her palms on her thighs. "Around there, yeah."

The house vibrates as the garage door groans open. "Oh, it looks like your father's back. Guess I can take this out now."

Heat fills the room as she opens the oven and digs out some kind of casserole. My mouth starts watering.

"Is that—"

"Garlic cheddar chicken, your favorite."

"I'm back! I'm back!" Dad stumbles in from the door that connects to the garage with at least half a dozen reusable bags hanging from his arms. He kicks the door shut, then stands up straight and levels us with a wide grin. "I brought options. Smells great in here, honey."

Jacks's head whips back and forth as she takes it all in like she's witnessing an exhibit at a zoo.

"Oh, Jacks, it's nice to meet you!" Dad unloads his haul onto the kitchen island and offers her a hand to shake. "You can call me Dave."

"Nice to meet you," she murmurs.

Mom nudges him as she carries the casserole over to the

table. "Go wash your hands. Now, how long has it been since you two have seen each other?"

Jacks and I exchange a look, and I can't help the sudden drop in my stomach.

The heat, and fire blindingly bright against the night sky...

"I think...maybe nine years now?" she offers.

"How wonderful that you managed to track him down."

My eyes snap to my mom's face—something about the tone of her voice... But she's still smiling, pleasant as ever, as she situates the food in the middle of the table and slides into the seat across from me.

Jacks scratches at the back of her neck. "The listings for his camps online made it pretty easy."

Mom nods along as Dad takes the seat next to her. I might be imagining it, but it feels like she's avoiding meeting my eyes.

"Thank you," Jacks adds. "For inviting me to dinner. This looks amazing."

"Well, dig in!"

"You'll never guess who I saw at the store," says Dad as we all load up our plates.

"Who?" asks Mom.

Dad swirls the wine in his glass and spreads his hands wide like he's presenting something. "Julian Brooks."

My stomach flips.

"Doing his own shopping?" says Mom, her voice light, but she's peeking at me out of the corner of her eye now. "How unusual."

I busy myself cutting the casserole on my plate.

"That's what I thought! Standing at the self-checkout in a suit that must have cost at least a thousand dollars. A sight to see."

Jacks shoots me a questioning look.

I clear my throat. "You might have noticed a lot of the businesses around here have the name Brooks on them? He owns them."

"And he puts his name on *all* of them? Classy," she mutters.

I chuckle under my breath.

The dinner passes fairly uneventfully, though Mom can't seem to stand the silence for more than a few seconds before she jumps in with another question for Jacks—does she play any sports? What kind of TV does she like? How is she liking Sweetspire so far? And on, and on, and on.

When Jacks mentions how much she likes cars, Dad just barely stops himself from leaping up from the table. He turns to me, betrayal in his eyes as if I was purposefully withholding this information. "You didn't tell me she likes cars."

I shrug. I didn't know. I make a mental note to introduce her to Leo. He might be willing to help get her a job, though I don't know if appreciating cars necessarily translates to wanting to work on them.

My dad waves for her to join him as he all but skips to the garage. "You're going to love this."

Mom gives me a small smile and rolls her eyes as Jacks follows him. That piece of junk—or classic, depending on who you ask—has been sitting there since the day I got here nine years ago.

And it's not any closer to running now than it was back then.

Once the two of them disappear through the door, Mom slides into the seat beside me.

"How are you doing?" she asks.

"I'm sleeping fine, Mom," I say immediately.

"I don't just mean that."

I frown, but when I turn to her, she's not looking at me. Her gaze is trained on the garage door.

"This is about Jacks?"

Her eyes find mine again, and that worried crease in her forehead doesn't relent. "I just...I just want you to be careful."

"Careful? Of what? Do *not* tell me this is about her aura or something."

She makes a *now that you mention it* face, and I scoff.

"But it's not just that!" she insists. "Something feels...off here, Fletcher. Like, how did she look you up now that you have a different last name? And did you forget that she *broke into your house* when she first got here?"

Okay, so it sounds kind of bad when she puts it like that. And I know Mom thinks she understands since she's been a foster parent, but being on the other side of it is something else entirely. In my experience, she was the anomaly. No other placement I had comes close. She's heard the horror stories, read my file. But nothing replaces experiencing it for yourself, what it does to you. How it changes you.

As far as Jacks breaking in...I mean, I was picking locks myself by the time I was ten. And she hadn't wanted to wait outside in the dark—especially after she'd just run away from home. She was worried if someone called her in for looking suspicious, they might send her back there, a legal adult now or not.

I force myself to keep my voice low. "You're practically a professional at taking in strays, but *this* is where you draw the line?"

"I know you two have a history. But you were children, and that was a long time ago. People change. How much do you really know about her? A lot could've happened since you last saw her."

I shake my head. I can't believe this. "What I know is I'm not going to turn her away when she needs help."

"And I'm not saying that you should. I'm just worried about you."

"I got lucky and got out. She never did. That's not her fault."

Mom sighs. "I know you think that's your responsibility, but—"

The garage door opens.

I force a smile as I turn. "So what did you think? Piece of junk, right?"

Jacks steps through the door first, her eyes a little wide. "Not at all." For the first time tonight, she smiles.

Chapter Thirty-One
CHRISTINE

I stare at the ingredients laid out along the counter for French toast. I *will* make something edible today. There will *not* be any fires. And there is *no* backup cereal left, so I have no other choice.

Casey shoots me a supportive thumbs-up from the table, but before I can dip the first piece of bread in the egg mixture, the doorbell rings.

I frown and motion for Casey to wait here. It's my weekend with him, so Julian—or rather, *Dina*—shouldn't be here, but after the fiasco at the skate park...

I peek through the window, and my shoulders sag in relief.

"What are you doing here?" I ask as I swing the door open.

Fletcher smiles sheepishly from the porch as the sound of little footsteps galloping toward us grows.

"Fletcher!" Casey launches himself to hug him. "You came!"

I raise an eyebrow and meet Fletcher's eyes over my son's head.

That sheepish smile grows. "He may have texted me earlier to see if I'd help with breakfast."

"I—he texted you?" I pat down my pockets to find that my phone is, indeed, missing.

Now it's Casey's turn to look sheepish.

Not that I can blame his doubt in my abilities, but still. "How'd you even know my passcode?"

He rolls his eyes. "It's my birthday. You use that for everything."

This kid is too smart for his own good. I'm never going to make it out of his teenage years alive.

"So." Fletcher rubs his hands together, still crouched down at Casey's level. "What are we making?"

Casey leans forward as if to whisper something conspiratory to him. "French toast."

"You know what? That's my favorite."

Casey beams. "Mine too!"

I press my lips together against my smile. This is the first I'm hearing of this, and I'm willing to bet anything else that's a favorite of Fletcher's, coincidentally, is also his favorite.

Casey sprints back to his spot at the table as Fletcher follows me to the stove.

He glances around appreciatively. "Seems like you've already got things under control here."

I hold back my wince and stand up straighter. "That's right. I do."

I flip on the burner closest to me, set a flat pan on top, and submerge the first piece of bread in the egg mixture.

Fletcher clears his throat behind me.

"What?" How could I possibly *already* have done something wrong?

He steps up behind me, close enough that I can feel the heat from his skin, and winds an arm around my waist to ease the heat down to medium.

"Butter?" he murmurs, his lips right beside my ear.

I turn, and it places our lips dangerously close to each other.

This whole *no sex while we get to know each other* idea is great and all, in theory.

How long he's going to make me wait, he didn't specify.

And that vibrator in my nightstand, yeah, it's not cutting it these days.

It takes me a moment to peel my gaze up to meet his. "Hm?"

His lips tug into a half smirk. "Butter in the fridge?"

I nod and watch with my eyebrows dug in as he turns to retrieve it. Butter? For what?

I finish coating the first piece of bread, but before I can throw it on the pan, Fletcher hurries over, a hand held up for me to wait, and plops a generous spoonful of butter onto the pan.

"I—I already sprayed it with that oil stuff," I say.

He makes a clicking sound with the corner of his mouth. "Yeah, not the same. Trust me."

"Maybe you should do this," I mumble.

"No, no, you're doing great." He spreads the melting butter around with a spoon, then gestures to me. "Go ahead. Put it in."

My gaze snaps to his, and it must take a moment for what he said to click, because then his eyes widen. Suddenly I feel like I'm fourteen again because it is taking everything in me not to laugh.

I set the toast in the pan, and his hand brushes my lower back as he passes to my other side, whispering "Filthy mind" as he goes.

I bite my lip to hide my smirk, then nod at the cabinet above him. "Mugs are in there if you'd like some coffee."

While I wait for the toast to be ready to flip, I hunt down my phone—beside Casey at the table—to see what exactly he texted Fletcher that made him get over here so fast.

Can you show mom how to not burn breakfast?

Maybe I'd be embarrassed if it weren't fucking hilarious.

And thank God the string of messages above it were PG.

Casey shrinks into himself as I read, as if waiting to be reprimanded. I smooth a hand over his hair and plant a kiss on the top of his head.

"I'm going to get better at this. I promise."

"I know! You just haven't had practice. Like with my skate camp. I wasn't good at first either."

Fletcher watches us from across the kitchen, his hip propped against the counter and a steaming cup of coffee in his hand. A soft smile rests on his lips, and it grows as he meets my eyes.

He nods toward the pan on the stove. "Ready when you are."

"Oh!" I hurry over and snatch the spatula off the counter.

"I'd test the edges all around first—helps it not stick too."

I do as he says, marveling at how easily it lifts. Plus, there's no smoke or thick burnt scent in the air. I flip the bread, and a perfectly toasted side stares back at me.

I've never gotten this far before.

Once the first piece is ready to go, Fletch takes it over to Casey, who eagerly digs in.

"I can take over," Fletcher offers.

"Absolutely not." I swat him away with my spatula. "I'm on a roll now."

He retreats to the table with a smirk, and peers at my laptop I left out. "Oh! Is this the new site Gracie made?"

"Yes! She just sent over the final version today."

"Do you mind if I…?" He waves a hand at the screen.

"Oh yeah, of course."

He scrolls through each bit slowly. It's fairly basic since I'm still starting out—a home page, portfolio, testimonials, and contact form—but it's a million times better than anything I could've come up with on my own. I haven't officially started accepting clients, but thanks to Marti's party, I've got a generous little waitlist going already.

"Wow, this looks amazing," Fletcher murmurs.

I beam. "Doesn't it?"

CC Events fades from the center of the screen when you first click into the site, then the rest of the design swims into view. I wanted a subtle color scheme—something that felt luxurious. Gold, black, and white, mostly.

I thought coming up with the name would be the hard part, but I'd settled on it almost immediately. For obvious reasons, I didn't want the Brooks name anywhere near it. And my maiden name doesn't hold any fonder memories for me. And maybe it's a little vain, but I wanted my name on it in some way. Something unequivocally mine that I built by myself. The answer seemed obvious from there.

CC. Christine and Casey.

Between this and helping Jacks study nearly every day for the past week, it feels like the cloud that's been following me around since the divorce has finally lifted. Each day feels a little less aimless, a little less pointless. I feel more useful, hopeful. Like this new phase of my life has a direction.

That reminds me. I cock my head as I slide another finished piece of toast onto a plate. "Where's Jacks this morning?"

Fletcher shrugs. "She's a runner now, apparently. Has been going for a run on the beach every morning."

"Are you working at the bar today?"

He nods and checks his watch. "Need to be there at ten thirty to open."

"Well, thank you," I say as I carry my coffee and the rest of the toast to the table and take the seat beside him. "For sharing your morning with us."

He smiles, slides a piece of toast onto his plate, and meets my eyes as he says, "I wouldn't want to be anywhere else." He lifts his cup toward Casey. "What are you two up to today?"

Casey practically starts vibrating in his seat. "Rollercoasters!"

A hint of concern pinches Fletcher's eyebrows together as he looks at me, but the unspoken part is clear. *You're going on a rollercoaster? Even when heights leave you no better than an opossum playing dead?*

There are enough other rides in the park to distract Casey, and when it comes to the handful of big ones, I'm hoping being strapped in against my will and closing my eyes will suffice.

But I have a budding daredevil for a kid, so I know he'll love it. And if I don't ride them with him, I don't think he'll do it—don't think they'll even let him on. And I'm not going to be the reason he can't. His height was a good excuse…for a while.

I shrug and feign nonchalance. "Promised him we'd try the amusement park down in Beach Haven once he grew some more…"

"And we measured last night!" Casey jumps in. "I'm fifty inches!"

The concern doesn't ease from Fletcher's expression. "What's the requirement?"

"For most of the rides, forty-eight," I say.

"Which means I'm tall enough now!" Casey's expression sobers a bit. "I wish you could come too."

"Me too, bud. That sounds like a lot more fun than work. Next time."

Casey thrusts his pinky across the table. "Promise?"

Fletcher chuckles and wraps his pinky around Casey's. "I promise."

"Do you think Jacks would want to come?"

Fletch's eyes shoot to mine. "You don't have to do that…"

I shrug. "I know she's still finding her groove around here, and I want her to feel welcome. Plus, she could probably use a fun day before her test next week. Especially with how hard she's been studying. And the more the merrier, right, Case?"

He nods vigorously.

Fletcher's eyes soften as they linger on my face.

"You can ask her so she doesn't feel too much pressure to say yes to me if she doesn't want to."

"Casey," says Fletcher, though his eyes stay locked on me.

"Yeah?"

"I'm gonna need you to look away for a few seconds."

"Why?"

Fletcher's lips tug into a crooked smirk. "Because I'm about to kiss your mom."

"Ew!" Casey slaps both hands over his eyes as Fletcher wraps one hand around the back of my neck and pulls me in to kiss me. It's brief and sweet, but he keeps his hold on me even once he leans back, his eyes studying my face like he's deciding something.

He digs his phone out of his pocket and his thumbs rapidly dart across the screen. "Hold on."

"What?" I murmur.

He waits for a moment after he finishes typing, and as his phone buzzes with a response, he looks up, grinning widely. "Anna's gonna cover my shift."

"You're coming with us?" Casey asks.

He turns his smile on Casey. "How do you feel about bumper cars?"

Chapter Thirty-Two
CHRISTINE

"Get him, Mom! Get him!" cries Casey.

"No!" Jacks's head whips around in her and Fletcher's bumper car, sizing up the narrowing distance between us. She repeatedly taps Fletcher on the shoulder as he steers. "Stand your ground! Stand your ground!"

He swerves to avoid getting stuck in the corner, but that just gives me the perfect opportunity to T-bone him.

Jacks lets out a little shriek as our cars collide and theirs spins in a full circle. Casey laughs and claps beside me. I don't at all like that look in Fletcher's eyes as he smiles up at us.

"Go!" cries Casey. "Go, go, go!"

I steer us away, the neon lights drenching the rink flashing before my eyes as we swerve in and out of other cars.

"No!" screams Casey, right before they crash into us from behind, shooting us forward into the wall.

The buzzer goes off, announcing our time's up, and Casey sighs.

"We can get in line to go again," I say as we climb out. "But I thought you wanted to try the slides?"

His eyes light up and he grabs my hand to drag me to the exit.

The massive rainbow slides are just next door, and a group of teens speeds down on their burlap sacks as we approach, screaming and laughing. I gulp audibly as I stare at the stairs that lead to the top.

Fletcher crouches next to Casey. "So are we racing, or do you want to go down with me? I think your mom should stay here so she can get a good picture of you."

Casey blinks up at me. "Is that okay?"

I can't help my relieved smile. "Of course."

"I'm going to sit this one out too," says Jacks. She waits until Fletcher and Casey start up the stairs before adding, "Last thing I want is rug burn on my ass."

I snort out a laugh. "I'm really glad you decided to come with us, Jacks."

Her smile turns a little shy. "Me too."

Not only does Fletcher seem happier with her here, but she and Casey have gotten on surprisingly well too, despite the big gap in their ages. To be honest, I think Casey might have a bit of a crush on her.

I whip my phone out as Fletcher and Casey inch toward the front of the line. They settle together on a sack—Casey in front, Fletcher's arms around him—and the sight of it has my heart aching in a way I don't quite understand. Casey grins from ear to ear the entire way down, no trace of fear to be found.

If I'd gone up there, someone would've had to shove me down. Seriously, where did this kid come from?

"Can we go again?" asks Casey as soon as they reach the bottom. "I want to race this time!"

Fletcher smirks. "Sure thing."

I turn to Jacks. "You hungry?"

She shrugs. "A little."

I nod at the stand across the walkway. "Want to grab some funnel cake?"

Another shrug, but I *think* that's a hint of a smile on her lips now.

"We'll be right back!" I call to Fletcher, and he waves to let me know he heard me.

"I've never had one of these," Jacks admits as we get in line.

"Haven't you ever been to the fair before?"

"Once, with my boyfriend. But we really just did the rides."

My eyebrows shoot up, but I try not to let my excitement show on my face. Despite how much time we've been spending together these past few weeks, she hasn't exactly been forthcoming with many personal details, especially things about her past. And I haven't wanted to push her. So her voluntarily offering this information can't help but feel like a win.

"Boyfriend?" I ask innocently.

She winces. "Ex, I meant."

"Oh, I'm sorry."

I hand over my card for the food, but I don't miss the way her expression darkens. "Don't be. He was an asshole."

"Well, *that*"—I smile at the cashier and lift the funnel cake between us so Jacks can try it first—"I can relate to."

She eyes the plate before cautiously breaking off a piece. I wait, gauging her reaction as she chews. Her eyes snap to mine.

"Good?"

She breaks off another piece.

I smile as we head toward the slides. "Well, I hope he's not still giving you trouble, your ex."

"Oh, no. I don't have to worry about him anymore."

"Mommy, did you see me?" Casey sprints toward us. "I won!"

"I'm gonna need some of this for my wounded pride," laments Fletcher as he breaks off a piece of the funnel cake.

Luckily, there's enough to catch Casey's eye that keeps us on the ground for the next hour—the ring toss, the teacups, the water gun race. I'm beginning to think I'll make it out of today alive when Casey stops in the middle of the walkway—the teddy bear wearing a cowboy hat that Fletcher won for him clutched to his chest—and cranes his neck to take in the massive rollercoaster overhead.

"That one." I watch him point his little finger as if in slow motion. Then he turns his best puppy dog eyes on me. "Will you do this one too?"

"Oh, Jacks or I can ride with you," Fletcher starts.

Casey stays focused on me.

And somehow, I find myself saying, "Yeah, let's all do it."

Fletcher's gaze snaps to me, and I force a smile. Jacks looks between the two of us before directing her attention to Casey.

"Will you ride with me, Case? I'm a little scared."

Casey smiles and tries to make himself taller. "Okay!"

The two of them head into the line first, and Fletcher lays his hand on my arm as we follow. "Are you sure about this?"

I nod, faking far more confidence than I feel. "I think it'll be good for me to do at least one before we go." That had been the original plan, after all, before Fletcher and Jacks joined. If it were just me here, I'd have no choice. I can do this. I can.

He links his fingers through mine and squeezes. "All right."

The coaster looms in front of us as we inch along in line. Fletcher never lets go of my hand, even though it's definitely clammy now. My heart is already pounding in my chest and we're not even on the damn thing yet.

He leans close and murmurs in my ear, "You're allowed to change your mind."

I give a firm shake of my head, and he chuckles under his breath.

"Good to see where Casey gets his stubbornness from."

I glare at him, but that easy smile never falters.

All too soon, it's our turn. Jacks and Casey take the seats in front of us, and I focus on my breathing as the teenager working comes to pull the bars over our heads. I immediately grasp the handles.

I know I must look ridiculous, but Fletcher doesn't laugh. He rests his hand on my knee and strokes his thumb back and forth.

Then we start to move backward. Casey giggles, and I try to focus on the absolute joy radiating from him rather than the ground rapidly growing farther away from us as the coaster prepares to slingshot us forward.

"You're doing great," Fletcher says.

"How are you so calm right now?" I manage to squeeze out, my eyes already shut as tight as they can go. "It doesn't bother you *at all* being up this high?"

There's a slight pause before he admits, "Okay, so it's a little high."

My response turns into a scream as we fall.

I think I black out. All I know is my stomach is in my throat, my hands are cramping from holding on so tightly, and I don't open my eyes a single time.

But I hear Casey's laughter and delighted screams in front of me, and that alone makes it worth it.

When it's finally over, Fletcher has to pry my hands from the bars.

"You can open your eyes now," he murmurs.

Casey and Jacks climb out first, both grinning with their entire faces. Casey's practically jumping up and down as we head down the ramp and back to the rest of the park.

Fletcher throws an arm around my shoulders and tugs me in close as we walk. "You all right?"

"Mm-hmm."

His breath stirs my hair as he kisses my temple. "Knew you could do it."

"Just don't ask me to do it again."

He chuckles. "Come on. That Strength Tester has my name all over it. Let's get you a bear like Casey's."

I turn to him with wide eyes. "Maybe I wanted the mermaid."

He nods seriously. "Mermaid it is." He presses his face against the side of my neck and takes a long, deep breath before letting it out on a sigh.

"What?" I ask.

A bemused smile tugs at the corners of his lips, but when he meets my eyes, there's much more than amusement burning behind them.

"One of these days," he says, almost too low for me to hear, "I'll have some alone time with you again."

My blood heats, but I keep my expression impassive. "Oh, so that whole *taking it slow* speech really was all talk, huh?"

His smile turns crooked like he sees right through me. "If you'd prefer, we can keep on—"

I tighten my fist around his shirt and give it a small tug. "I absolutely do not prefer."

He chuckles and presses a kiss to the top of my head. "You. Me. Tomorrow. I'll pick Jacks up from studying. She's starting her new job at the movie theater tomorrow night, so I'll have the house to myself. And Casey will be with his dad. I'll cook you dinner, and…"

I grin and lift my eyebrows at him. "*And…?*"

He brings a hand to his chest in mock offense. "And nothing. I have absolutely no ulterior motives."

"Uh-huh."

He squeezes me tighter to his side. "So is it a date or what?"

I slide my hand into his back pocket and bite my lip to keep from grinning. "It's a date."

Chapter Thirty-Three
CHRISTINE

So it's a little over-the-top. Overzealous, some might say.

Maybe I should be embarrassed.

But honestly, it's a miracle I managed to put on a dress instead of showing up in lingerie and a trench coat.

Not that I was *actually* going to do that.

But I may have considered it.

Only for a second.

Any lingering doubts or insecurities disappear the moment Fletcher opens the front door.

Because clearly I wasn't the only one. He looks *nice*. A black button-down shirt and matching trousers—I don't think I've ever seen him wear something like this. And honestly, thank God he doesn't work an office job or something because if I saw him in this kind of outfit on the regular, I don't think I'd be able to keep my hands to myself.

He doesn't say anything when he sees me, not at first. His eyes travel the length of me, starting with my face, then the dress straps that dangle off my shoulders, the fitted waist, the slit up the leg, revealing my black thigh-high stockings and the nicest heels I own. His throat bobs as he swallows, and he blinks rapidly before finding my face again.

And it's difficult to tell in this lighting, but I swear his pupils are a little dilated now.

Yeah, definitely worth it.

His usual carefree grin finally makes an appearance as he steps back and holds the door open. He presses a hand to the small of my back as I pass.

"You look...I don't have words. Truly," he murmurs.

I bump his chest with my shoulder. "Back at you. Smells amazing in here."

His smile widens as he leads me to the kitchen. "Word on the street is you appreciate a good chili and baked potato combo."

"Oh, the street, huh?"

He shrugs. "Casey."

A stupid smile fights its way onto my face at the sight of the table—draped with a tablecloth I've never seen him use, and perfectly set with two places, along with a single rose in a vase and three flickering candlesticks. Faint instrumental music trickles from somewhere.

Fletcher gestures for me to take the seat at the head of the table as he uncorks a bottle of wine. His eyes dart from me to the glass as he pours. "Is this too much?"

I blow the air out of my cheeks as I take the glass from him. "That depends. Did you make dessert too?"

He glances sideways at the kitchen, and I laugh.

"That part's store-bought, if it helps."

"Can I do anything?"

He shakes his head and squeezes my shoulder as he passes. "No, just sit tight. Should be ready in a few minutes."

I turn my chair, sip my wine, and watch shamelessly as he

bends over to check the oven. He rolls up his sleeves before pulling out the pan, and I am in *heat.*

I might not make it through dinner.

It's been two months since that first night in the hotel—not that I'm keeping track. My thighs involuntarily press together, and I quickly cross them. As Fletcher removes the oven mitts, his eyes find my leg—namely, the good deal of thigh showing from the slit in my dress. I smile a little as he quickly looks away. So the stockings were a good call.

"So," he says. "I've been meaning to ask you about next week..."

I dig in my eyebrows. Next week?

"Is it not your birthday?" he asks.

Oh. *Oh.* I picture a calendar in my head. Yeah, I guess he's right.

He laughs in disbelief. "Did you forget?"

I shrug. "Well...yeah."

It's not like there hasn't been plenty else going on. And I've never been a fan of my birthday to begin with. I've spent most of them alone. My mom didn't believe in birthday cakes—said they weren't worth the calories. And I didn't exactly have a lot of friends to invite for a party.

A look I can't read passes over Fletcher's face. "Well, I'd understand if you wanted to keep it with just you and Case or something, but if you'd be okay with me being there..."

"Of course I want you there, Fletch. Just—we really don't need to make a big deal of it or anything, okay?"

He nods, his lips pressed together like he's suppressing a smile. "Understood."

Once everything's ready, he brings over our plates and takes the seat beside me. It is, unsurprisingly, one of the best things I've ever tasted—as everything he makes seems to be.

"Where did you learn to cook like this?" I ask between bites, though it's difficult to hold back from shoveling the entire plate into my mouth.

He gives me one of those rare bashful smiles, the one that only comes out when someone compliments him. "Trial and error, mostly. Foster parents left us up to our own devices most of the time, and they did a shit job at grocery shopping, so I had to get creative." He smirks and sips his wine. "Got a lot better once I ended up with my parents and started using real recipes. My mom's an excellent cook."

I smile. "I like your mom. From what I've seen of her."

"Well, the feeling is mutual. She won't shut up about you."

"Oh really?"

He chuckles. "I believe her exact words when I told her you and I were officially dating were 'Well, finally. I was starting to think you had brain damage.'"

I wiggle my eyebrows. "You told your mom about us?"

"She would love to enlist your help with my backyard, which is apparently still unacceptable."

I glance through the window behind him, though it's too dark to see much. "I think what you're really missing is a jacuzzi."

His eyebrows slowly lift, and I have a pretty good idea of what he's imagining now. But I don't pull out the big guns yet. Not until the table is clear and he brings out the dessert—some kind of chocolate lava cake with vanilla ice cream. I'm practically drooling when he sets it in front of me.

I wait until he takes a bite of his own—his eyes closed, and a soft hum in the back of his throat—before I slide one foot from my high heel and glide it up the inside of his leg.

I catch the way his eyes snap open in my peripheral vision, but I keep my expression perfectly innocent, my attention on my own cake as I cut off a piece with my fork.

"Chris," he says, his voice coming out slightly strained.

My foot stops before it reaches his knee, then works its way back down.

"Mm-hmm?" I meet his gaze as I wrap my lips around the bite of cake.

His eyes track the movement.

"This is delicious." I lick the ice cream from my fork, then start my way up his leg again.

He pulls in a deep breath through his nose.

"Chris," he repeats, though this time it sounds like more of a warning.

I pause, my foot at his inner thigh now, and tilt my head to the side. "Yes?"

The last thing I see is his wolfish smile, then he ducks under the tablecloth.

"What are you doing?" I demand on a laugh, but then his hands are on my legs beneath the table, and I can feel his hot breath against my knee. "I—*oh*." He nudges my legs open in my chair, and it takes my brain a beat too long to realize his intentions. "*Fletcher.*"

"Keep eating the cake" is all he says, then he grabs my hips and pulls me to the edge of my chair.

My eyes threaten to bulge out of my head. Keep eating the...?

His mouth ghosts across my skin as he pushes my dress aside and works his way up my legs. His breath washes over me, but his lips barely make contact.

That is, until he takes the top of one of my stockings between his teeth and starts pulling it down.

I gasp, and he runs his hands up and down my legs, raising goosebumps in his wake.

"Big fan of these, by the way," he murmurs as he releases the stocking.

"I thought you might be." I laugh breathlessly as he presses his lips to the skin of my inner thigh that he just exposed. Agonizingly slowly, he works his way higher, higher, until I'm squirming in my chair. But once he's close enough that I can feel his hot breath against the place I want him most, he stops.

"Put the cake in your mouth," he says in a low voice.

I laugh again. "You're really going to make me—?"

"Yes. Do it now."

For some reason, I listen. And even though he can't see me from beneath the tablecloth, the moment that cake hits my tongue, he drags my underwear to the side and leans in to taste me.

I moan, the chocolate flooding my taste buds at the same time warmth shoots through my veins from the sensations of his tongue. God, that's…new.

I take another bite, and his hands tighten around my hips as his tongue works me faster. Fuck, I almost forgot how *good* he is at this. My head falls back with a shameless moan, and I comb my fingers through his hair, holding him to me.

But after a few moments—minutes?—he pushes my chair back, climbs out after me, and rises to his feet. I barely have a chance to catch my breath before he braces his hands on the chair arms, caging me in, and leans down until we share the same breath.

"Is it good?" I blink stupidly, and his lips twist into a grin. "The cake. Is it good?"

I bite my lip to hold back the girlish giggle threatening to break out and nod.

He brushes his nose against mine. "Do you want me here, or we can take this upstairs?"

"Why, are there rose petals upstairs?"

He narrows his eyes. "You making fun of my setup?"

I laugh, take his face between my hands, and kiss the corner of his mouth. "Not at all. I love it." I cock my head to the side. "But you're saying the kitchen counter is out of the question?"

He gives me that crooked grin again. "Oh, be careful what you ask for. I will give you the kitchen counter."

His mouth lands on mine before I can respond. All the kisses leading up to this these past few weeks, I'd known he was holding himself back, but *fuck*. Now, he kisses me with abandon, and I'm dizzy with it, drunk on it—his teeth, his tongue, his lips, his breath.

"Take me upstairs," I breathe against his mouth, my fingers already desperately working at the buttons on his shirt.

The entire house starts to vibrate.

My eyes snap open at the same time his do.

"Is that—?" I start.

His eyes fall shut. "The garage."

"I thought she—"

He lets his forehead fall against my shoulder with a defeated exhale. "She's home early."

We stay like that for a beat before breaking apart and adjusting our clothes.

His expression turns stricken. "I'm so—"

"I know," I sigh.

Jacks steps through the door a moment later, bringing the smell of movie theater popcorn with her. "Oh, hey," she says as her eyes land on me, then widen as she takes in the leftover cake on the counter. "Ooo."

"Help yourself," says Fletcher.

Jacks practically skips to the kitchen for a plate. Her eyes flick between us, then to the candles on the table, as she cuts herself a piece. "Hope I'm not interrupting."

"No. We were…" Fletcher clears his throat. "Just getting into dessert. How was your first day at work?"

Jacks shrugs as she chews. "Could be worse. Apparently I get to see movies for free."

"You'll have to give us a heads-up on the good ones that are showing," I offer.

"Anyway." Jacks scoops up her plate and heads for the stairs. "I'll let you guys finish your...dessert."

Fletcher grimaces, and my face burns as I double-check nothing is out of place with my clothes. I discreetly tug one of my stockings up. Once Jacks has disappeared upstairs, Fletcher meets my eyes.

I shake my head. "I can't—"

"I know." He offers his hand palm up and nods toward the couch. "How about a movie?"

Chapter Thirty-Four
FLETCHER

"*More* flowers?"

Casey nods seriously and struggles to fit the new bouquet into the shopping cart. It's currently stuffed to the brim with a mix of fresh and fake flowers—pretty much every one the store has. My hand shoots out to grab it before it can topple to the floor, and I gently tuck it into the last remaining pocket of space.

"You sure these are the kinds she likes?"

Casey nods again. "She likes all of them."

He trudges forward down the aisle, and I push the cart after him as he points to other things we need—shimmery garlands, balloons, a happy-birthday sign.

I can't stop thinking about the flowers.

How do I not know her favorite flower by now?

When we reach the baking section, at least there I have a better idea of what I'm doing. Chocolate cake, chocolate frosting, chocolate sprinkles. I grab some little chocolate candy bars to add to the top for good measure.

"You wanna help me bake the cake when we get back?" I ask.

Casey's eyes light up. "Can I lick the spoon?"

"Of course."

Chris's birthday isn't for a few more days, but today's the last day she'll be busy helping Jacks study since Jacks is going to give the test a go tomorrow. And Casey's going to be with his dad for the next few days. Leaving today as the perfect—and only—opportunity for us to prepare.

Especially after seeing *her* abilities, this surprise party is probably going to be incredibly underwhelming in comparison, but at least I have Casey's help. I'm hoping the talent is genetic.

"What else do we need, Case?" I ask.

He purses his lips, considering. Then, very seriously, he says, "Games."

"Games?"

He nods. "Parties have to have games."

Of course. Genius.

Unfortunately for Casey, we take so long at the next store meticulously considering every game on the shelf that Christine and Jacks are done before we have a chance to get started on the cake. I make a mental note to save a little batter in a Tupperware bowl for him.

We wait on the porch as Christine drops off Jacks since the kitchen is currently a disaster zone with all of our finds from today and I can't risk ruining the surprise.

"How'd the studying go?" I ask Jacks as she climbs out of the passenger seat.

"Fine," she mumbles, already heading for the front door.

Chris gives me an amused smile through the window. "She aced her practice test."

"Jacks!" I whip around, but she's already slipped inside.

"What did you two get up to today?" Chris asks.

Casey's eyes go comically wide.

"Afraid I can't tell you that," I say as I open the door and help Casey into his seat.

Chris's mouth falls open. "We're keeping secrets now?"

God, she looks beautiful today. Her hair is pulled back in a messy ponytail, and she's not wearing any makeup—at least, I think she's not. I can see her freckles better than usual.

But I can't afford to convince her to spend more time with me the way I want to. There's far too much left to do.

I clip Casey's seat belt and pat him on the head. "Don't give in. Stand your ground."

He gives me a determined little nod.

I shoot Chris a wink before closing the door. I wave and linger on the sidewalk until her SUV disappears around the corner.

When I head back inside, Jacks is poking around at the various bags piled on the kitchen table.

"I was about to get started on the cake if you want to help," I offer.

She lifts an eyebrow. "*You're* making the cake?"

"I'll try not to take offense to that tone." I grab the bag of ingredients on my way to the kitchen, then search for a mixing bowl. "I made you a few birthday cakes over the years, if you remember."

"Yeah, and they were awful."

I sputter and stand up straight. They were *not*—

She smirks at me over the island. "So how are you planning on getting her out of the house to set up?"

I duck into the fridge to search for the eggs. "Gracie's job is to occupy Chris for a few hours, then bring her to the party. I think she's taking her to some kind of spa. Li, Leo, and Case are gonna help set up. I'd *love* another set of hands if you want to join. And your company, of course."

She rolls her eyes, slides onto a barstool, and tears into the cake mix box. "She doesn't really have any friends, right? Don't you think a mostly empty house will be a bit of a downer?"

I rear my head back. "I—no, I don't."

Sure, Chris doesn't have the widest circle of friends around here, especially since the majority of the people she used to call friends bailed on her once the divorce hit. But she has people. Liam, Asher, Gracie, Leo, Keava—and baby Rowan—me, Casey, Casey's friend Erin and her mom Gloria, Gracie's friend Carson—that's more than enough people for a party, isn't it? Plus, everyone knows they're welcome to bring a plus one.

I stare down at the mixing bowl in my hands. *Is* this a bad idea? The last thing I want is for something that's meant to make her feel special to do the opposite.

She blinks up at me and shrugs. "I'm sure it'll be fine. I just couldn't help but notice when she and I were out how people around here kind of..." She trails off with a wince.

"Yeah," I mutter. You'd think people would've moved on by now. How fucking bored with your own life do you need to be to—

"Okayyyy, I'm just gonna take these."

I blink back to the room as Jacks extracts the eggs from my bone-crushing grip.

"Mixing spoon?" she asks.

I turn and rifle through the drawers.

"So." I clear my throat. "Chris said you aced your test today."

"It was just a practice test."

She pours the cake mix into the bowl while I add the rest of the ingredients. "That must feel good though, right? Make you feel ready to take the real thing?"

She shrugs, attention entirely focused on the bowl. "I guess."

I sigh inwardly, wishing Christine were here to translate teenage girl for me. Jacks starts mixing while I preheat the oven. I can't gauge her expression at all—can't tell if she's in some kind of mood or this is her default.

She's the same in a lot of ways from when we were kids, but also, so much has changed. There's so much about her that I don't know anymore. And not from lack of trying. I've asked her questions about what her life in our time apart was like, but she's even better at deflecting than I used to be. And I'm worried the more I push, the more she'll pull away. Maybe I should do what my parents did for me and find her a therapist.

"You're coming to the party, right?" I try. "I mean, we'll have to celebrate after your test tomorrow too, so you may already be partied out... But at least swing by to get some of this cake."

Her eyes flick up to meet mine. "I'm invited?"

Is *that* what this is about?

I smile. "Of course."

She refocuses on the cake batter.

My smile falls. "Well, no pressure. I can hitch a ride with Liam or something so I can leave the car here for you. I'm thinking I might end up staying with Chris, so I don't want to leave you stranded."

Her head snaps up. "You're going to *stay* there?"

I blink at the intensity in her voice. "I—well, it'll depend on how Chris feels about it, but maybe, yeah. Unless...if you're not comfortable spending the night here alone, I can come back."

"Forget about me. You don't think that's a bad idea? With her having a kid and everything?"

Truthfully, I don't know. I've never dated someone with kids before. I know me staying over is much more complicated, and ultimately, it's up to her, and I'll respect whatever she wants. But it's not like I haven't already spent a ton of time around Casey, and she and I are on the same page that this isn't some casual thing. Hell, I'm not above sneaking in and out of her window so Casey doesn't know, if that's what she wants.

"I don't know. *You* clearly think it's a bad idea though. What is going on with you?"

She shakes her head and sticks the spoon upright in the batter. "Nothing." She turns and heads for the stairs.

"Jacks!" I call after her.

She pauses at the foot of the stairs, her eyebrows pulling together as she looks at me over her shoulder. But all she says is "I'm just tired. I'm gonna go lie down. You can count me in for the party."

"You remember those snacks?"

Jacks glances at me sideways from the passenger seat. The weird mood from last night seems to be gone. She hasn't mentioned it, so neither have I. She shuffled downstairs this morning as she has each day since she got here, eyes barely open as she scavenged the kitchen for a cup of coffee. She even accepted the omelet I made her without any snarky comments about my cooking.

"You mean the *five-course* meal you packed?" She holds up the brown paper bag. "Yeah, I've got it."

I bristle in my seat. "It's an eight-hour day. Just thought you might get hungry."

She smirks but is gentle as she tucks the bag in her backpack. "It's not a prison. We're allowed to take breaks between the tests and leave."

"How *are* you feeling about the tests?"

She shrugs and frowns at the building in front of us through the windshield—the local community college. It's a gray, dreary morning, with heavy layers of fog lingering in the air. A good day to be trapped inside all day, I guess. "As ready as I'm going to be."

"Well. No pressure. Just do your best, and text me when you're done. If I can't pick you up, Chris said she could."

"Fletcher."

"Yeah?"

"You don't need to dad me."

I clear my throat. "Right. Uh, get the hell out of my truck."

She taps the tip of her nose with a smirk, throws the door open, and climbs out.

I drum my fingers against the steering wheel as I wait for her to make it inside. I think I'm more nervous about today than she is. But I was never a good test taker. School in general wasn't my strong suit. Something about it always made me feel…restless. Just the thought of being stuck at one of those tiny, rigid desks all day has my skin crawling. If I hadn't come to Sweetspire—if I hadn't ended up with my parents—honestly, I probably would've not finished school like Jacks.

If she's nervous, she doesn't show it. She hunches beneath the hood of her sweatshirt and strides through the doors without looking back.

My phone buzzes in my pocket.

Christine: Just dropped Casey off. Julian was actually there *gasp*

Christine: Do you want me to make a reservation to celebrate Jacks tonight?

Christine: Or do you think she'd rather do something at home

Christine: Or maybe she'd prefer just the two of you

I grin like an idiot and shake my head as the notifications flood in rapidly.

Fletcher: Please be there too. A reservation's a good idea. Something nice, but not too nice, you know?

Christine: I'm on it

Chapter Thirty-Five
CHRISTINE

"Maybe this was a bad idea," I whisper.

Fletcher lays a hand on my arm as Jacks pauses a few steps into the parking lot, craning her head to take in the structure in front of us.

The Shoreline Stage glows against the night sky backdrop as waves crash in the distance. String lights wind around their outdoor seating area, along with warm yellow lanterns on either side of the entrance.

I've only been here once—with Julian, unfortunately—and he hated it, so we never came back.

But I *loved* it.

He said it was too small, too cramped, the food too *ordinary*.

But I found it cozy, personable, and charmingly eclectic. None of the furniture matches, the walls are covered in rich velvet tapestries, and between the roaring fireplace in the corner and the mood lighting from the lanterns in the center of each table, it makes the whole place feel homey, welcoming.

Then there's the stage in the back. Sometimes there's live

music, poetry readings, stand-up comedy—a different theme for each night of the week.

The couple who owns it does the cooking themselves, and they change the menu on a monthly basis.

I gave Fletcher and Jacks a brief rundown of the place on the drive here, and she hadn't said anything...just like she's not saying anything now. In fact, she's been quiet since she got back from the test. Though, to be fair, I'd probably be pretty exhausted and nonverbal after eight straight hours of test-taking too. I didn't take it all in one day like she did.

Finally, she asks, "What night is it?" She looks at me over her shoulder. "For the theme—what is it tonight?"

"Comedy."

She turns back to the restaurant, but I *think* she just smiled. She shrugs and heads for the front door. "Cool."

I raise my eyebrows and meet Fletcher's eyes.

Cool, he mouths and gives me a thumbs-up.

It's crowded when we step inside, nearly every table filled, and the waiting area is standing room only. Fletch heads to the hostess to give her our reservation—which I put under his name instead of mine to avoid any potential...hiccups. Luckily his height makes him easy to keep track of in the crowd. He gestures for us to follow as the waitress collects the menus, and as I pass, his fingers gently tug on my wrist, then slide down and weave through mine.

I tense, hyperaware of every eye in the room, though none seem to be on us. Not that there's much to see in the first place, but despite how fourth grade it would be, I wouldn't put hand-holding above the Sweetspire rumor mill these days. Then I remember this isn't a secret anymore.

I'm not willing for this to be a secret anymore.

He loosens his grip like he can sense my discomfort and is

meaning to let go, but I tighten my fingers around his before he can.

He looks so goddamn handsome in the dim light—his skin tanned from working on a house in the sun with his dad all day, his hair lightly tousled, his button-down open at the collar, exposing the long column of his throat.

We end up at a booth in the back corner, and we all slide together on one side so we can see the stage, with Fletcher in the middle.

But even once we're sitting, he doesn't let go of my hand.

Jacks flips through the menu while she chews on her thumbnail. Her leg bounces restlessly beneath the table.

"You guys want an appetizer?" asks Fletcher. "Or skip that so we have room for dessert?"

My eyebrows inch up as I spy the chocolate cake at the bottom of the menu.

Fletcher leans over to Jacks and murmurs under his breath, "Get whatever you want. It's on me."

That, at least, makes her leg stop.

The waitress comes around for our drink order, and I glance at the empty stage, then the time.

"I think the show's supposed to start in fifteen minutes." I lower my voice and lean closer. "Don't get your hopes up too high though. There's no cover charge, and it's mostly an open mic night for locals, so this could be really bad."

Jacks snorts and nudges Fletcher in the ribs. "You should go up there."

He groans and rubs a hand over his face. "You're never going to let me live that down."

"Live what down?"

Jacks turns to Fletcher with her eyebrows raised, waiting.

He sighs heavily and shakes his head. "I might have done a stand-up comedy act for our school talent show when I was ten. Which *you*"—he turns to Jacks—"shouldn't even remember! You were like five!"

She taps her temple. "I remember it *all*."

"Please tell me you remember some of your jokes," I say.

He quickly shakes his head. "Absolutely not. You couldn't waterboard them out of me."

I try to picture a younger Fletcher like that—on stage, under the lights, the center of attention.

I can't.

"I never took you for a performer."

He glances at me sideways. "Oh, I learned my lesson. I never did it again."

"You might as well tell me the jokes. You know I'm just going to get them out of Jacks later."

Jacks nods seriously. "It's true."

I smile and thank the waitress as she circles back with our drinks. By the time she disappears to put in our order, Jacks's mood has shifted again. She's slumped against the booth now, eyes glued to her phone screen.

"So how long until you get your scores and everything?" asks Fletcher as he sips his beer.

It's hard to tell in the dim lighting, but her cheeks look a little red. "Um." She sits up straight and puts her phone away. "I have them now, actually."

"What?" Fletcher puts the cup down. "Why didn't you say!"

Jacks's eyes flick from him to me, but she focuses on her hands as she says, "Because I didn't pass."

"Oh—I—well, that's all right." Fletcher sets a hand on her shoulder and hurries to comfort her, but I can't help but cock my head.

Didn't pass?

There were a few sections she was stronger in than others

for sure. And the tests vary—it's never exactly like the practice tests.

But she wasn't just *passing* during our study sessions. She was college level in most things, scoring even high enough to qualify for college credits.

And not just once.

Every time. Every practice test.

With how well she was doing, she could've skipped a fourth of the questions and still have been fine. She was a million times more prepared than I was.

The chance of her not passing didn't even occur to me. Didn't seem possible.

I blink back to the table.

"You know what? No one passes it the first time," Fletcher is saying. "So this is basically a rite of passage."

Jacks quirks an unconvinced eyebrow, then turns to me. "How many tries did it take *you* to pass?"

I open my mouth, but nothing comes out.

"The *point* is," says Fletcher, "you can take it as many times as you need to, and now that you've got one under your belt, you know better what to expect. Maybe we rushed into this one. You only really studied for a week or so. Maybe you need more time than that."

She relaxes a bit, her smile more genuine now. "Thanks, Fletch. I'm sorry—you guys tried to do all this to celebrate, and I…"

"We're *celebrating* because you're my sister, and I'm happy to have you around again." He throws an arm around her shoulders and tugs her into a headlock until she bats him away, laughing.

When he looks up, grinning and so fucking happy and at ease, I force myself to smile back.

The comedians are, indeed, horrible. But in a *so bad it's fun* kind of way, and the food is as good as I remembered. And no meal can be that bad if it ends with chocolate cake.

On the drive home, Jacks is in the best mood I've seen from her yet. Very noticeably so. Like a weight has been lifted from her shoulders.

A weight that has now, apparently, been transferred to mine.

Because try as I may, I can't shake this feeling that something is off.

But as Jacks takes off inside when we reach Fletcher's house, it's clear he doesn't feel it too. He opens my door and braces his arms on the car's frame overhead.

"Still up for staying here tonight?" he murmurs.

It was something we'd agreed on earlier since Casey is with Julian—I even packed an overnight bag and a certain adult accessory in anticipation—but now his smile is full of promises I don't know that I can muster the mood for anymore. Not with my stomach in knots like this.

"I don't know…"

"I won't push you on it. Only if you want to."

I roll my eyes. "Of course I *want* to."

Staying here sounds much more appealing than going back to that empty, everything-is-falling-apart house right now. I bite my lip. I don't know why something about it feels like it might be…inappropriate. Jacks is eighteen, and his sister—not his kid—but still. This is new territory, and I'm not quite sure how I'm supposed to navigate it.

"Stay. Please."

I sigh like this is a major inconvenience. But before I can

say anything else, he pulls me from the car, throws me over his shoulder, and fireman-carries me toward the door.

I let out a breathless laugh. "Put me down!"

Doing no such thing, he pushes into the house and heads straight for the stairs.

To my mortification, Jacks is lingering in the kitchen. My face burns as we pass her, and I offer an awkward wave as I dangle against her brother's back.

"Night, Jacks!" Fletcher calls as we disappear upstairs.

"Fletcher!" I hiss.

"Almost there," he says cheerfully as he carries me straight to his bedroom, then deposits me on his bed and hovers over me with a crooked grin.

"Fletcher!" I slap his chest, my eyes darting to the door he left wide open. "We are *not*—"

He presses his lips to my forehead. "I know. I just wanted that worried look off your face. This one is much more fun." He kisses me before I can respond, slowly, gently, then tucks my hair behind my ears. "Thank you for helping me with Jacks. Not just tonight. With everything. The studying, talking to her. You have no idea... I don't know what I would've done without you."

"You would've figured it out. There's a reason you're the person she went to when she needed help."

He ducks his head, never able to take a compliment, and pushes to his feet. "Let me find you something to sleep in."

He rifles through his drawers, carefully selecting what to give me. And I wish I could just sit here and gawk at how good he looks and how good it *feels* to be here right now, but that gnawing feeling is still in the pit of my stomach.

He sets my clothes on the bed, and I drift to the other side of the room and quietly close the door.

I open and close my mouth at least three times before I

manage to get the words out. "Can I talk to you about something?"

Fletcher sets his watch on the nightstand and peers up at me. "Of course."

I tuck one leg under myself as I sit on the foot of the bed again, weighing my words, but there's no getting around what I mean.

"What is it?" he presses.

"Jacks failing the GED test…"

"Oh." He sighs and comes to sit beside me. "Look, that's not your fault, *at all*—"

"No, I don't mean…" I hold up a hand to stop him as I fight to get the words out. "I don't think her failing was…an accident." I stare at my hands in my lap before peeling my gaze up to meet his.

His brow furrows as he searches my face. "You think she failed on purpose."

It doesn't sound like a question, but I nod anyway.

"Just listen. I studied with her. I quizzed her. I graded her practice tests. She was *ready* for that test. She was ready to ace it. She's *smart*. The margin that she failed by…it's like someone else entirely took it. It doesn't make any sense."

The lines in his forehead deepen as he shakes his head. "I—well, people have test anxiety, right? Maybe it was the pressure."

I chew on my lip. Maybe I shouldn't have brought this up. And maybe I'm wrong.

"Why would she do that? Fail on purpose?" he continues.

I shrug. That I don't have the answer to.

"People self-sabotage for all sorts of reasons. Maybe she's just afraid of not knowing what's next if she did pass," I murmur. "You know—just forget I said anything—"

"No." He rests his hand on my leg. "I believe you. If you think something's off here, I believe you."

The relief from hearing those words is unexpected and immediate. "Thank you," I whisper and lay my hand over his. He immediately flips his over to link our fingers together. "Are you sure it's okay if I stay here tonight?"

His hand tightens around mine. "I will be absolutely heartbroken if you don't."

I smirk and roll my eyes.

"How are you feeling about Casey being with his dad?"

"I hate it," I admit on a pitiful little laugh. "I miss him. I'm worried Julian's not being nice to him. And I'm trying not to hover and call every five minutes."

He smiles and runs his thumb along the back of my hand. "He's a good kid. I miss him too."

I can tell he means it—means everything he says, really. There's something so earnest about him, the conviction in his voice, the openness in his eyes. Not someone saying what they think they're supposed to, or what'll get other people to like them. Maybe spending so much time around Julian left me jaded—always searching for that hollow kind of charisma, that glint in someone's eye that signals an ulterior motive.

"What are you thinking so hard about?" he murmurs.

I smile and squeeze his fingers. "That you're a good person."

His gaze drops to my lips, and when his eyes meet mine again, there's a question in them.

To answer, I lean in first. And my lips just brush his when—

"If I'm going to need earplugs tonight, can you at least give me a heads-up!" Jacks shouts from down the hall.

I laugh breathlessly and press my forehead to his shoulder instead. His chest rises and falls as he lets out a deep breath, and he rubs his hand along my back.

"Let's go to bed."

Fletcher's bed is even more comfortable than the one in his guest room. Maybe I'm just exhausted, but I pass out almost immediately. At some point in the night, I roll over, half awake, and reach for Fletcher's side of the bed, but it's cold.

I must fall back asleep because the next thing I know, the bed shifts, and I feel the warmth of his body curl against my back. Sighing, I lean into him, and his arm winds around my waist. When his face presses against the crook of my neck, I can feel him smile against my skin.

"You smell so good," he murmurs in a voice so low it raises the hairs on my arms.

I nestle farther into his chest. The muscles in his arms flex as they tighten around me, and I let out another involuntary sigh, all too aware of every point of contact between us—his legs tangled with mine, his hips flush against my ass, his lips lightly trailing along the back of my neck.

My head falls back against his shoulder as his hand slips beneath the hem of my shirt and his fingers explore my stomach. I can't think when he touches me like this. I just need more, *more*. His fingers drift higher, until his knuckles skim the undersides of my breasts, and my breath hitches. But he stops there, then trails them back down, following the curve of my waist until he reaches my hips, then starts up again.

I skim my fingertips along his thigh, and when he hums low in his chest, I feel the vibrations against my back.

He seems perfectly content to torture me like this all morning, so taking matters into my own hands, I turn enough to grab his chin and pull his mouth down to mine.

Thankfully, he doesn't need any more convincing than that. He grabs the back of my head as his tongue delves into my mouth. I melt into the bed as he rolls himself on top of me and nudges my legs open with his knee. I run my hands up his chest before letting them weave into his hair, my lips never breaking from his. When he rolls his hips against mine, I moan against his mouth.

"Shh." His lips curl into a smile. "Can you keep quiet for me?"

My breath hitches as reality trickles in—that nothing but a thin wall separates us from Jacks right now. His fingers hook beneath the waistband of my sweatpants before I can respond, and he follows them to the edge of the bed as he pulls them down.

"I really can't make that promise," I gasp as he lies on his stomach and settles his head between my legs. Then his mouth is on me, and my head falls back with an involuntary moan.

He starts slowly, in a way that has my body going lax against the mattress, and my eyes close at the warmth that floods every inch of my skin. Once my hips start to lift of their own accord, desperate for more friction, he throws one of my legs over his shoulder, wraps his arms around my hips, and presses down on my stomach as his movements shift from exploring to ravaging.

"Fletcher—*oh*—I can't—fuck—" I don't know what I'm saying. I grasp for his arms just for something to hold on to, and he never breaks his pace.

I pant, desperately trying to catch my breath, and prop myself on my elbows to watch. He looks up at me through his lashes, and Jesus Christ, it's the hottest fucking thing I've ever seen. His eyes hold mine as he leads me straight to the edge at a dizzying, violent speed. I expect for him to ease off, to make me wait for it, but no.

I fall onto my back and grab the other pillow to hold over my face as the orgasm rips through me. I arch off the bed and bite the pillow to quiet the noises trying to claw their way out of my throat. My legs shake as I come down from it, somehow already desperate for another one.

"Fletch," I say breathlessly as I let the pillow fall to the side.

He presses a gentle kiss to my thigh, my hip, then pauses, his forehead resting against my stomach. I comb my fingers through his hair, and he leans into my touch.

Then I hear the distinct thud of the front door closing downstairs.

My head shoots up.

"Fletch?"

He climbs out of bed and peers out the window that overlooks the front of the house. "It's just Jacks heading out for a run. She always heads out around this time."

My face burns. She was *awake*? If she heard—well, I think I might just put that pillow right back over my face. Permanently.

He smirks when he turns and sees me stewing in my mortification. "I doubt she heard anything. You were very quiet. I was impressed. Had me second-guessing myself for a minute there."

I slide my legs over the edge of the bed, and his eyes track the movement.

"How long is she usually gone for?" I murmur.

He swallows hard as I join him by the window and lightly tuck my fingers beneath the waistband of his pants.

"Half an hour."

"That seems like plenty of time." Before he can lean in to kiss me, I pull his pants down with me as I lower to my knees.

"Chris," he breathes.

"Mm?" I hum as I wrap my hand around him.

His eyes flutter shut as if it's involuntary, but it's nothing compared to the groan he tries to stifle as I slowly run my tongue along the tip.

"Wait."

I pause, and there's a glint in his eyes I can't quite read. "Did you bring what I asked you to?"

I bite my lip. "In my purse."

He goes to where it's hanging off his desk chair, fishes around, then pulls out the little pink vibrator.

"Stay on your knees, but spread your legs," he says in a low voice.

The soft buzz fills the room as he crouches in front of me and switches it on. Instead of using it himself, he slides it into my hand, then guides it until I'm pressing it to my clit. My breath hitches, and my body jerks.

"Keep it there," he orders, then rises to his feet.

It's going to be a whole lot harder to focus on the task at hand now. He brushes my hair back from my face, his touch light as I grip his dick with my other hand and ease the tip between my lips.

His abs flex, and he lets out a harsh breath as I work him slowly, gently, the opposite of what I know he's desperate for. But he doesn't move a muscle, doesn't guide my head. He just swallows hard and watches me, rapt.

I try to keep a steady pace, I do, but it's hard when my body is shaking and I'm moaning around him. I was *intending* to take some of the control back here, but now I am a panting, quivering mess at his feet. I know from experience this toy can get me there in under sixty seconds, and we are already well past that. I ease it away, my heart hammering in my chest.

"I don't think so." Fletcher crouches down again, his hand covering mine, and brings the vibrator back to my clit. He holds my eyes as he grinds it against me over and over, and I cry out, every cell in my body begging for release.

He pulls it away abruptly, and I sag forward, panting and desperately needing relief. He gives me a second to catch my breath before returning it to its original position. I gasp, but manage to keep it there as he stands and waits for me to continue.

I take him deeper into my mouth, hoping the distraction will help me hold out. If anything, it just turns me on *more*, especially when I hear the labored way he's breathing above me. His fingers weave in my hair, though his touch is gentle.

I don't know if he's worried about hurting me or what, because I don't remember him being this careful last time. I pull back, meet his eyes, and open my mouth wide as an invitation.

His eyelids fall to half mast, and his fingers tighten slightly in my hair.

"Let me know if I go too far," he murmurs, then slides his dick into my mouth.

I keep my eyes locked on his as he presses inside inch by inch, testing, waiting to see my reaction. I gag when he hits the back of my throat, and he starts to pull out, but I grab his thigh and yank him toward me.

He curses and shakes his head a little. "More?"

I nod and moan around him.

He mutters something under his breath that sounds a lot like *You're going to fucking kill me* before pushing deeper into my throat. I dig my fingers into his thigh, holding on as my body fights against the intrusion. He coaxes out a gargled noise with each thrust, and my jaw starts to ache. Of course I remembered his size, but I hadn't really considered how much harder it would be to take him in my mouth.

My legs tremble, and it takes everything in me to keep the vibrator in place. I can feel how fucking wet I am—feel it dripping down my thighs.

He pulls all the way out, and I gasp in a breath. His brow furrows as he looks down at me and strokes my hair, his chest rising and falling rapidly with his breath.

"You okay?"

I nod quickly, but my head falls back of its own volition with a breathless moan.

He drops to his knees, his hand layering over mine and shaking the toy against me as if I fucking need any more stimulation down there.

"Fuck—Fletch—I can't—"

"I know." He grabs my jaw and crushes his lips to mine as the orgasm tears through me—abrupt and explosive, leaving me completely undone. I feel his lips curl into a smile as he kisses me, then finally, *mercifully*, lets me drop the toy.

The break is short-lived.

Because then he's scooping me up and positioning me on the bed. He settles himself between my thighs on his knees and rolls a condom onto himself.

He pauses as he leans over me, his eyes searching my face in question. To answer, I skim my hands up his arms, his chest, his neck, then draw his mouth to mine.

He pushes inside an inch, then another. My head falls back on a moan, and I cling to his shoulders as he slides the rest of the way in.

"Fuck," he mutters under his breath, then grabs both of my hands in his, links our fingers together, and presses them to the mattress over my head.

And this—this is not what I'd been expecting. This gentle, slow roll of his hips against mine, filling me all the way, then almost leaving me completely. He stares into my eyes, so close we share the same breath, but neither of us speaks. It's a delicious, sweet agony of its own. The eye contact is almost too much, but I can't look away.

I lock my ankles around the backs of his thighs as if I can pull him in deeper even though there *is* no deeper.

"This time when I make you come, you're going to look me in the eye," he whispers.

I don't blink. I can barely breathe.

I nod.

I feel like I shouldn't even be able to do it again after the last one, but I'm already close. My hips rock up against him involuntarily, matching his pace. His forehead presses to mine, and I can feel his every muscle tensing around me.

My breaths turn into pants, into moans.

And the *sounds* he makes. It's nearly enough to push me over the edge alone.

But is that—are those footsteps on the stairs?

He must notice it at the same time because we both freeze.

I blink up at him, breathless. "You said thirty—"

He flattens his lips into a tight line and shakes his head. "She's back early."

I slump against the pillow, defeated, but he doesn't move. "Fletch…"

"Shh." He brings his mouth to mine.

He keeps kissing me, and I can't help it—my desperately horny, traitorous body melts into it—and slowly, his hips start to move against mine again.

"Fletcher," I manage between kisses.

"She'll get in the shower in a minute," he breathes.

Sure enough, the bathroom door shuts down the hall, followed by the sound of the water turning on.

I giggle as he runs his nose along the side of my throat. I feel like a fucking teenager sneaking around. Or, what I imagine that would've been like, seeing as my mother couldn't have cared less about what I got up to.

He grins down at me, but it softens into a smile as he meets my eyes. "I love your laugh."

I smile back, but falter at the words on the tip of my tongue. He doesn't seem to notice though, because he resumes his earlier pace, his hands tightening around mine.

My breaths quicken as the tension in my body winds tighter, but those three unspoken words linger in the back of my mind. The impulse to say them came out of nowhere. It was just a knee jerk response, right? Not—

My eyes roll back as he thrusts into me harder, and it forces that line of thinking away.

"Please don't stop," I gasp. "Fuck, Fletcher, *please.*"

"Come on, Chris. I need at least one more. Give it to me."

His hands tighten around mine, and I have no choice. The orgasm rolls over my body, stealing my breath and my voice.

"Eyes on me," he orders through his teeth.

I hadn't even realized I'd closed them.

They fly open and lock on his staring down at me. He keeps the same pace until the last of it ebbs away and I go limp against the bed.

He rolls off of me, and my head whips up. Did he even finish? But then he's propping me on my side and sliding in behind me.

Oh God, more?

I strain my ear—the shower is still running.

One hand wedges beneath me and winds around my breasts, holding me to his chest. The other grips my thigh as he pulls my leg up and repositions himself.

"You can lean back on me," he murmurs. "I've got you."

I'm too exhausted to do anything else at this point. My head falls against his shoulder as he slides his length along my pussy a few times before pushing inside.

"Tell me if you need me to stop," he grits out through his teeth.

I think I've lost the ability to speak, so I shake my head and moan as I reach around for any part of him I can get my hands on—behind his neck and his wrist.

His pace is faster this time, harder. Each thrust has me gasping for air.

"Think you've got one more for me?"

I let out a breathy laugh because I have no fucking idea. I'm a little delirious and just hanging on for dear life.

"You already had enough?"

I immediately shake my head, because I might be out of my mind, but God, I don't want him to stop.

"I want...you to...come," I gasp.

He grabs my face and crushes his lips to mine, his thrusts hitting harder, deeper. I moan against his mouth.

"I wish you could see yourself like this, Chris," he breathes. "God, look at you."

His movements get increasingly jerky, his muscles tensing beneath my hands. I didn't think I'd come again too, but the fucking sounds he makes push me right over the edge with him.

I'm left shaking and gasping and like fucking putty in his hands, but he doesn't let me go. He holds me tightly against his chest, breathing hard, his forehead coming to press against my temple.

Distantly, I register the sound of the shower shutting off. We both laugh a little breathlessly, but even once several minutes pass, neither of us moves.

"Well, shit," I whisper.

"What?"

"I was kind of hoping the first time was a fluke, how good it was."

He squeezes me closer. "And was it? A fluke?"

I laugh and shake my head. "God, you even upped your game this time."

I feel his smile against my neck. I start to disentangle myself to go clean up in the bathroom but pause. He falls onto his back with a sigh, and I roll over and brace my arms against his chest so I look down at him.

"Fletch?"

He hums, still smiling with his eyes closed.

Because as good of a job as he just did at distracting me, it all comes rushing back now—the empty side of the bed, the covers pushed back, the door slightly ajar.

I hadn't checked the time, but I'd be willing to guess it was sometime around 4:30 AM.

Just like the last time I was here. Just like that night in the hotel.

I study his face, the bags beneath his eyes dark despite the happiness currently softening his features.

"Talk to me about this morning," I murmur.

His eyes snap open, and immediately, there's a wall over them. He opens his mouth, already poised to brush it off.

"Don't tell me you're an early riser or it's nothing. Talk to me."

He sighs and rubs his eyes.

But he says nothing.

I prop my chin on my arms. "Your mom told me about the nightmares."

He presses the heels of his hands into his eyes, something between a sigh and a laugh coming out. "Of course she did."

"She's worried about you. *I'm* worried about you. You're having these every night, aren't you?"

I wait for him to brush it off again, to deflect, but after a few moments of silence, he gives a small nod.

"And they're always the same?" I try.

Another nod.

I push the hair from his face. Finally, he meets my eyes. And the pain behind them cuts right through me. This is more than a couple of bad dreams. This is something big, something heavy, that he's been carrying around. For a long time, it seems.

"Fletch." I prop myself up so my face hovers over his. "Talk to me. Please."

He shakes his head. "I can't." And the way his voice breaks around the words *kills* me.

I run my fingers through his hair again. "You can."

Silence falls around us for several long moments. Long enough that I wonder if pushing him right now is doing more harm than good. But then so quietly I almost don't hear it, he says, "There was a fire."

I stay completely still, as if any sound or movement will make him stop.

"At my foster house when I was thirteen. There were five kids there, including me. I was the oldest. It was in the middle of the night, and it was already bad by the time I woke up. Both of the adults died."

Both of the adults. Interesting that he doesn't refer to them as parents, but that detail's not important now.

"You were thirteen," I repeat. The age he said he was when he ran off before coming here. "You left after that fire."

He nods.

"And that was the house you lived in with Jacks," I realize.

He nods again.

"But you were having these nightmares even before she showed up, right? So that's not what triggered them."

Another nod.

"I don't know what causes them," he murmurs. "I've gone

years without having them. Sometimes it's just every once in a while. Sometimes..."

"It's every night. How long has it been going on this time?"

He shrugs and lets out a long breath, his gaze focused on the ceiling. "I've lost track. Since before we met."

"Fletch," I breathe.

His brow furrows. "It doesn't usually...they don't usually last this long."

"Have you ever talked to anyone about them? Like a doctor?"

"My parents put me in therapy for a bit when I was a kid, but it never helped with them."

"And the dreams are always the same? Always of that night?"

He nods.

I run my thumb along his cheek, and he leans into my touch. "I'm sorry." The words sound even lamer aloud than I thought they would, but I don't know what to say, how to help. "If you ever want to talk about it more, I want you to know that I'm here."

He smiles a little.

"And coming from someone with no background on the topic at all, it sounds to me like your subconscious is trying to tell you something."

He lays his hand over mine on his face. "What do you mean?"

I shrug. "Our brains don't ever do something to hurt us. At least, that's not the intent. It always serves some kind of biological purpose—it's trying to fulfill a need. So maybe the dreams are trying to tell you something."

Finally, some of the tension eases from his forehead, and a slow smile spreads across his face. "You're too smart for me. Maybe you're right."

"But it could also be a perfectly reasonable trauma response to something terrible that happened to you," I rush to get out, realizing how insensitive that may have come across. "So don't listen to me."

"Don't do that." He tightens his hand around mine before I can pull away. "I love listening to you."

My brain goes blank for a moment. *That word again.* I plant a quick kiss on his cheek before pushing myself out of bed. "Come on. Get yourself decent and meet me downstairs."

"Oh?" he asks on a laugh.

After pulling myself together in the bathroom and throwing on a pair of Fletcher's sweats, I make my way to the kitchen. The stairs creak as he follows me down, and I glance over my shoulder as he rounds the corner.

"You. Sit."

He raises his eyebrows at me in disbelief. "Excuse me?"

"You heard me." I jut my chin at the barstool and reach for the fridge.

"What do you think you're doing?"

"Wooing you with my cooking skills, obviously."

He watches in amusement as I hunt through his cabinets for a pan. "Do you want some help?"

Finally, I find the right one and straighten a little too quickly in my excitement. My head hits the inside of the cabinet with a dull thunk.

"Chris—"

"No. You always do it. So just go sit over there and let me make my boyfriend breakfast for once, okay?"

I compile my finds on the counter—eggs and bread. I can handle eggs and toast—but turn when I realize how uncharacteristically quiet he's being now.

He's sitting on a barstool, arms crossed over his chest and watching me with a soft smile.

"What?" I demand.

He shakes his head, and his eyes trace over every detail of my face. Quietly, he murmurs, "I like hearing you call me your boyfriend. And I like having you stay over, that's all."

I smirk, my face heating a bit. "That's just because you haven't tasted my eggs yet."

"Please tell me you guys aren't doing it on the kitchen counter right now!" Jacks calls from the stairs.

"The coast is clear," Fletcher deadpans.

She appears a moment later with wet hair and slides onto the barstool beside Fletcher. "Why are you up so early?"

I meet his eyes, but that haunted look behind them is gone now, replaced by his usual easy smile. "I don't know. Keep hearing about this early bird getting a worm or something. Thought I'd give it a shot."

Chapter Thirty-Six
FLETCHER

I doubt Sweetspire's tiny costume shop has seen this much business in years. When I tell the little old man behind the counter I need thirteen costumes, his eyes all but fall out of his head. He doesn't have enough to match the theme, so I take the eight he has and figure we can pick and choose a few pieces for everyone and get creative with the rest.

Casey tears into one of the bags the moment we're in the truck and slips the eye patch on. He whips toward me with a hooked finger. "Aaarrgggg!"

"Don't forget the pet monkey."

He slips that over his shoulder next. "Are you going to be a pirate too?" he asks.

"I don't know." I start the car and throw a hand over the back of the passenger seat as I reverse out of the parking lot.

Casey and I got the idea for a costume party while we were browsing for games, but it was Jacks who suggested we make it one of those whodunit murder mystery parties instead.

A few minutes of internet searches later, I found a script to print with a list of characters and instructions on how to host.

Murder among the Mateys it's called, so they're all pirate themed. Casey's clearly vying for the pirate captain.

"I figured I'd let everyone else pick their characters and I'd take whatever was left," I add. "Who do you think we should save for your mom?"

He sifts through the costumes in the seat beside him and I see him pull up the big dress in the rearview mirror.

"That's for the governor's wife. Kind of boring. Chris needs something more badass than that."

Casey's eyes go wide, and it takes me a moment too long to realize what I said.

"Sorry!" I whip around as we pull up to a stop sign. "Don't tell your mom I said that."

Casey covers his mouth with his hand and giggles.

"And if you repeat that, you did *not* hear that from me, right?" I say as I turn and pull forward.

He salutes me in the rearview mirror, and I smirk. He must've picked that up from Liam.

"I'm thinking we should make her the innkeeper."

"What's an innkeeper?"

I flip the blinker on as we pull into Chris's neighborhood. "Someone who runs an inn—it's like a hotel."

Casey screws up his face in a way that's also eerily similar to Liam.

"Hey, hey, I wasn't done. The innkeeper is a cool character because she's also secretly a vigilante."

"What's a vig-il-ante?"

I smile as he struggles to pronounce it.

Luckily, there are several cars outside the house when I pull up. I knew Liam would already be here, but didn't have a ton of faith in Leo's punctuality. And we have only so much time to set up.

"Uh, it's someone who fights crime. But not like a police

officer. They take matters into their own hands. Kind of like a secret superhero."

Casey *ooo*s. "Mom would be a good superhero."

God, I wish Chris were here to hear that.

"Look!" Casey squeals, pointing.

I squint through the windshield, and sure enough, the decorating crew has gotten started. A wooden sign hangs from the door with a skull and crossbones and the words *Enter at Yer Own Risk* in black paint. Beside the door hangs a tattered pirate flag, along with a cheap Halloween skeleton "door man" with an eyepatch, a pirate hat, and a lantern.

I stare at it for a second, then scan the surrounding cars. There is *no way* this is Liam's or Leo's doing, and Gracie's busy occupying Chris right now, so then who…? I do a double take when I reach the car parked along the curb across the street.

Casey's already climbing out of the car, trying to carry the twenty pounds of costume pieces himself even though the load is bigger than he is.

"Here, bud." I throw the larger garment bags over my forearm and the strap for the bags over my shoulder. Once I have a free hand, Casey links his fingers through mine and starts pulling me to the door. I smirk when I realize he's still wearing the eye patch and monkey.

"Let's *go!*"

The front door is unlocked, and Casey bursts through it first, eyes bright.

"Oh my God," I breathe.

If I didn't know any better, I would've thought Christine did this herself.

There must be a speaker somewhere—the kitchen, if I had to guess—playing a soundtrack of creaking wood, crashing waves, and slightly eerie nautical music. It even *smells* like we're in the middle of the ocean—a mix of salt water, wood, and...is that vanilla? How are they *doing* that?

Everything from the hall to the living room to the kitchen is loaded with decorations. Fish nets, thick ropes, and loose woven fabrics are draped over the furniture, and lines of candles waiting to be lit cover every hard surface. Some random pieces are added here and there on the floor and walls—a starfish, a treasure chest overflowing with plastic gold coins, a parchment scroll.

Mom's head pokes into the hall from the kitchen. "Oh good, you're back! I could use some help in here!"

I blink at her, stunned. "Mom?"

Casey hesitates and looks up at me. "That's your mom?"

"I still have a few more clue stations to set up, and I could use an extra set of hands for the food!" Mom calls.

"Hey, Case!" Liam appears at the top of the stairs with a wide grin.

"Liam!"

Li jogs down, arms full of scraps of paper and bottles of fake blood. "Your parents have been a *lifesaver*."

As he says it, the back door to the kitchen swings open, and Dad steps in, dusting off his hands. "Done!" he announces.

What is going on?

Liam turns to Casey. "You want to help me hide some treasure?"

"*Yes.*"

"Don't spoil the whole game for him," I whisper.

Liam waves me off. "I know."

The two of them disappear upstairs as I set the costumes on the living room couch and make my way to the kitchen. The table is covered in plastic goblets, rustic silverware, and mini signs with cheesy names on them—Dead Man's Fingers, Shark Bait, Seaweed Dip. The room is warm, like the oven's on.

"Mom, Dad, what are you doing here?"

Mom waves me off. "Oh, don't worry. We're not sticking around for the party. But we thought you might need some help setting up."

I'd only mentioned the party in passing, mainly to explain why I couldn't help Dad with the house today. "How did you...?"

She shrugs unapologetically. "I happened to run into Liam the other day, and he mentioned what a big undertaking it was going to be..."

I cross my arms, unable to hold back my smirk. "Oh, you just ran into him, huh?"

"Well, go on, take a look around," says Dad. "Tell us what's missing. Give me a new job." He rubs his palms together. "I'm ready."

Casey's laughter echoes from somewhere upstairs, and Mom hands Dad another box full of decorations. "By the fireplace," she instructs, then he's off again.

"Have you already assigned everyone a character?" she asks.

"Loosely," I mumble.

Her hand shoots out. "Which in Fletcher language means not at all."

I dig the instructions from my pocket and hand it over. "You really don't have to do all this."

She pulls out a kitchen chair, plucks a pen from behind her ear, and waves for me to join her. When I do, she finally slows down for a moment, and her eyes meet mine.

"I like her." Her soft smile is gone just as fast, replaced by a stern expression as she clicks her pen and smooths out the paper in front of her. "So don't screw it up."

I smirk and lean forward so I can see the names too. "I'll try not to."

"Shh! Everybody, get down!" I let the curtain fall back into place and hurry away from the front door as Gracie's car pulls into the driveway. I crouch behind the couch with Liam and Casey, the others tucked behind the walls in the kitchen.

"What is *that?*" comes Christine's muffled voice through the door.

I ended up with the treasure hunter character—leaving me in a ridiculous loose shirt with no neckline to speak of, a leather vest, fingerless gloves, and a thick belt full of loops and pouches. The absurd amount of fake leather packed into my costume squeaks with my every movement, and Casey whips around to hold a finger to his lips.

The security system beeps as the door opens, and the moment the light flips on, we all jump out and shout "Aaarrrggg"—per Casey's request.

Chris grabs Gracie's shoulder to steady herself.

"Happy birthday!" Casey darts forward and throws his arms around his mom's waist.

"Thank you!" She grins and squats down to inspect his costume. Her head cocks as she lifts the stuffed monkey's tail. "Was this your idea?"

"It was Fletcher's. But I helped!"

Her eyes find me next, and my lungs fill with air, like it's the first breath I've taken all day. Her eyebrows skyrocket as she takes in my outfit. "Pirates?"

"Aaarrgg!" Casey raises his plastic hook. "There's been a murder on the ship!"

Her jaw drops open in fake shock. "A *murder?*"

"The murder mystery part was Jacks's idea," I say.

Chris rises to her feet, her lips curled in a smile that crinkles her eyes now, and she's fucking breathtaking. I drift a few steps closer, and I don't care that everyone is looking at us right now—don't care about anything else at all other than this need to be close to her.

"Happy birthday," I say, but before I can kiss her, Gracie tugs Chris back a step.

"Save it, lovebirds! Our costumes are upstairs, and we have a murder to solve!"

Chris presses her lips together and gives me a bemused smile over her shoulder as she follows Gracie upstairs. My eyes stay locked on her until she disappears around the corner, then a hand claps me on the back.

Leo flashes his crinkled-eye grin as he glances from me to the now-empty staircase. "You gonna wait here all night?"

I blink back to the surrounding room—everyone else has already ventured to the kitchen for snacks and drinks.

I cough and look Leo up and down. "Who are you supposed to be again?"

He stands a little taller and straightens his ridiculous ruffled cravat. The suit itself is long and fitted—and *velvet*. "You can call me Your Highness."

The monarch, right.

"If you need to head out of here early, don't worry about it, all right?" I murmur.

He gives me a tired smile, accentuating the dark circles under his eyes. Last I heard, he was taking all the night shifts, and it's starting to show. I was surprised he showed up at all, to be honest. I can count on one hand the number of times I've seen him this summer. I knew getting Keava here, too, would be a stretch with a two-month-old at home.

"How are Keava and Rowan?"

"Oh, good. They're on the rocker in the nursery."

I lift an eyebrow.

His smile turns a little sheepish as he holds up his phone. "There's an app that connects to the cameras in there."

"What are you two gossiping about?" Liam appears on my other side, double-fisting the punch my mom made—The Captain's Poison, I think she named it.

"I cannot take you seriously with that thing on," Leo deadpans.

Liam ended up with the commodore character, so his outfit isn't that different than Leo's. Apart from, of course, the pointed hat with a giant white feather.

He grins and offers one of the drinks to me. "I think I'm going to keep it."

I take a sip, expecting something like root beer, and sputter at the fire that immediately rages down my throat. Liam discreetly flashes the flask in his breast pocket, then pats it twice and pops his eyebrows.

Laughter echoes through the house as Casey chases Erin out the back door with a plastic sword.

Leo clears his throat and nudges me with his elbow. My head snaps back to the stairs. Gracie appears first, dressed as the governor's daughter in a gigantic hoop skirt. Liam beams when he sees her and slips past us to wait for her at the foot of the stairs.

"Nice hat," she says as she reaches him.

"Nice corset." He offers his arm. "If you need help getting that off later, just let me know." He lowers his voice as he says it, but not enough.

Leo chokes next to me, his complexion going red as he looks from his sister to Liam. Before Leo can get any words out, Liam grimaces and whisks Gracie toward the kitchen.

But my attention is locked on the stairs. Time slows as Christine rounds the corner. She bunches the layers of her skirt in her hand as she heads down, and her soft blond curls bounce around her shoulders with each step. She catches my eye and gives me one of those coy little smirks of hers.

"Do you like it?"

She has a corset like Gracie, though hers is covered in thick leather buckles that match the tool belt hung low on her hips. It's layered over an off-white blouse with puffy sleeves and strings cinching it together at the neckline. Despite my best efforts, I can't help but stare.

Role-play has never been my thing in the past, but this… this is making me question things about myself.

"You have to stop looking at me like that," she says lowly.

"Believe me, I'm trying."

"Help! Help!"

A chorus of screams breaks out in the living room. Christine hooks her arm through mine as we hurry to join them.

In the center of the room lies Jacks, a mess of fake blood covering her throat.

"Arrrg!" cries Casey. "There's been a murder on the ship!"

Chapter Thirty-Seven
CHRISTINE

Watching Fletcher explain the rules to the room in pirate garb should absolutely not be a turn-on, and yet... I think he needs to start wearing more leather. Like, all the time. The neckline of his shirt is lower than mine, and I am absolutely not staring at the planes of his chest every time he moves.

Once the first round of the game is underway, everyone breaks off to interrogate each other and search for clues. Instead of Casey being glued to my side like he usually is in group settings, it's like he can't get away from me fast enough as he and Erin take off, more interested in their sword fight than the details of the game.

The party itself is...impressive, to say the least. Every detail was clearly carefully thought out—the food, the decorations, the costumes, the game—and it almost brings tears to my eyes.

The birthdays I spent with Julian were...cold. Fancy, but hollow. Expensive restaurants, expensive gifts. But they were the kinds of places he could've taken anyone, the types of jewelry that held no personal touches. Nothing that ever suggested he knew a damn thing about me.

"Please save me from myself. I can't stop."

I blink back to Gloria as she stuffs another handful of the Pirate Booty popcorn in her mouth. I narrow in on the M&Ms mixed in, and I quickly scoop up a handful for myself.

"I should warn you, there *is* a cake coming up you'll want to save room for." Fletcher slides in on my right.

My eyes dart around the rest of the kitchen—the table, the counters. No sign of a cake.

He chuckles and rests his hand against the small of my back. "Tucked away for safe keeping."

Gloria nods knowingly. "Erin and Casey."

Fletcher chuckles again, his eyes flicking to me. "Not who I was thinking of, actually."

I swat him on the chest.

He clears his throat, his expression suddenly serious. "Now, if you'll excuse us, ma'am, I have some questions for the innkeeper."

I have to press my lips together to keep from laughing at the way he's talking out of one corner of his mouth. And what even is that accent?

"Is your pirate from the South?" I whisper.

"Hey now, I am a *treasure hunter*." He offers an arm, then leads me from the room. I wave to Gloria over my shoulder before we turn and head upstairs.

"Should I be nervous about this interrogation?" I ask. "If it requires privacy?"

He nudges me into my bedroom, closes the door behind us, and grins. "Very."

"Fletcher," I hiss as he closes the distance between us, grabs my face with both hands, and pulls my mouth to his.

He hums against my lips, and I can't even pretend to offer resistance. I melt against him.

"We have a house full of people," I murmur.

"Mm-hmm." He kisses me harder and backs us up until I'm pressed against the wall. "We agreed to end the round in"—he pulls back to check his watch—"twenty-three minutes. I can get *a lot* done in twenty-three minutes. And there are no clues in here. I made sure to leave a sign on the door so people wouldn't be in your stuff."

My head falls back against the wall as he kisses me again. *This is a bad idea...*

"The lock on my door doesn't work."

He pauses, looks around, then grabs my hips and pivots us toward the bathroom. "What about this one?"

I laugh. "You can't be serious."

But he's already tugging me inside. I'm still laughing as he closes the door behind us, locks it, and hurriedly pulls my face to his.

"I've been out of my fucking mind since the moment you walked down the stairs in this," he says against my lips.

"Oh, you like this?" I lift the layers of my skirt. Before I can drop them, his hand covers mine, and he yanks them up farther.

"I do."

My breath hitches as his hand slips beneath the fabric and his fingers glide along my thigh, higher, higher.

"You should see yourself." He spins me around to face the mirror. His face dips in the crook of my shoulder, and his lips brush my ear as he murmurs, "Hands on the counter. And I want you to watch."

I meet his eyes in the reflection, breathless as his chest presses against my back and he holds me to him with one hand around my waist, the other buried beneath my skirt. I jolt as his fingers reach my hip, and he trails them leisurely along the waistband of my underwear. A flush spreads across my skin as we watch each other, and I lift a hand to touch him too, but he freezes the moment I do, his hold on me tightening.

"Hands. On. The. Counter."

Slowly, I put my hand back.

He rewards me by finally sliding his hand between my legs.

My intake of breath feels loud in the small space. Fire spreads through me, and his lips trail along the side of my throat, my shoulder. The slight stubble dusting his jaw scrapes along my skin, and the sensation is *delicious*. I want more of it —I want it *everywhere*.

As if he can read my mind, Fletcher spins me to face him and lowers to his knees.

"Fletch," I gasp.

"Hold on to the counter." He grabs one of my legs to prop over his shoulder, shoves the layers of my skirt up, and—

The bedroom door creaks open.

"Fletcher," Jacks singsongs.

"Shit," he mutters, quickly lowers my leg and skirt, and pushes to his feet. He gives me an apologetic look as I whip around to check myself in the mirror.

"You two better not be *boning* in there," she calls.

Jesus Christ.

Wait. I cock my head. Is she—is she slurring her words?

Fletcher throws the bathroom door open as Jacks launches herself stomach-first onto my bed like she's diving into a pool.

"Have you been drinking?" he demands.

She rolls onto her back, her lower lip pushed out in a pout, and she squints as she pinches her forefinger and thumb together.

I curse under my breath and cross the room to close the door.

"Jacks, this is completely unacceptable."

"Oh, puh-lease. You can put the dad face away. Like you never drank at eighteen."

"We'll talk about this more later, once you've sobered up," he says.

She clamps a hand over her mouth, her eyes going wide.

Fletcher curses, grabs her arm, and hurries her toward the bathroom. Thankfully, they make it to the toilet before she retches. He kneels beside her and frantically gathers her hair out of the way. When she's done, Fletcher sighs and glances at me over his shoulder.

"It's okay, you can take her home," I murmur. "I'll handle everything here."

His expression turns stricken.

"It's okay," I insist.

He joins me in the doorway as she flushes the toilet and leans against the bathtub with a huff.

"I'm so sorry," he says.

"You have nothing to be sorry for."

"God, we haven't—we haven't finished the game. We haven't even brought out the cake yet."

"Fletch, it's *okay*. I've already had the best night—"

Something like resolve hardens behind his eyes. "No. I'm at least going to be here long enough to do the cake. Just hang on, okay? Can you stay with her for a minute?"

I nod, and he gently cups the side of my face before slipping past me and out of the room. Then it's just me and a nearly unconscious teenage girl on my bathroom floor.

Sighing, I take one of the little paper cups from the cabinet, fill it with mouthwash, and walk over to her. "Here."

She swishes it around, eyes still closed, and spits it in the toilet. I wince at the harsh stench emanating from her pores.

"Whiskey, huh?" I say lightly. "Hope you at least had something to eat first."

"You can stop pretending to be nice to me."

I blink and rock back on my heels. "What? Jacks—I—I'm not pretending."

She peels her eyes open just to roll them. "I'm in the way. I get it. You think—you think you can patch me up, put me on my feet, then shove me out into the world so I won't be a problem anymore." She squints and taps her nose a few times. "And you're good at it. You've got him wrapped around your finger for being so *helpful.*"

I blink rapidly, my eyes burning at the *venom* in her voice. Is that really what she thinks? Have I done something to make her feel unwelcome? "Jacks," I force out through the tightness in my throat. "No one is trying to get rid of you."

Footsteps grow louder as someone enters the room and heads toward us. Liam pokes his head around the corner, something between a smile and a grimace on his face. "I'm here to take over for you. *You* are needed in the kitchen."

I push myself up on shaky feet. Jacks's eyes are closed again, her head resting against the side of the bathtub. Of all people to leave her with, at least it's Liam. It's not like he doesn't have plenty of practice at this from Asher.

"Thanks, Liam," I murmur as I slip past him.

I force a smile onto my face as I reach the kitchen, where everyone else is already gathered around the counter. In the center waits a three-tiered cake that appears to be covered in every type of chocolate imaginable.

Fletcher smiles, takes my hand, and pulls me in front of it as the group descends into the obligatory Happy Birthday song. Casey squeezes in on my other side, standing on his tiptoes to see the cake.

"Make a wish! Make a wish!" he urges as everyone finishes the song and cheers.

I stare at the flames flickering on the candles for a moment.

They cast a warm glow over everyone's faces—faces that are smiling at me. No judgment, no impatience, no apathy. And I suppose if I have anything to wish for, it's just more of this.

I close my eyes and blow out the candles, and the room erupts in another round of applause.

"Happy Birthday, Mom!" Casey throws his arms around my middle and hugs me as tightly as he can.

I squeeze him back. "You want to help me cut the cake?"

"Oh, I'll do that!" Gracie steps in, giant knife in hand, and Leo spreads the plates out along the counter.

Fletcher presses a kiss to my temple. "Happy Birthday."

He gives me a soft smile, but I don't miss the tension in his brow, or the way his eyes keep flickering toward the stairs.

I squeeze his arm. "You can go get Jacks. It's okay."

He frowns and looks between me and the stairs again. "You're sure?"

I nod. "Just let me know when you two make it home okay. And thank you for all of this, Fletch. Really."

"I'll call you later, all right?"

"You're leaving?" Casey blinks up at him with puppy dog eyes.

"Yeah, bud. I gotta go." He crouches down to give Casey a hug.

"We'll save a piece of cake for you," Casey promises.

Fletcher's smile turns crooked as he rises to his feet and ruffles Casey's hair. "I'll hold you to that."

"For the birthday girl." Gracie presents me with a very generous slice, and Casey tugs on my hand to lead me to the table. By the time we're situated, Fletcher is already gone.

Chapter Thirty-Eight
FLETCHER

We spend the first half of the drive in utter silence. Jacks's eyes are closed, and she has her head leaned against the window, but I know she's not asleep. My knuckles ache from how tightly my hands are wrapped around the steering wheel, but I force myself to think through what I'm going to say. Letting my anger win out here won't help.

Because the fact of the matter is, I'm not her dad, and she's not wrong. I wasn't a saint at eighteen. And under different circumstances, I might not have been as bothered. But Christine deserved for this night to be perfect, or at the very least, not cut short like this. Not to mention I'd been hoping to spend more time with her after the party was over. And Jacks knew that.

I can't help but feel like this was intentional. But maybe it wasn't.

We're a few minutes to the house when I finally manage to calmly ask, "Do you want to explain to me what happened tonight?"

"Not really," she mumbles.

"It was a rhetorical question."

"Then you didn't need an answer."

I let out a short breath through my nose. "Explain what the hell happened, Jacks."

"Okay, party police. So I had a few drinks. Calm down."

"You just puked your guts out, and I can smell you from here. Why did you do this? If being there tonight was so painful for you that you couldn't do it sober, you could've stayed home."

"Right, how *dare* I mess up *Christine's* night."

I rear my head back at the way she says Chris's name. "What's that supposed to mean?"

"Nothing," she mutters.

"Jacks, I'm *worried* about you. You've been acting weird for days. What's going on?"

"You clearly weren't too worried if cutting the fucking cake was more important," she spits.

"What the hell is the matter with you?"

"Just forget it."

"No, Jacks, I'm not going to forget it. What is your problem? Is it Christine? Did something happen?"

"Of course not," she drawls as I pull into the driveway, her words dripping with sarcasm. "She's too perfect for that."

Where the hell is this coming from? Have I been completely blind? I'd thought—I'd thought things were going so well. The dinner, the amusement park, their study sessions. They seemed to be getting along. And I can't tell if this is some nonsense drunken tirade or if she's been bottling all of this up for a while.

"Jacks—"

"I heard you two, okay!" She whips around to face me, and

fire burns in her eyes. "I know she thinks I failed the test on purpose."

The test?

All of this is about the damn test? I sigh and rub my eyes. "She was—we *both* were just surprised—"

"God, are you really that dumb? She wants to get rid of me! And now she's trying to turn you against me."

My head spins, and I feel like I have whiplash. "Okay, Jacks, that's not true at all."

"It's all she talks about! How *exciting* it was for her to get her first place, and she *can't wait* until I get to experience that. How *exciting* it'll be for me to find some job I'm passionate about. She wants me *out*. Why the hell do you think she's going through all the trouble to get me to pass this stupid test?" She throws her door open, stumbles out, and slams it behind her.

"Jacks!" I hurry after her and grab the front door before she can slam that too. "That's not what she's—God—if you'd just—"

"I'm going to bed." She heads for the stairs, and I sigh, watching her go.

Maybe it's best if she sleeps this off and we try again in the morning. It'll give me a chance to cool off too.

"We're not done talking about this," I call.

She slams her door in response, leaving me alone and utterly mystified in the kitchen.

Hours pass, and despite trying to fill the time and burn off this energy by tidying up the house, checking in with Chris, and restlessly pacing around, my mind won't rest.

This is all my fault. Of course Jacks is looking for any scrap of evidence that I'm going to abandon her.

Because I've already done it once.

Her blaming Chris though...I don't know what to do with that.

There's still so much I don't know, so much Jacks won't talk about, no matter how hard I try. But I see myself in her. The fourteen-year-old version of me who didn't know how to process anything, so he took it out on people who didn't deserve it. My parents were saints back then. Liam too.

I don't know how to help her. Hell, I don't even know how to help myself. Jacks thinks I'm all *shiny and normal* now, but I haven't slept in months. And no amount of therapy or time away from that night has helped. I couldn't even talk to Chris about it—she had to drag it out of me.

Something else she said that day comes back to me.

Maybe your subconscious is trying to tell you something.

If it is, it hasn't been doing a very good job. Nine years of trying, and all I've got is reliving the worst night of my life a hundred times over.

I don't know if it's my intuition or the sleep deprivation is finally catching up with me, but something inside of me is insisting that it's important right now.

I sit on the edge of my bed, force down a deep breath, and close my eyes. A shiver runs through me as if my body is trying to physically repel the memory.

The dreams aren't always the same. Some end sooner than others. Some have details I haven't noticed before, but I've always chocked those up to my imagination twisting the memory into fiction.

But the one thing they always have in common is: they always, *always* cut off by the jump from the window as if my brain knows it wouldn't survive digging any deeper.

It's not that I don't know what comes next, but living it once was more than enough.

The moment I drop into the memory, my throat tightens as if my lungs are filling with smoke in real time. Sweat breaks out along my skin as if feeling the heat from the flames.

The dreams always start the same—the moment Jacks woke me up. We went looking for our shitty foster parents, then the other kids...the fire had started downstairs...

I shake my head and shove to my feet. This isn't helping. I know every goddamn detail of that memory inside and out.

My gaze lands on my laptop sitting on the desk across the room.

Maybe I need more than just what I can find in my own head.

Steeling myself with a breath, I sit at the desk and search for fires in the area that year.

Unsurprisingly, a news story from that night is the first result. The picture was taken from the street. Giant orange flames climb toward the night sky, and the firetruck sits off to the left.

Tragic House Fire Takes Three Lives.

I close my eyes. Maybe I can't do this.

But when I focus on the screen again, what catches my attention is the article below it. I scroll and reveal a news article from about five years later—another fire, this one at our old middle school.

My heart beats a little faster in my chest as I skim the article. No one was hurt, but the fire started in the classroom of an eighth-grade science teacher.

I return to the results and scroll farther.

I cover my mouth with my hand.

Another one. Two years after the school. A car fire, this one killing the person who owned it—a seventeen-year-old boy.

I promised myself I would never look back after the night of the fire. I just took off. Never checked in. So I guess I shouldn't be surprised that I hadn't heard about any of this. But for such a small town—three fires in seven years? Is that normal?

I return to the first article about the house.

Thought to have started somewhere around two in the morning... owners of the home, Joan and Bob Wilcox, were found dead on the scene. One of their foster children also died on the scene from smoke inhalation. The fire started from a stove left on...

I blink back to the room around me and sit up straighter. From the stove? I think back. I vividly remember seeing all of the cigarettes discarded on the living room floor. I guess I always assumed that's what had done it.

But the stove? I was the one who cooked dinner—a good eight hours before the fire. Bob and Joan were out for most of the night, and they never bothered with cooking when they stumbled in drunk. Raiding the fridge and pantry, maybe. But I'm not entirely convinced either of them even knew *how* to work the stove.

I sigh and rub my eyes. It was a long time ago. My memory isn't exactly the most reliable.

But I have this nagging feeling. Something urgent enough that I go back to the second article, find the teacher's name, and search again.

Former Middle School Science Teacher Joshua Burgess Arrested for Multiple Sexual Abuse Against Minors Charges.

The first image to appear is his mugshot. I recognize him immediately from when I went there. I wasn't in his class, but I'd see him in the halls. He had the beady eyes even back then.

I search for the kid who died in the car fire next.

There are a few articles about the accident, and a memorialized social media page. I flip through his pictures, not sure what I'm hoping to accomplish, but I freeze at one dated exactly a month before the fire.

He's standing in a suit that's too big for him, a corsage pinned to his chest.

And standing beside him is Jacks.

Chapter Thirty-Nine
CHRISTINE

Once Fletcher left, Gracie and Liam jumped in to help finish the game. Liam was the only one to guess the killer right. Considering it was his girlfriend, he had a bit of an advantage. She was shocked when he figured it out, but he just laughed and said, "Gracie, I love you, but you have the worst poker face in the world."

Everyone stayed around for about an hour once we were done to mingle and finish off the snacks, and by the time the house was empty, I was practically asleep on my feet. Casey was *literally* asleep, his little head slumped on the kitchen table, and I had to carry him upstairs.

It feels like I've just barely crawled into my bed, my brain already slipping in and out of consciousness, when a piercing shriek jars me fully awake. I roll over in bed and cover my ears. At first I think it's the security system, but no.

What *is* that?

When I try to open my eyes, they burn. And when I suck in a surprised gasp, I cough.

Smoke.

Oh my God that's smoke.
Fire.
Casey.

I trip over the sheets wrapped around my legs as I stumble out of bed and hit the ground on my knees. The air is already so thick it feels impossible to breathe. I pull up my shirt to cover my mouth and nose, but it does little to stop the coughing.

Casey. I have to get to Casey.

When I make it to the hall, the smoke is thicker, my surrounding visibility getting worse by the second. *Where is it coming from?*

Casey.

He must be awake. There's no way he could sleep through this alarm.

I shove through his door.

The bed is empty.

No. *No.*

"Casey!"

I turn a full circle, looking for every place he could hide. I check under the bed, in the closet.

"Casey!" I scream, and it takes all of the air from my lungs and rips through my throat. I double over as the coughs turn violent.

Where is he?

I stumble into the hallway. The smoke is growing thicker by the second. I think it's coming from somewhere downstairs.

I'm about to circle back and check Casey's room again when the house makes a horrible groaning sound.

I barely have time to process what I'm hearing before the ceiling caves in.

Chapter Forty

FLETCHER

I don't breathe for a full minute.

My mind jumps to an answer that's impossible.

It's *impossible*.

A coincidence at best.

It's a small town. The probability of Jacks being the common denominator in all three fires doesn't mean anything.

But when I dig more into each story, I don't find any answers, because neither did they.

The house fire was labeled an accident, and based on the state Joan and Bob were in at the time, everyone else did exactly what I had—assumed it was them.

The school fire started with a Bunsen burner during lunch. The teacher, Joshua Burgess, was the only person inside. He made it out, but not easily. There was something blocking the door and he ended up jumping from the second-story window and breaking his ankle.

And the car…inconclusive. The kid was also from a foster home, so I'm guessing he didn't have anyone who cared enough to push for answers.

I'm being ridiculous. Maybe there's no connection between the three. They happened years apart, and they could all have been freak accidents.

And yet. *And yet.*

Maybe your subconscious is trying to tell you something.

It feels just out of reach, like trying to catch smoke with my hands. A detail, a moment. *Something* from that night that I just can't remember.

Something that twists incessantly in the pit of my stomach until I feel like I'm going to be sick.

I shove back from the desk and pace into the hall. The house is dark, quiet. I don't know what I'm doing, what my plan is. I pause outside Jacks's room where the door is propped open an inch.

I ease it open a few more. I should just ask her about it. We promised we'd be honest with each other, and—

Her bed is empty.

I backtrack and glance in the bathroom across the hall, then head downstairs. But no—not in the kitchen, the living room, on the deck.

Jacks is gone.

I grab the keys and head for the garage before I realize what I'm doing. If she took off because of our fight and something happens to her, I'll never be able to forgive myself. I don't know when she left, but if she's on foot, she couldn't have gotten that far. Hopefully it's too late for her to be able to grab a bus. I try to think of where else she would go, who else she knows around here.

Maybe she went for one of her runs on the beach to blow off steam.

The roads are empty this time of night, and I speed down them, my head whipping back and forth for any trace of her. I'm a few minutes from the water when I see the smoke in the air, billowing up toward the night sky.

Everything stops.

My heart.

My breathing.

I yank the steering wheel in that direction and slam my foot on the pedal.

"No," I breathe aloud as I get closer and a spark of light in the distance swims into view. It's far too bright. Too large. And where it's coming from...that area...

No.

My tires squeal as I round the corner and find Christine's house up in flames.

My vision blurs as I shove myself out of the car. I blink hard, trying to dispel the memories.

This is not one of my nightmares. I'm awake right now. *I'm awake.*

The neighbors are gathered on the surrounding lawns, hands held over their mouths.

There's no fire truck.

"Did someone call 911?" I ask the first person I see—a woman crying in a bathrobe. She nods.

"Are they out? Christine and Casey? Are they out?"

She lets out a little sob and shakes her head.

The man standing beside her tries to grab my arm as I head for the house.

"You can't go in there—"

I shove him off and sprint toward the front door.

"You should wait for the fire department—!"

After finding the spare key under the rock, I try the door, but it won't open more than an inch. Something's blocking it.

"Fuck." I throw my shoulder against it, and it opens an inch more. Smoke and a wave of heat pours out.

"Chris!" I shout through the opening, but she either doesn't respond or the roar of the fire drowns it out.

This isn't happening. This isn't happening.

Not them. *Not them.*

I ram my shoulder into the door again and again, putting my entire weight behind it until each jolt sends a flash of pain through my bones.

Finally, the door gives way.

Parts of the ceiling have caved in. A massive beam is crossed diagonally in front of the door, and I duck under it.

The smoke is already thick, the air unbearably warm.

I don't have much time.

The upstairs is in even worse shape. It seems the entire attic came down. The floor is utterly covered in debris.

And in the center of the hall—it's her hair I see first.

"Chris!" I fall to my knees and shove bits of plaster away. She's utterly buried in it. I dig out her face. Her eyes are closed, and her hairline is saturated with blood.

And she's so, so still.

"Chris!" I dig her the rest of the way out and pull her toward me. I don't have time to worry about any other injuries. I have to get her out of here.

But no matter how much digging I do, I don't find Casey.

I scoop her into my arms. She doesn't wake up. I don't think she's breathing.

I have to get her outside.

But Casey.

I call out for him and stumble over the debris toward his room.

Coughs rack my body, and my vision darkens at the edges. I feel myself getting sluggish.

Chris stirs in my arms.

The relief that tears through me as bright blue eyes look up at me nearly brings me to my knees.

"Casey," she rasps.

"I'll find him."

The house groans around us, and I have less than a second to crouch and try to cover Chris's body with my own before more of the ceiling rains down on us.

"Fletcher," she whimpers, and I tighten my arms around her.

But no—

That's not Christine's voice.

I whip my head around.

Casey.

He's standing in the doorway to the bathroom. I hold one arm out for him, and he rushes in. All the breath leaves my lungs at once as I crush him to my side and close my eyes for a second.

But only a second.

"Can you walk?" I ask Chris. She gives a shaky nod.

The stairs are completely blocked off. Which means the only way out is…

I pull them both into Casey's room and beeline for the window.

"Chris, you're going down first, then I'll hand you Casey—"

"I can't," she says in a small voice.

I kick at the screen until it falls, then poke my head out. My head spins—from vertigo, déjà vu, or the smoke inhalation, I'm not sure. A two-story drop. Nothing to break the fall but grass.

I reach a hand for her. "I need to get you out of this smoke, *now.*"

"Fletcher, I—" Her eyes are round, wide. Fucking terrified.

Heights.

"Okay. I'll jump. Then you hand me Casey, then you jump, and I'm going to catch you, okay?"

She shakes her head. "We could—"

"Chris, we don't have time. Now."

I climb over and hang on to the ledge to try to get myself as low as possible before the drop.

I don't hesitate. I just let go, bend my knees, and pray I don't break anything.

"Fletch!" Chris calls, her voice shrill. "Are you okay?"

I drop into a crouch. The impact zings up my bones, but it's not unbearable. I reach my arms up. "Casey."

Chris disappears from view, then returns with her son in her arms. Tears stream down Casey's face as he coughs uncontrollably.

"I'm gonna catch you, Case. You'll be fine. Now, Chris."

She lets him go.

I grunt as he falls against my chest, and he tucks his face against my neck. "You're okay," I murmur before setting him beside me. "Now your mom. Chris!" I call.

She bites her lip and peers at me over the edge.

"Just don't think about it. Close your eyes and jump. I've got you."

"Fletcher—" Her voice trembles.

The fire rages behind her. I don't know how much time we have. And every moment she's in there, she's breathing in more smoke. I know she's scared, and I don't mean for my voice to come out as hard as it does, but I can't help it. "*Now*, Chris. I need you to trust me."

"Mommy," Casey wails beside me.

She throws her legs over the edge, closes her eyes, and jumps.

She sobs as I catch her, and I drop to my knees, all of us

breathing hard. She's shaking so badly. I cradle the side of her face with my hand and tuck her against my neck.

"You're okay, baby," I breathe. "I've got you. I've got you both."

Finally, sirens and flashing lights flood the street.

Chapter Forty-One
CHRISTINE

The firefighters are working away, but their hose doesn't seem to be doing much. I stare at the orange flames climbing higher and higher toward the sky, eating away the home I spent months trying to build.

And I feel absolutely nothing.

Paramedics poke and prod at me and force an oxygen mask onto my face, and my eyes lock on Casey as a few more do the same to him. Fletcher hovers around us both with his arms crossed over his chest, his eyes bloodshot and almost manic as his gaze darts between me and Casey.

"You checked the back of his throat?" he asks the paramedic with Casey.

The man looks like he's barely holding on to his patience. "Yes—"

"And he doesn't need to be intubated?"

"No, he doesn't."

"You're absolutely sure?" Fletcher pushes.

"Sir, let me do my job—"

"He inhaled a *lot* of smoke—"

"And his airway is clear," snaps the paramedic.

Fletcher opens his mouth, and I lower the mask from my face before he can say whatever he's preparing for.

"Fletch," I rasp.

His eyes snap to me, and he hurries over. "Hey. How are you feeling?" He looks up at the medic behind me. "Is she okay?"

"She'll be fine," says the woman like she's bracing for the same interrogation her colleague got.

I smile a little and wrap my fingers around his wrist. "Leave the poor paramedics alone."

His lips flatten into a tight line. "I'm just checking."

"I know." My eyes flick between his, and my eyebrows tug together. "How did you know? How did you get here so fast?"

He lets out the heaviest sigh I've ever heard, kneels in front of me, and roughs a hand through his hair. When he meets my eyes again, the pain in his is breathtaking. He wets his lips, but before he can speak, two firefighters burst through the front door with a body slung over the larger man's shoulders.

"We've got another one!"

My head snaps up as the paramedic behind me takes off at a run toward the lawn.

Another...who else was in the house?

Fletcher pushes to his feet like he wants to go to them, but he stops after a single step as the firefighter hands the person off to the medics.

Is that...?

"Jacks," he breathes.

Jacks? When did she—why was she—? Oh God, is she—?

The paramedics put her on a stretcher, but she's not moving. I can see the burns on her arms from here, and my stomach twists. They put an oxygen mask on her though, so she must be alive.

I look up at Fletcher...but he isn't going to her. He's standing frozen on the lawn, his face ashen.

"Fletcher," I say gently. "We're okay. You can go with her."

When he turns to me, anguish rolls like waves behind his eyes, and he shakes his head. "You don't understand," he rasps. "Chris—I—I think she did this."

Chapter Forty-Two
FLETCHER

I've always hated hospitals. It's the smell. It feels stale, and it's always so strong you can taste it.

I shouldn't even be here right now. I should've gone with Christine and Casey.

But the moment I saw them carry Jacks out of the house, I knew what I had to do. I called my parents. My mom was a nurse for nearly ten years before she met Dad and decided to change careers, so leaving Christine and Casey with her at least lessened some of my anxiety. She'll know what to look for, what to do.

And this is something I need to do on my own.

I hang my head between my shoulders and sigh. A headache pounds in my eye sockets.

I did this. I let her back into my life, let her around the people I love.

Mom tried to warn me. She saw something I couldn't. She's always had good instincts. *Why didn't I listen to her?*

A nurse leads me back minutes—hours?—later. She tells me the police haven't been in to see her. Yet.

Jacks gives me a tired smile as I step through the door. Her hair is bloody and matted, and both arms are wrapped in bandages.

"You came," she breathes.

I stop a pace inside the door, and her smile falters.

I cross my arms over my chest and fight the sudden urge to cry. This entire night has been a fever dream. Every time I blink I feel like I'm slipping in and out of reality. One moment I'm in the present, the next, I'm in a memory of that night. I look at Jacks, and I see an eighteen-year-old. I blink, and she's eight again.

It's so fucking confusing.

A part of me feels like I raised Jacks. She was basically Casey's age when I knew her. And our foster parents were intoxicated in one way or another the majority of the time, so the responsibility in the house fell to me. If I didn't cook, the kids didn't eat. If I didn't hound Jacks to do her homework, it didn't get done. If I didn't help with hair and shoes in the morning, they missed the bus.

I may have left that place, but a part of me has always stayed there.

And having her back in my life, I admit, I'd started to imagine things. I'd started to *hope* for things. *Family* has always been an evolving word for me. But maybe it was fate that had brought us back together after all these years. A second chance. And she seemed like maybe she could fit in with my life here. That maybe this tangled, complicated family situation I've built for myself could include her too. And I'd *wanted* it to. She's the closest thing I've ever had to a real sibling. And having her back was the first time it seemed like maybe those two versions of my life could coexist. That I hadn't needed to leave everything behind and have a clean slate here.

But now—

"Why were you at Christine's house, Jacks?" I ask, and my voice barely sounds like it belongs to me. Her eyes shift, and she opens her mouth. I recognize that look immediately and cut in, "Don't lie to me. I know about the teacher at your school. Your old boyfriend. *Our house.* Tell me the truth, Jacks, or I swear to God I will walk out that door right now and you will never see me again."

She looks down at her lap and bites her lip. She murmurs something too low for me to hear. I drift forward another step.

"What?"

Her forehead wrinkles as she says, "I tried to stop it."

"Stop what?"

She meets my eyes. Hers are desperate, pleading. It makes my stomach feel like it's full of ice.

"The fire," she whispers. "I regretted it right away and I tried to stop it."

The ice cracks.

I rub a hand over my face and pace along the end of her bed.

I wanted her to deny it, I realize. *Needed* her to. I wanted an explanation. An excuse. Something even remotely believable to latch on to. Anything, *anything* other than this.

"How could you do this?" I ask, and my voice comes out hoarse.

"I tried—"

"How could you do this?" I demand and whip around. My hands clench into fists at my sides, and I have to take a deep breath to keep from yelling. "*Why* would you do this to Christine? She tried to help you. She was *good* to you."

"She wanted me to leave, okay! That's the only reason she was helping me with the stupid GED anyway, to get me out of your house as fast as possible."

"I—Jacks, she was trying to *help* you. She knows better than anyone what struggling is like, especially at your age. To have no one to fall back on, to have nothing." My voice breaks, and I suck my teeth for a moment. "She was trying to help you so you could help yourself and not have to get help the way she did." I sigh as something occurs to me. "You did fail on purpose, didn't you? Because you thought if you passed, you'd have to leave."

And I'm sure catching on to that made Christine look like even more of a threat in her eyes.

Jacks drops her gaze.

"And *Casey*?" I demand. "Was he collateral damage? He's just a kid."

A tear rolls down her cheek. "I know, okay? I know I screwed up. I didn't—I got scared. I didn't have a backup plan. I found you online years ago. And the idea of getting out and finding you after I turned eighteen was the only thing that got me through these past few years. You're the only person who's ever looked out for me. So when I thought you'd...that she was...that I'd have to leave..."

I hate the way my stomach drops, the way my heart twists.

I go back to pacing.

"Fletcher," she gasps, her voice breaking around my name. "I don't—I don't know why I do the things I do sometimes, okay? I know I'm all messed up. I just—"

I stop at the foot of her bed. "Lucy."

She flinches and looks away.

"*Lucy*," I say through my teeth.

"I know," she croaks.

"She was *five*—"

"I know!" Jacks shouts, tears running down her face now, and she breathes heavily through gritted teeth. "And I've carried that with me my entire life—"

"But you still did it again!" I'm shaking. Head to toe I am

vibrating with rage. The piece of that night that I never dare to think about, that every cell in my body has been fighting to keep out of my memory floods back.

We made it out the window. I got her out. *I got her out.* But by the time we were on the ground, she wasn't breathing.

I remember an ambulance in the street by then. I'd sprinted for it with her in my arms.

They tried everything. CPR. Oxygen. Her throat was so swollen they couldn't get a tube down it.

I couldn't hear anything. My ears were ringing. But I was on my knees at her side begging them, *begging them*, to keep trying.

All these years I've blamed myself. I let her go. I didn't get her out fast enough. I didn't wake up soon enough. So many little things I could've done differently and maybe today she'd still be alive.

I blink back to the room. To the face of the person who started the fire.

Because that noise, that itching that's been in the back of my mind for months, I remember it now.

It wasn't Jacks shaking me that woke me up. It was footsteps on the squeaky stairs.

Coming up from the kitchen, down the hall, and then into my room.

Because the cigarettes didn't start the fire. And I didn't leave the stove on.

She went down there and set it herself.

"You know what? I might have been able to forgive you for that. We were kids, and you were going after Joan and Bob. I know you didn't mean for that to happen. But Christine and Casey?" My voice breaks around their names.

For a moment, when I saw Chris buried under the ceiling, I'd thought she was dead. That I was too late.

"Please, Fletcher, you have to forgive me."

"You tried to *kill them*." The heat rises in my chest like my voice is aching to scream, to yell, but the words come out low and quiet and shaking. "Even if we set aside for a second"—I can't help but laugh because I can't fucking believe these words are coming out of my mouth—"that killing people, inherently, is wrong. What about me, Jacks? Someone you supposedly care about—"

"I *do* care about you—"

"Do you have any idea what losing them would've done to me?"

I can't even fathom it. The moment my brain tries, everything inside of me repels it with a vicious desperation.

My life wasn't bad before Christine. And maybe I could've gone on that way forever. But once she stepped into my life, there was no going back. Because knowing what life looked like with her in it—everything was different. The way I breathed, the way I walked, the way my heart beat. She was a vital organ I didn't know I had, one that had been living outside of my body for the first twenty-three years of my life.

Losing her wouldn't just devastate me. It would *destroy* me.

"I know it was wrong. Fletcher, I tried to stop it—"

I bark out a laugh again and pace the length of the room. My entire body is vibrating with restless, uncontrollable energy. My nostrils flare as I meet Jacks's eyes, and a violence I have never felt floods my veins. I have *never* thought I'd be capable of hurting someone until now.

Lowly, I force out, "I will *never* forgive you for this. And if you have even a shred of a soul left you will tell the police exactly what you did when they come in here."

Her chin wobbles. "Fletcher—"

"Don't ever speak to me again. Don't ever come near me or the people I love again. You and me, we are done, Jacks."

"You're all I have," she cries.

I pause in the door. She looks so small surrounded by all those machines. Footsteps echo down the hall as a pair of police officers makes their way toward us.

My face feels wet, and my throat is tight.

The last thing I say to her is "The Jacks I knew died in that fire with Lucy."

Chapter Forty-Three
CHRISTINE

"Can I have another?"

Jodie beams at Casey over the kitchen counter, then slides another pancake onto his plate. "Of course."

As he inhales it, she turns her attention on me, her smile softening. "How are you feeling?"

I force myself to smile back as I sip my coffee. Truthfully, everything inside of me aches—my lungs, my throat. Every breath hurts. But we both got out without any burns, so I'm more thankful for that than anything.

The state of the house on the other hand... It doesn't sound like there's going to be much left.

"Just tired," I say. "Thank you again for letting us stay here."

"Of course." She smiles fondly at Casey as he guzzles some orange juice.

When Fletcher insisted we stay at his parents' house, I assumed he'd come join us after going to see Jacks in the hospital. He left around midnight. That was more than nine hours ago.

And still no sign of him. I texted a few times, but he hasn't responded.

The police did call to let me know that Jacks confessed.

The fire had started in the kitchen, which was also where they found Jacks, along with the garden hose, like she'd changed her mind and was trying to stop it.

I haven't even begun to process that.

I haven't begun to process any of this.

"Give him some time."

I meet her eyes again, and she gives me a sad, knowing smile.

"Hey, Casey, you know how to play catch?" asks Fletcher's dad.

Casey wipes the back of his hand across his mouth and nods vigorously.

Dave winks at me over Casey's head as he grabs a little foam football and the two head to the backyard.

"I don't understand any of this," I murmur.

Jodie sighs and rounds the counter to take over Casey's seat.

I should be angry. And part of me is. The mother inside of me is murderous, in fact. But mostly I'm just...stunned. I'd felt something off about Jacks, but I never imagined it would lead to this, especially since things seemed to be going well between us. I thought she was warming up to me, something beyond mild tolerance.

I *never* could have imagined...

"Has Fletcher spoken to you about the fire at his old foster home?" she asks slowly.

"A little. That's what the nightmares are about. He said his foster parents died that night." The police had mentioned it too, that Jacks admitted to starting that one, as well as two others in their old town.

Something flutters across her face—so quick I barely catch it. "Is that all he said?"

I frown. "I know he left after that. Was out on his own with a few other kids for a year before he ended up with you."

She nods and rolls her lips together. "It wasn't just the parents who died that night. A little girl did too. She was five years old. Her name was Lucy."

I suck in a sharp breath. No, he had most certainly not told me that part.

"Fletcher jumped out of the window with her to get her out, but the paramedics couldn't resuscitate her. The smoke inhalation closed off her airway. She died on the scene."

Last night. Fletcher had been so worried—out of his mind in a way I'd never seen before—because of the smoke. He kept asking them to check our throats...

God, that must have dug up so much for him.

I cover my mouth with my hand. "Why are you telling me this?"

"Because I'm afraid." Her frown carves deep lines into her face, and she wrings her hands together in her lap. "I think there's a lot in his past that he hasn't processed. We've tried to help him as much as we can. And this...he won't make it easy on you, but he needs someone. He never likes to be the one getting taken care of. He hasn't let me in a long time. But I'm hoping he might let you."

"You don't think he's coming back here," I realize.

She shakes her head. "Dave drove to his house this morning to see if he'd gone there after the hospital."

"Where else would he go?" I ask, but I already know the answer, don't I?

It's a four-hour drive to Northumberland, squarely in the middle-of-nowhere Pennsylvania. But the moment Fletcher's mom helped me dig up the address for his old house, I jumped in the car. Luckily they agreed to watch Casey until Liam could come pick him up later in the morning.

I just hope I'm right about this.

When I finally turn into the neighborhood, I slow to a crawl and take in the houses around me. Many falling apart or boarded up. A sad park sits in the center—two swings, one of them broken, and a metal slide. All of the surrounding grass is dead.

My heart aches as I inch along, trying to picture a younger Fletcher growing up here.

It's not that different from what my neighborhood looked like at that age.

It's not the house I see first.

It's his truck.

I let out the breath I've been holding the entire drive here.

He's parked across the street from the shambles of what used to be his home. It's clear it was never fixed after the fire. Condemned. Left behind to rot.

I can't help but wonder which window it was. I'm guessing one on the side of the house. They all have boards over them now.

I park a few feet away and climb out. I don't think he's noticed me, not until I round to the passenger side and knock on the window.

He jumps, and his eyes soften in surprise when he sees me. He immediately unlocks the door and leans over to open it.

"Chris," he breathes. "What are you—?"

His eyes are bloodshot, and the shadows beneath them are a darkness I've never seen on him—and that's saying something with the amount of sleep he's been getting lately.

"You shouldn't be here," he murmurs as I climb in. "You should hate me."

My heart cracks in half in my chest. "*Fletcher.*" I lay my hand on the side of his face and force him to meet my eyes. "I don't blame you for a second."

"This is because of me. I brought her into your lives, and I put Casey at risk—"

"This isn't your fault." I make my voice as firm as I can manage. "Please don't take this on. *You* got us both out. You're the reason we're okay."

He shakes his head a little and faces forward. A muscle in his jaw jumps, and a tear rolls down his cheek.

"Fletch," I say quietly. "Why didn't you tell me about Lucy?"

His eyes fall shut, and he says nothing for a long time. "I got her out," he whispers. "I got her out, and she still died." He hiccups, his chest rising rapidly with his breath. "I got her out. She shouldn't have died. I got her—I got her—"

"Fletcher." I reach for him, desperately wanting to help but not knowing what to do. I touch his face, the back of his neck. He doesn't even seem to be aware that I'm here anymore.

"I got her out," he gasps. "I got her—I got her out. It doesn't make sense. I got her out."

I climb over the center console, into his lap, and take his face between my hands, forcing him to look at me.

"Breathe."

"I got her—I got her out," he whispers. Tears stream down his cheeks.

"I know. I know." I wrap my arms around him and hold him as tightly as I can.

"I got her out," he says, and it sounds like a whimper.

"You did everything you could for her. You did everything you could. It wasn't your fault." I press my face against his shoulder and murmur in his ear over and over. I don't even know what I'm saying at this point, but he's holding me back just as tightly.

"I thought you were dead," he gasps. "I thought I lost you."

I kiss his temple and tighten my arms around him. "You have me."

I hold him until his breathing slows. When I pull back, I frame his face again and search his eyes. They stare back at me, and I've never seen him this open, this vulnerable.

This broken.

And I want so desperately to put the pieces back together for him, but I can't fix this. It's just the kind of pain you have to suffer through until it doesn't hurt as much anymore.

I know nothing I can say will make this better, but I settle on "I love you."

His eyelids shutter, and he swallows hard. "I love you," he says roughly, and his hands mirror mine, one coming to each side of my face.

I wipe the tears from his cheeks. "Lucy—do you know where she is?"

His eyebrows pull together, and he scrunches his nose like he's trying not to cry again. He shakes his head.

I run a hand down the back of his hair. "Would you like to go find her?"

The records aren't that hard to find, and the cemetery is only a few blocks from the house. With no family, she was cremated and buried here among other unclaimed bodies.

I start to worry this was a very bad idea as I hold Fletcher's hand and follow him through the rows. Maybe seeing such a small, sad burial for her will make him feel more guilty.

But when we find her, he sighs, and the tension in his shoulders seems to ease.

I gently lay down the flowers we picked up on the way, then turn my face as I rise to my feet so Fletcher can't see the tears already streaming down my cheeks.

He clears his throat, lowers to a knee, and runs his fingers over the tiny stone in the ground. "Hey, Goose."

I press my lips together, the tears coming in earnest now.

"You were always asking when I was finally going to get a girlfriend," he continues, a small smile in his voice. "So I brought someone to meet you. This is Christine."

"Hi, Lucy," I murmur.

"I want you to know that I've never stopped thinking about you. I'm sorry I didn't make it here before now."

I take in the surrounding graves. Small, unkempt. No flowers or candles or teddy bears. Has anyone *ever* been to see her?

"Christine has a son, Casey," Fletcher continues. "I think you would've liked him."

My heart feels like someone is crushing their fist around it. I lay my hand on Fletcher's shoulder from behind and squeeze.

He says nothing else, and neither do I. But we stay like that until the last of the daylight bleeds from the sky.

Chapter Forty-Four

CHRISTINE

It's late by the time we leave the cemetery, and neither of us is up for the four-hour drive back to Sweetspire, so we find a hotel for the night. I wait in the car to call Casey and tell him goodnight while Fletcher goes inside to book a room.

It's the nicest place we could find around here—which isn't saying much. It's a glorified motel, at best.

I text Fletcher's mom while I'm at it to let her know I found him, he's all right, and we'll be back tomorrow. She sends me a string of what I'm assuming are excited emojis—a smiley with hearts around it, fireworks, three thumbs-up, a rose, a peace sign, and what I think is two people hugging. I smirk at the screen, and it softens into a smile as I catch sight through the windshield of Fletcher heading this way.

I don't know his mom all that well, but I know that I like her. A lot. After everything he's been through, I'm so glad he ended up with someone like her.

He offers me a tired smile as I climb out of the car and meet him halfway in the parking lot. And that smile…even on a day like today, even after watching my fresh start literally burn to the ground before my eyes, this feeling of unwavering peace washes over me, and I know everything's going to be okay as long as he keeps looking at me like that.

I follow him to our room at the end of the line and take the second key card he offers. Despite the slightly scary exterior, the room itself is fine, if a little plain and outdated. It's not a far cry from the place I used to work.

Fletcher seemed okay leaving the cemetery earlier, like having a proper chance to say goodbye to Lucy had lifted at least some of the weight from his shoulders. But after driving here in separate cars, I'm having a hard time gauging his mood. I can't tell if he wants me to talk to him or leave him to his thoughts.

He silently takes a seat at the foot of the bed and hangs his head between his shoulders.

I hesitate before sinking next to him and laying a hand on his thigh. He immediately puts his hand over mine.

"I'm so sorry, Chris," he whispers.

I tighten my hand around him. "Fletcher—"

He flattens his lips into a tight line and shakes his head. "Your *house*. And after you put so much effort into trying to have a fresh start for you and Case—"

"Fletcher—"

"This is all my fault. I didn't *think*—"

"*Fletcher.*" I frame his face with my hands and force him to look at me. He stares back with sad, pleading eyes that cut straight through my chest. "Stop," I say quietly. "Everything in there was replaceable. It's just stuff. It doesn't matter to me."

"The house..."

"I hated that house." I let out a small, pitiful laugh as I realize how true it is. "It's been falling apart since the moment I bought it. I was starting to think the Realtor had it out for me."

He chuckles too, and his expression sobers as he meets my eyes. Something about it has me holding my breath.

"I wouldn't survive it," he whispers. "If something happened to either of you. I wouldn't survive it."

"I know the feeling."

He closes his eyes and presses his forehead to mine. "I'm going to say something, and you're going to think I'm crazy, so just don't respond right away, okay?"

My eyebrows fly up.

"I want you and Casey to move in with me."

I stare at him. Usually my brain is running a million miles an hour, but right now, it goes completely blank.

"I know it's fast," he continues. "And under different circumstances, I wouldn't…but you guys need somewhere to go, and I have the space. At least until you can figure out what you want to do. Figure it out with me."

I swallow hard. With the whirlwind of the past few days, I hadn't even begun to think about next steps. I don't think I've even really started to process the fire. Casey can't stay at Liam's forever. And the last thing I want to do is give Julian an opportunity to swoop in and take Casey for an extended period of time.

But something about it has my entire body feeling clammy.

Fletcher's eyebrows tug together as he searches my face. "You hate the idea."

"No. No. I just…" I trail off, not sure what to say. Not sure what I'm even feeling right now.

Fletcher's expression softens like he's figured it out though. "This isn't anything like that."

I frown. "Like what?"

He tilts his head. "Like your mom."

Like my…

That's exactly it, I realize. My mom's Band-Aid for every

problem growing up was *always* to find a man to move in with. There were so many I lost count.

"Isn't it?" I whisper.

His grip on my face tightens. "No. Chris, you are more than capable of finding another solution, I know that. I'm not offering you a handout. You're not taking advantage of me. I'm not some random guy who only wants you and doesn't give a shit about your kid. I'm in love with you. I've been in love with you since that first night at the bar, I think. And I love Casey. And I'm asking you because I *want* you there. I want you both."

I blink rapidly to get rid of the building tears.

"Chris…"

I bite my lip and look down.

A few moments of silence pass before he releases me. "I won't push you on it. But the door is open."

My eyes flick up as a wave of déjà vu washes over me.

Another night. Another hotel. His final words to me before he slipped out the door, and I wondered if I'd ever see him again.

His gaze is trained on his hands in his lap now. There's something so much softer about his face from this angle.

"You won't like living with me," I murmur. "I'm messy. And I'll take up the entire closet. And I always forget my hair in the shower."

He stills. Looks at me.

"And you can't keep candy in the house or I'll eat it all. I don't have any self-control," I continue, my voice getting wobbly.

His hands weave into my hair and pull me close.

"But Casey likes to have fruit snacks around. I know they're not the healthiest, but they're his favorite. And I'm not above bribing in some situations—"

Fletcher crushes his lips to mine.

"And I always forget my key—"

"I will hide as many spares as you need," he says against my mouth.

He kisses me slowly, deeply, the kind of kiss that makes my head spin.

"I'm a terrible cook—"

His lips curl into a smile against mine. "I love cooking."

When I say nothing else, he pulls back an inch and waits. He lifts an eyebrow. "Anything else?"

I sniffle. "That's all I can think of right now."

"Thank God." He pulls my mouth back to his.

Chapter Forty-Five

FLETCHER

They were able to salvage more from the fire than any of us expected. Pretty much nothing from downstairs, but a lot of Chris's and Casey's personal belongings from their bedrooms survived, which I think is what they cared about the most anyway.

We set Casey up in the guest room. Luckily my parents chipped in and helped gut it so I didn't have to—disposing of every personal touch we'd made for Jacks.

Even thinking her name hits like a punch to the gut.

Everything about this house now feels tainted with memories of her. Mom and Dad have been trying to get me to take on another house project for months, and now maybe it's time. I could find something bigger, something Chris and Casey like too. Then we could sell this place and have a fresh start.

I know Chris thinks this is a temporary solution while the two of them get back on their feet.

But I plan to spend every moment they're here proving her wrong.

Maybe it's fast and impulsive and immature.

But I've always been a man who knows what he wants.

Instead of scaring me off, the situation with Jacks only made it that much clearer. Life is unpredictable. And I don't know how much time I'll get with them, so I'm not planning on taking a single moment for granted.

Chris is quiet when I enter the kitchen, sitting in the same chair at the table as she has been all morning, eyes glued to her laptop screen. At first I thought she was just processing Casey starting school again today, but that deep line etched between her eyebrows makes me pause.

I circle the table and place a hand on the back of her chair as I peer over her shoulder.

I suck in a sharp breath as I take in what's on her screen. She has a million tabs open and pulled up side by side—news articles about the fires, research about serial arsonists, psychology journals. There's enough of a backlog that it's clear she didn't get started on this today.

She swallows hard and closes the laptop. "It looks like she'll probably get a minimum of thirty years," she says quietly. "Potentially a life sentence. Especially with Pennsylvania's laws, how bad the property damage was, and how many deaths there were—those are first-degree felonies. They might try her as an adult for those too."

I sink into the chair next to her, my mouth suddenly dry. We haven't really talked about Jacks since the fire a few weeks ago. The only time she's come up is when we've been dealing with the insurance company or the cops. They held off arresting her until the hospital cleared her medically, and they've been holding her without bail due to the judge considering her a danger to society with her repeat offenses.

I try to gauge Chris's expression, but I can't. I feel like this should be good news for her—make her feel a little safer if she knows Jacks will be locked away for so long. But her face as she looks at her hands...she looks *gutted*.

"I don't know how to feel about this," she whispers.

I sigh and pull her chair closer to mine. "I know. I don't either."

"She—she had her whole life ahead of her." Finally, she peers up at me and searches my face. "How are you doing?"

I shake my head and run a hand under my jaw. "I haven't let myself think about it much."

It sounds like a lame blow-off, but it's the truth. And it's been all too easy to distract myself with all of the logistical nightmares we've been wading through—moving Chris and Casey in, salvaging what we could from the house, the insurance, the cops, Casey's address changing right before he started school.

Because if I do, if I start thinking about her, then I start to wonder.

What would have happened if I hadn't left. If I hadn't left her behind. If she'd had someone there for her after the first fire. Maybe I could've...I don't know. Guided her in a different direction. The guilt from accidentally killing Lucy—and at eight years old—that alone... And then to tack on everything else she endured, God, she didn't stand a chance.

And I did that. I left her there.

"I want you to know that it's okay if you need to talk about her."

I blink back to the table to find Christine's wide blue eyes peering up at me, her eyebrows pinched together in concern as she searches my face.

"I know this is...complicated," she adds.

I don't respond at first and focus on the table in front of me. Talking it out has never been my way of processing things —much to the dismay of the many therapists my parents got for me as a teen. But my usual methods haven't been doing me much good these past few weeks either. There were only so many odd jobs around the house to fix.

Maybe doing things with my hands has never been about helping me process things though. Maybe it's always just been a distraction.

"You know what the really fucked-up part is?" I whisper.

She rests a hand on my leg and waits for me to continue.

"The part I keep getting hung up on is she went after you and Casey. And I can never forgive her for that. But if she hadn't... If we hadn't fought that night, if she hadn't lashed out, and I'd found out about the other fires some other way... I think that I...I think maybe—"

"You would have been able to forgive her."

"Maybe," I whisper, but I shake my head at myself the moment the word is out there. "Four people. She's killed *four people*. She's only eighteen years old, and she's already killed four people."

Chris scoots her chair closer and runs her hands up and down my arms, but I can barely feel her. I blink rapidly, but the tears build in my eyes just the same. I can barely see the kitchen, the house. I could be anywhere. Any time. Even back when—

"I used to make her mac and cheese for dinner," I breathe, and I can practically smell it in the air. Usually burnt and dry—at least the first few times I tried. "I'd help her braid her hair before bed. It always got tangled if I didn't—then we'd be late trying to brush it out the next day. And she *hated* being late. We'd sit at the kitchen table doing her math homework in the afternoon. I always had to pack her lunch directly into her backpack, otherwise she'd forget it."

I shake my head, coming back to the room. I can't look at Chris. I can't see her face without being back in that house, the air unbearably hot, the ceiling collapsed on top of her and blood seeping from her hairline.

She keeps her hands on my arms, but it feels numb, distant.

"I thought I would regret leaving her behind my whole life. That I'd done something selfish and unforgivable. Then she showed up here, and I—" I practically choke on the words trying to get them out. "I started to picture—I started to picture the future. And I could see her at my wedding. Could picture her being an aunt to my kids." My voice breaks, but now that I've started, I can't stop. "I could picture her as a part of my life again. But now..." Silence falls between us, heavy and thick. When I manage to speak, the words are barely audible. "I just wish this didn't happen."

Her hands find the sides of my face. "I know."

"I know I shouldn't, but I miss her. And seeing how good you were with her—seeing her with Casey—I guess I just really believed it was all gonna work out."

I squint, trying in vain to stop the tears, and Chris wipes them away for me. "So did I," she whispers. "Fletcher, I need you to hear me when I tell you this. You are allowed to miss her. You are allowed to be heartbroken over this—*devastated* over this. Please don't think you're not allowed to feel however you feel for our sake."

I let out a shuddering breath, and my eyes fall closed like they're suddenly too heavy to keep open.

"Do you...do you want me to try to find her a lawyer? I don't know how much of a difference it'll make, but I doubt a public defender is going to do her any favors."

My eyes snap to her face. *Find her a lawyer?* Jacks could have *killed* her, could have killed Casey, and still, she's trying to help. "I would never ask you to do that," I whisper.

She sighs and wraps her hand around my wrist. "Don't get me wrong. I'm angry, Fletch. And I don't know if I would ever be willing to let her around Casey again." She presses her lips into a hard line and shakes her head. "But...she showed remorse. She almost killed herself trying to stop it. Cold-blooded killers don't do that. That's not what a lost cause looks like. I don't...I don't think she's a bad kid. I think life dealt her a real fucked-up hand and she never learned how to deal with it. And no one ever helped her learn. And she's important to you. And *you* are important to me. So I'm asking you, how do you want to handle this? Because I will help you however you need."

That feels like the most fucked-up part of it all. I wish I could be consumed with this rage. But the lingering empathy I have for her, it feels like it's eating me alive.

I lean forward, take Chris's head between my hands, and bring our faces a few inches away. "You are too good for me."

She lays her hands over mine as more tears threaten.

My throat thickens as I say, "And I would protect you and Casey with my life. I need you to know that."

"Fletch." She gives me a small smile and wipes the tears from my face with her thumbs again. "You ran into a burning building for us. I know."

I clear my throat, scrub a hand across my cheeks, and lean back in my chair. "I don't think I'll ever be able to forgive her for this."

She lays her hand on my arm.

My breath leaves me all at once as I hang my head between my shoulders. "But."

She squeezes my wrist. "But you don't know if you'd be able to forgive yourself later if you do nothing now."

I nod.

She takes a deep breath, squeezes my arm once more, then opens her laptop. "Okay. So we'll see what we can do for her. That doesn't mean you have to forgive her, or go see her, or ever speak to her again. But we'll give her her best shot. And then what she does from there will be up to her. Okay?"

"Chris?"

She hums, eyes glued to the screen as her fingers fly across the keyboard. When I say nothing else, she glances at me.

And with that one look, all of the chaos vibrating inside of me goes still. Calm. This woman who has been tossed around by life more than anyone I've ever met—who's gotten so much worse than she deserves. But she hasn't let it harden her. Not even close. She has more compassion and understanding than anyone I've ever met. Even for people who might not deserve it. "I love you."

She smiles, just a soft, small turn of her lips. The kind I usually only see her give Casey. "I love you too."

Epilogue
CHRISTINE—FOUR MONTHS LATER

In all the years I've lived here, we've never had snow on Christmas Eve. At least not the kind that lasted long enough to stick to the ground. But today, the lawn is absolutely covered in it.

Casey squeals in delight and bursts through the back doors the second Fletcher finishes helping him with his gloves. He sinks into the snow with each step, slowing him down, as he passes the swing set and tree house Fletcher finished building a few months ago. Then, once he reaches the center of the yard, he plops onto his back and fans his arms and legs out to make a snow angel.

Liam darts after him, and Gracie sputters and tries to grab him, but he's already slipped through the door.

"You're not even wearing your jacket!" she calls.

I see a flash of Liam's grin as he falls to the ground beside Casey in nothing but his jeans and T-shirt.

I stay in the kitchen with Keava, who has Rowan in her arms. The snow is awfully pretty to look at—from here. Near the heating vent. With a cup of hot chocolate in my hands.

"I cannot believe you put our daughter in that," says Leo as he presses a kiss to Keava's temple and ducks into the fridge for the eggnog.

I, for one, think she looks adorable. The Santa hat is slightly too big, and the red and green tulle tutu is just ridiculous enough without being over-the-top. Rowan watches his every move, the way she always does when he's in the room. It doesn't matter how many other people are around, her eyes always find Leo.

"You're just lucky I didn't make you a matching one," says Keava.

Fletcher snorts as he slides in behind me and wraps his arms around my waist. "Green *is* his color."

"What do you think, Row? Maybe we can match next year." Leo lifts her from Keava's arms and hoists her up in the air, and she erupts in giggles.

"I said we should all get matching ugly sweaters," offers Gracie as she slides onto one of the barstools.

I crane my neck to see what's going on in the backyard. "Are they still just lying there?"

Fletch shakes his head. "Looks like Liam's teaching him to make a snowman."

I meet his eyes over my shoulder and slowly raise my eyebrows. "Are you thinking what I'm thinking?"

His smile turns catlike. "Ambush?"

Liam and Casey are so engrossed in building the bottom of their snowman that they don't even hear Fletcher, Leo, Gracie, and me sneak out onto the deck. It isn't until we're at the edge of the stairs, first snowballs ready to go, that Liam glances up.

"Fire!" calls Fletch.

"Take cover!" yells Liam.

Casey sprints for the playset as Liam scrambles to make a snowball of his own while taking the brunt of the attack. One of Gracie's hits him square in the chest, and he looks up at her with betrayal in his eyes.

"Whose side are you on?" he demands.

She shrugs and throws another, this one hitting him in the leg.

"Nice aim," says Leo.

"Thanks."

Casey emerges from behind the slide with a battle cry, his little arms loaded with a stack of snowballs. Our group erupts in screams and pivots for the door.

Fletcher shields me as Casey and Liam fire, and Leo and I hurry back inside. I watch through the glass as Fletcher and Gracie exchange a look, nod, then plunge down the stairs and into the fight.

I laugh as I join Keava in the kitchen, and she shakes her head.

"They're all going to be soaking wet, cold, and complaining in a minute."

Leo smiles and kisses the top of her head. "You sound like such a mom."

She exchanges a sideways glance with me. "Imagine that."

"Are you guys heading over to your parents'?" I ask Leo.

He bobs his head as he inhales yet another sugar cookie. I think he's cleared half the plate on his own. "We'll go in a bit. Are you going to Fletcher's parents?"

"Not tonight, but we're doing brunch there tomorrow."

"I'm surprised that—" Leo stops midword and winces.

I offer him a tight smile and sip my hot chocolate. "You can say it."

That Casey's dad didn't even put up a fight to spend any part of Christmas with him? That he's out of town God knows where yet again? I shouldn't have been surprised, considering he did the same thing for Thanksgiving, but a part of me was. I didn't exactly expect him to hang around with us sipping eggnog—but seeing Casey for just an hour or two? I didn't think that was too much to ask.

Instead, he had a gift delivered with a premade card and his business signature at the bottom. What's worse is Casey didn't even ask about him. Even he knows what to expect by now.

After the fire, Julian had pleasantly surprised me. He kept checking in—*him*, not his assistant—and he showed up to help clean up the wreckage, brought over food, spent hours with Casey each day. It got to the point where I thought it may have been a wakeup call for him, that he would start prioritizing Casey more.

That lasted about a week.

Instead of stewing about it, I'm choosing to see it as a blessing. A little less drama in our lives, and more time for me with Casey.

The glass door slides open, revealing a breathless and dripping-wet Fletcher with Casey slung over his shoulder.

"Must have been quite the battle if you're taking prisoners," I say.

"It was a close call," says Liam with a lift of his chin as he steps in after him, looking even worse for the wear.

Gracie pats him on the back comfortingly as she slips inside last and closes the door behind her. "Denial is normal." She reaches for Rowan before he can respond. "Is it time to go to Grandma and Grandpa's? Is it time?" she asks in a baby voice.

Rowan reaches right back and eagerly wraps her arms around Gracie's neck.

My heart melts at the sight, but it's bittersweet, in a way. Seeing the entire village Rowan has in a way Casey never did at that age. But I suppose it's better late than never. He certainly has a village now. With our friends, but also, Fletcher's parents have been such a big part of that.

Casey's never had a grandparent presence in his life—Julian's parents are both dead, and mine might as well be. But Dave and Jodie have embraced Casey in a way I didn't even know to hope for.

And me too. They're the type of kind I thought didn't exist outside of movies.

I actually think it scares Fletcher a bit, how well Jodie and I get along. We've already been talking about bringing her in to help on some outdoor parties CC Events has coming up. She's also been working me down for months about talking Fletcher into finding a venue of my own—just a fixer-upper around town that we could all pitch in to flip, that way we'd have a consistent space to use during the busy seasons, and we could rent it out the rest of the year for another source of income.

Admittedly, the idea of taking a tiny piece out of Julian's monopoly on commercial real estate around here brings me a small thrill.

Fletch, Casey, and I stand on the front porch and wave them off as their brake lights disappear down the snowy streets. And it takes all of twenty minutes until Casey can't keep his eyes open anymore and Fletcher carries him up to bed. Then suddenly the house that was so full of warmth and laughter is utterly and completely quiet.

The virtual fireplace flickers on the TV. That paired with the Christmas tree beside it give the room perfect mood lighting. I settle myself on the couch and snuggle beneath a blanket as Fletcher's footsteps descend the stairs. He leaps over the back of the couch, eagerly slides in next to me, and throws an arm around my shoulders.

"Promise we'll have a real one of these in the new house," he murmurs.

I smile and lean my head against his chest. We closed on the new place just after Thanksgiving, but since Fletcher wants to do most of the work himself, it'll be several more months before it's move-in ready.

But as lengthy as the process is turning out to be, it'll still be faster than the situation with Jacks. It's a particularly complicated case with the jurisdictional questions and multiple offenses—she was arrested four months ago but could be waiting over a year until her actual trials. We found her the best lawyer money can buy, and despite Fletcher not being any more willing to speak with her than he was after the fire, I know he's stayed up-to-date on the proceedings.

We don't talk about it much. I think sometimes he needs to pretend it isn't happening. But every once in a while, he'll offer up a detail he heard from the lawyer that day.

He thinks they'll be able to try her as a juvenile for the first trial since she was under ten.

They're going to do a mental health evaluation.

He wants to file a motion to suppress her confession.

"So, Rowan's giving you baby fever, huh?"

"I—what?" I blink back to the room, and my face burns as his words sink in. As a matter of fact, I couldn't take my eyes off her all night. But he was so busy with Casey he shouldn't have noticed.

"Well, she was giving it to me," he says lightly.

My head whips around. When I do manage to speak, my voice comes out small. "Really?"

He keeps his gaze trained on the fire, but he's smiling now. "I know we haven't talked about it yet. And I'm not traditional about most things, but I am here. So I very much intend on marrying you first. And letting us get settled in the new house. But after that...I guess I just wondered what you thought about it. I know your business is really taking off now too, so I don't want to derail that. But if you do...want to, I mean..." Finally, he looks over at me, and there's so much unease in his expression, uncertainty, like maybe this is something he's been wanting to talk about for a while. "Well, I could take as much time off as we need. So I don't want you to worry about that side of things."

Tears build in my eyes. I always thought I wanted more than one, but then after having Casey with Julian...that changed. I had to do everything on my own, even when he was right beside me, and I never wanted to experience that again.

But now...

"We might not have that much time," I murmur. "Chances for complications will start going up for me in just a few years."

He tucks a strand of hair behind my ear. "I don't want to rush it, and I wouldn't ever want to do something unsafe for you. So we could see a doctor, go from there. I don't care how it happens. If we adopt, foster—anything. But however we do it, is that something you'd—?"

"Yes," I whisper.

His entire body deflates in relief with his exhale. "Really?"

I nod, the tears clouding my vision now, and I *laugh*.

He smiles, uncertain. "What?"

I shake my head, unsure how to put it into words. The last seven months with him have been an absolute whirlwind. Thinking about how different my life was a year ago makes my head spin. But everything feels so...certain. Right. It doesn't even feel like we've been moving fast. It just feels like something inevitable finally clicked into place.

Six months ago, hearing someone talk like this, it would've had my heart racing, my fight or flight in overdrive. Promises, plans for the future. It would've felt too fragile, too slippery to hold on to. To count on.

Too scary to even try.

I don't know what it is about Fletcher. I think he's the first person in my life that when he says things…I believe him. And I don't have to convince myself to. I just do.

"You just came out of nowhere," I whisper. "And now I can't imagine my life without you."

He frames my face with his hands before pulling me close. "You won't ever have to."

He'll leave, my mother's voice echoes in my head. *And you'll be left with nothing.*

Instead of shoving her in the corner as I've always done, I let myself imagine her fully. To picture the cruel curve of her poorly drawn lipstick, her overly tanned skin, her disapproving eyes. And I meet them head on.

He won't, I say calmly. *And if he does, you're wrong. I won't be left with nothing. I'll be left with me. And she's done a pretty damn good job of taking care of me so far, so I trust her to figure it out then too if it came down to it.*

Then I turn away, and I let her go.

Not into the corner—not in my mind at all. She doesn't get to stay anymore. I leave her in her lawn of dead grass behind some moron's house who's already drunk at one in the afternoon, and I don't look back.

See What Happens Next

Thank you so much for reading *Tell Me It's Wrong*! If you enjoyed it, **it would mean so much if you left a review!**

Have you read book one in the Sweetspire series yet? If you love banter, secret pining, brother's best friend, and employee x boss, check out Gracie and Liam's story in *Tell Me It's Right*.

Continue the Sweetspire series with book three, expected 2026. Subscribe to Katie Wismer's newsletter or follow her on social media for updates!

About the Author

Katie Wismer writes books with a little blood and a little spice (sometimes contemporary, sometimes paranormal.)

Be the first to know about upcoming projects, exclusive content, and more by signing up for her newsletter at katiewismer.com. Signed books are also available on her website, and she posts monthly bonus content on her Patreon (including a Patreon-exclusive book!)

When she's not reading, writing, or wrangling her two perfect cats, you can find her on her YouTube, Instagram, or TikTok.

- patreon.com/katiewismer
- tiktok.com/@authorkatiewismer
- instagram.com/authorkatiewismer
- youtube.com/katesbookdate
- goodreads.com/katesbookdate
- amazon.com/author/katiewismer
- bookbub.com/authors/katie-wismer